MAYAN FOLKTALES

MAYAN

FOLKTALES

FOLKLORE FROM
LAKE ATITLÁN, GUATEMALA

Translated and Edited by James D. Sexton

ANCHOR BOOKS
DOUBLEDAY
NEW YORK LONDON TORONTO SYDNEY AUCKLAND

An Anchor Book
PUBLISHED BY DOUBLEDAY
a division of Bantam Doubleday Dell Publishing Group, Inc.
666 Fifth Avenue, New York, New York 10103

Anchor Books, Doubleday, and the portrayal of an anchor
are trademarks of Doubleday, a division of Bantam Doubleday
Dell Publishing Group, Inc.

BOOK DESIGN BY CLAIRE N. VACCARO

Library of Congress Cataloging-in-Publication Data

Mayan folktales: folklore from Lake Atitlán, Guatemala / translated
and edited by James D. Sexton. —1st Anchor Books ed.
p.   cm.
Includes bibliographical references.
1. Mayas—Legends.   2. Tales—Guatemala—Atitlán, Lake, Region.
3. Folklore—Guatemala—Atitlán, Lake, Region.   I. Sexton, James D.
F1435.3.F6M38   1992
398.2′097281′6—dc20   91-37813
CIP

ISBN 0-385-42253-9
Copyright © 1992 by James D. Sexton

ALL RIGHTS RESERVED
PRINTED IN THE UNITED STATES OF AMERICA
FIRST ANCHOR BOOKS EDITION: May 1992

1   3   5   7   9   10   8   6   4   2

Contents

MAYAN FOLKTALES

Introduction

Traveling through the region in the mid-1800s, Frederick Catherwood eloquently described Lake Atitlán as having "a surface shining like a sheet of molten silver, enclosed by rocks and mountains of every form, some barren, and some covered with verdure, rising five hundred to five thousand feet in height" (Stephens 1969:157).

Lake Atitlán is as majestic today as it was then. Lying 5,100 feet above sea level in a basin about ten miles wide and twenty miles long, the freshwater lake spans about eleven miles from east to west and six miles from north to south, reaching a maximal depth of 1,122 feet (Serrano 1970 in Sexton 1990:8). The shore of the southern side of the lake is dominated by three immense volcanoes: *Nimajuyú* to the Maya, San Pedro to the Ladinos, rising 9,925 feet; Atitlán, reaching a height of 11,500 feet; and Tolimán, 10,350 feet in elevation. On their steep slopes, each of these volcanoes now has cornfields reaching nearly to their peaks, since all available land is used for slash-and-burn horticulture.

The highlands of Central America above 5,000 feet enjoy a cool tropical climate with well-marked dry (November through April) and wet (May through October) seasons. Natives commonly refer to the rainy season as *invierno* [winter]. The climate around the lake is semitropical and of a monsoonal character; the temperature rarely drops below fifty degrees Fahrenheit, and this happens only very early in the morning. In the shade the temperature rarely reaches eighty degrees, and this generally happens exactly in the middle of the afternoon (Tax 1968:20).

Surrounding Lake Atitlán are fourteen towns, all of them predominantly Maya Indian and all at various stages of development. Santa Cruz la Laguna, with 99 percent of its population Mayan, is the least developed, and Panajachel, with 74 percent of its population Mayan, is the most developed (Sexton and Woods 1982).

Lake Atitlán dominates the landscape of the department of Sololá, which, excluding Belize, is one of the twenty-two departments of the republic. Within the department of Sololá there are nineteen *municipios* [political and geographic subdivisions of departments], with their own subdivisions of *aldeas* [villages] and *caseríos* [hamlets]. Each *municipio* has its own *cabacera* [main town]. Normally, each *municipio* elects its *alcalde* [mayor], syndic, and *regidores* [councilmen]. During the 1980s, however, military presidents suspended elections, and town political officials were appointed. For example, the military governor, residing in the governmental seat that also is named Sololá, appointed the mayor for each of the nineteen *municipios*. In 1985, municipal and national elections were resumed and a civilian, Vinicio Cerezo, was elected to the presidency.

In all the towns, the Indian population share a general Mayan heritage. They still speak a dialect of Maya-Quiché as their native tongue and they share Mayan cultural patterns of brightly colored, indigenous dress and traditional beliefs and practices. Colors, styles, patterns, and particular *costumbres* [customs, rituals], however, vary from town to town. Guatemalan highland towns differ more in the way traits are combined and emphasized than in the presence or absence of certain traits (Nash 1969 in Sexton 1990:8).

Individual towns in the lake region are known for the specialized economic pursuits whether they be rope-making, fishing, cash cropping, or trade. They also participate in a system of economic exchange that involves rotating market days in each town. Most of the inhabitants also engage in subsistence horticulture, growing New World crops such as corn, beans, squash, tomatoes, potatoes, and avocados and Old World crops such as onions, chick-peas, garlic, carrots, lemons, and coffee. While campesinos consume most of what they grow, they sell surplus produce either on the open market or to middlemen, bartering for the best price they can get. For many of them, coffee and onions have become the most important source of cash.

Of the seven countries that make up Central America (Guatemala, Belize, El Salvador, Honduras, Nicaragua, Costa Rica, and Panamá), Guatemala is third in size with 42,044 square miles. It outranks the other countries in population, which was estimated at 8,900,000 in mid-1988, of which over half were Maya Indians, the largest percentage and absolute number of Indians in the region.

While there isn't fast agreement among linguists on the number of Indian dialects in Guatemala and the extent to which they are mutually intelligible, most agree that they all fall into the Maya-Quiché family. Guatemalan teachers instruct their students that there are six main groups comprised of different dialects: Quiché (Quiché, Cakchiquel, Tzutuhil, and Uspantec); Mam (Mam, Aguacatec, Jacalteca, Kanjobal, Chuj, and Ixil); Pocomam (Kechí, Pocomchí, Eastern Pocomam, Central Pocomam); Chol (Chortí, Chol Lacandón); Maya (Northern Lacandón, Yucateco, Mopán); Caribe (Arguaco Caribe, and Spanish Kekchí) (*Geografía Visualizada*, n.d.).

Most of the inhabitants living in the towns surrounding Lake Atitlán are Cakchiqueles and Tzutuhiles, with the Cakchiqueles concentrated in the eastern pueblos and the Tzutuhiles residing mainly in the western ones. Two easterly towns high above the lake are predominantly Quiché, and a smaller number of Quichés live mainly in eastern *aldeas*, or villages. While these three dialects are similar, there are some lexical items peculiar to each community.

The ancestors of the Quiché, Cakchiquel, and Tzutuhil Maya elite were a Nonoalca-Pipil-Chichimec mixture of war-like groups who migrated from Mexico into the highlands of Guatemala along the river routes during the early postclassic period (A.D. 1000–1200). They competed with earlier Mexican immigrants, the Pipil-Nicarao, who had established commercial relationships with the original inhabitants, the Pokomom and Mam. Eventually, the more recent Mexican Indian migrants extended their influence over the entire central highlands and became warring rivals for political and economic dominance of the region (De Borhegyi 1965 in Sexton 1990:5).

Lords and leaders settled in three major areas—the Cakchiquel at Iximché (also known by the local Indians as Patinamit), just outside of Tecpán; the Quiché at Utatlán (in Nahuatl, Gumarcaah in Quiché), near Santa Cruz del Quiché; and the Tzutuhil at Atitlán (in Nahuatl, Chiá in Tzutuhil), a former settlement on top the hill of Chuitinamit, a short distance across the bay from Santiago Atitlán. Rather than resembling the true urban centers in Mexico, these ancient cities were more like European castles and fortress towns. During peacetime, they were temporary quarters for festivals and market activities. In war they were strongholds for the warrior classes and served as a refuge for the outlying populations and satellite villages.

While the classic lowland Maya regions were in a state of decline at the time of the Spanish conquest in the early 1500s, the highland Maya areas were flourishing. Because of their expansionist policy and an interest in the rich cacao lands of the Pacific slopes, Mexicans from Tenochtitlán (Nahuatl-speaking Aztecs) founded a colony named Sonconusco on the southern coast. The highlanders traded with traveling merchants from Mexico (Aztecs). In exchange for copper, cloth, and wooden products, the highland Maya gave the Mexican merchants cacao (the chocolate bean), coastal cotton, and beautiful iridescent feathers of the quetzal bird. In an attempt to control the trade, the Quichés, Cakchiqueles, Tzutuhiles, and Pipiles frequently formed and broke alliances with one another (Sexton 1990).

If the Aztecs had not been conquered by the Spaniards and their Tlaxcalan allies, who were enemies of the lords of Tenochtitlán, it is conceivable that the Aztecs might have conquered the highland Maya. Montezuma worried about the appearance of the Spaniards in the Caribbean and sent urgent messages to the rulers of the Pipiles and the Cakchiqueles, who responded to his notices. The Pipiles had been sending tribute twice annually to Aztec leaders for forty years (Miles 1965:282).

When Pedro de Alvarado entered Guatemala from Mexico in 1524, he was able to play these rivalrous groups against each other, just as he and his commander Cortés had done in Mexico though not without initial fierce resistance on the part of the Quichés. Led by the warrior prince Tecún Umán, a large army of enraged Quiché warriors engaged the Spaniards in hand-to-hand combat. In battle, Tecún Umán sought out Pedro de Alvarado. Tecún's obsidian sword felled Pedro's horse, but it was no match for the latter's sword of steel. Despite the belief that Tecún was accompanied into battle by his guardian *nagual,* a beautiful quetzal bird, the Indian was fatally pierced by the Spaniard. According to legend, the quetzal, the bird of liberty, fell over the inert body of Tecún Umán. After the Spaniards recouped from the battle near Quezaltenango [the place where there are quetzals], they marched on to the Quiché capital of Utatlán, executed the high-ranking lords there, and burned the city. Pedro de Alvarado and his Indian allies then marched into Iximché without resistance, partly because the Cakchiqueles, like the Aztecs before them, mistook the light-complected Spaniards for returning gods.

Subsequently, the Cakchiqueles joined ranks with the Spaniards to march against their old enemies, the Tzutuhiles, who resided on the shores of Lake Atitlán. After an initial battle, the Tzutuhiles fled, but when the Spaniards threatened to cut down their cacao groves and burn their city, they returned subdued (Bernal Díaz in Mackie 1972). After conquest they were organized into Pedro de Alvarado's large *encomienda* [a colonial system exploiting the goods and services of the Indians] and were resettled to the present site of Santiago Atitlán, which today is the largest Tzutuhil town.

Throughout Central America, the Spaniards replaced Indian nobility at the top of the indigenous social hierarchy. They formed a plural society composed of different ethnic elements in a single social structure. Ethnic differences placed the Spaniards in the upper levels and the Indians in the lower ones.

By the time Guatemala and the rest of Central America declared their independence from Spain in 1821, culture, class, and race had become the criteria used to define an Indian from a non-Indian. The Indian spoke an Indian dialect as his or her mother tongue; the Spaniard spoke Spanish. And while the Indian wore native dress, the Spaniard wore Western-style clothing. The Indian generally was a campesino, a rural peasant or farmhand; the Ladino an administrator. And while the Indian was thought to have Mongoloid genes, the Ladino was believed to be more Caucasoid.

Although these criteria were more clearly marked after conquest and during the colonial period, today they have become more blurred. Now, class and occupation are important variables. While there is some upward social and economic mobility, it is still the exception to find Indians enjoying middle-class positions and jobs. Especially in rural pueblos, Indians are often found working as artisans as well as farming nearby milpas. Where towns such as Panajachel cater to tourism, many Indians work in service occupations. Such towns tend to be more ethnically mixed, and in them Indians clearly occupy inferior social positions. Even the term *indio* [Indian] carries a negative connotation, and it is not used in polite or official language. The words *natural* [native] or *indígena* [indigene, or native inhabitant] are preferred instead. The term Ladino, in contrast, carries no negative connotation.

Today, many Indians speak Spanish as a second language and have adopted Ladino material culture. Thus, the best description of an Indian is one who identifies himself or herself and who is identified by others as being Indian. Those who wish to pass as Ladinos often must move to towns larger than those of their birth. In these bigger urban centers, such as Quezaltenango and Guatemala City, the upper stratum of society is mostly of European descent. Spanish emigrants tend to own grocery stores, bars, and money-lending businesses. Several owners of *fincas* [farms], especially those growing coffee, are of German descent.

Before the conquest, the family was the basic social and economic unit. Providing they could afford it, patriarchs might have had more than one wife, and a typical household might consist of the adult male head, his wives, unmarried daughters, and both married and unmarried sons (Miles 1965 in Sexton 1990:16). With the arrival of the Spaniards, the Indian family changed little with the exception that plural marriages were less common. The more contemporary tendency, however, is toward nuclear units (the married couple and their children) rather than the consolidation of an extended family in one home. Occasionally there are polygamous unions, but monogamy is the norm. The comparative wealth of the parents of a newly united couple determines largely whether the couple will live with either set of parents. When a newly married couple lives in the *sitio* [homesite] of one set of parents, they usually have their own cooking hearth (kitchen), and in such cases may be considered independent units. As soon as the couple can afford it, they establish their own home, usually, though with some exceptions, near the groom's family.

Today, the Quiché-Maya trace kinship and inherent property according to the European legal system introduced by the Spaniards. That is, property and descent for male and female children are traced through both the father's side and the mother's side. Surnames, however, are traced in a patrilineal fashion with a child receiving the first surname of his father and the second surname of his mother's father.

Within the family, labor is divided by gender. Men do the heavy work in the fields. They also may work at numerous additional occupations such as mason, baker, and foot-loom weaver. Women, however, play critical domestic roles. They cook, weave on back strap looms, clean house, take care of the children, help weed and harvest the crops, and sell surplus vegetables and weavings in the marketplace. Although equal under the law, in a number of ways women are subordinate to men. Women often learn less Spanish than men, stay closer to home, and wear more traditional clothing. While they contribute equally to the well-being of the family and are consulted in most matters, their husbands often make the final decisions.

The ancestors of the Quiché-Maya of Lake Atitlán were under the religious influence of the Mexican Indians. They identified their god with Quetzalcoatl, the Azteč god; they called a class of priests and the coastal Pipil "Yaqui," or sacrificers; and they believed that local lords of mountains and Day Lords were capable of interceding with celestial gods like the sun, moon, and stars (Miles 1965 in Sexton 1990:13). But there was a solid foundation in the midwestern highlands that was more Mayan than Mexican. That is, much of the religion was concerned with curing, divination, witchcraft, and gods of various types and functions. There were *dueños* [owners or patrons or gods] of land, hills, mountains, water, rain, wind, and other natural phenomena. Both ancestors and gods were consulted in sacred caves. Prevalent was a belief in each person's having an animal form [*nagual*], and important persons might have more than one form that could be used on different occasions.

Among the ancient Quiché-Maya, rituals were both private and public. Public rituals involved the offering of incense, turkeys, blood, flowers, liquor, precious metals and stones, and sometimes even humans to the gods. Compared to the Mexican Indians, human sacrifice apparently played a minor role. During the public ceremonies, the images of gods were richly dressed and paraded through the towns to the accompaniment of trumpets and drums, usually ending at the ritual ball courts. Dance dramas celebrated historical events such as a victory in war or the reenactment of local myths (Miles 1965 and Thompson 1970 in Sexton 1990:14).

In all the towns surrounding Lake Atitlán, almost all of the native religious elements have survived with the exception of human sacrifice and parading images of gods, though the sacrificing of animals such as chickens and roosters and parading images of saints continue. The blending of native religion and the early Catholicism introduced by the Spanish friars is most obvious in the *cofradías* [religious brotherhoods that have as a major obligation the sponsoring of saints]. Each *cofradía* has an *alcalde* [head], and the more active *cofradías* have a *juez* [vice-head] and a first *mayordomo* [a liaison between the *juez* and secondary *mayordomos* who are the rank-and-file members]. Men climb the ranks by periodically bearing a cargo, or office, for a year. Holding such an office requires them to redistribute their wealth because they are expected to spend their money on food and drink for fiestas that honor the saints. Thus, a member's financial responsibilities may make him poor in wealth but rich in social status.

Men who successfully fulfill both high religious and political offices may become known as *principales*, or town elders, who are consulted on civil and religious matters. Although the *principal*'s whole family shares the prestige of his high status, wives and children enjoy this status only vicariously.

In the predominantly underdeveloped Indian towns, a large number of Mayans still accept traditional beliefs, including the following. Campesinos should perform *costumbres* before and after harvesting to honor the *dueños* of the land. Travelers and fishermen should perform *costumbres*, asking permission from the *dueña* of the lake before traveling and fishing. The winds of the lake are sacred and will cause the death of sinners by drowning. Drowning victims are the result of the water goddess's wanting more souls as servants. Fire is sacred and contains a holy spirit and spitting on it results in a dry mouth for the spitter. Placing fruit in the same basket with corn will by association result in smaller fruit during the next harvest. With personal items such as clothing, photographs, and hair, special precautions must be taken because witches may use them to invoke curses on the persons with whom they are associated. Humans, especially *brujos* [witches], can assume the form of their *naguales*, or animal forms, and powerful individuals like *brujos* may change into more than one animal form. There are *dueños* of the volcanoes and hills. Shamans can divine and witches can send misfortune and death. If a pregnant woman chances to go out of the house during an eclipse, her child will be born deformed.

Today many Indians believe that bad luck is more likely to occur on certain days and at certain hours; Monday, Wednesdays, and Fridays are bad luck days, and midday and midnight are bad luck hours. A person's general fate or luck depends on the day on which he or she is born. For example, a person born on the day of Ajpub, one of the twenty Day Lords, will have a strong *nagual*, or spirit, and may not want to die before someone else dies first. A person born on the day of Cauok, the lord of the lake, will have good luck, but only if the necessary *costumbres* are performed. Other Day Lords with

xxi

special significance are: Aj, Ey, Ix, Batz, Quemel, Tziquin, Imox, Bakbal, K'ik, Tijax, Can, Kjánel, Toj, Ajmac, Kat, Quej, Tzi, and Noj.

Many Indians think that particular *secretos* [magical or sacred rites] should be performed such as washing the sins from the deceased and throwing the water out in the cemetery so that the departed present themselves to the other life clean, without the filthiness of this world. And when a person dies away from home, his or her spirit will stay at the place of death until a shaman performs a *costumbre* to carry the spirit of the dead person from the place of death to join his or her body in the town cemetery. Many of these beliefs and similar ones seem to be vestiges of an ancient Mayan world view.

Folklore is a universal phenomenon which is an important part of the culture of any people. While folktales, jokes, and texts to dance dramas are enjoyable in their own right, they also serve a number of other functions. They expand our vision of the native world view, including beliefs, values, and thought systems. Folklore also gives us insight into how cultures rationalize behavior, especially rituals, and justify religious, social, political, and economic institutions. Finally, folklore offers a great deal of information about the environmental setting of a culture, particularly with respect to the plants, animals, and material culture found in it.

In 1941, Robert Redfield collected three folktales from Francisco Sánchez in San Antonio Palopó, a Cakchiquel Maya town, titled, "The Story of the Two *Compadres* Who Went Together on a Business Journey," "The Story of Three Brothers," and "*Ejemplo* [Example] of the Dogs." He placed these tales on deposit in the Microfilm Collection of Manuscripts of Middle American Cultural Anthropology at the Regenstein Library of the University of Chicago, but to my knowledge, he never published them (Redfield 1945). As early as 1949, Sol

Tax published an article in *The Journal of American Folklore*
suggesting that anthropologists could easily collect folktales in
the Lake Atitlán region of Guatemala simply by asking the
natives. As he reported, these highland Maya do not impose
taboos surrounding the telling of folktales as do many North
American Indian tribes such as the Navajo. Unlike Indians of
the Southwest, the Maya of Mexico and Central America tell
stories when they think of them, regardless of the season, time
of day, or whether the teller is indoors or outdoors (Tedlock
1983:14). Also, no one individual in a village or town is designated the only storyteller, although some individuals know
more stories than others.

Since Tax's 1949 publication, anthropologists have published some selected tales in English (Orellana 1975; Townsend 1980; Shaw 1971), but at the time of the writing of this
introduction, not a single book-length treatment of folktales
has been published from the Tzutuhil and Cakchiquel Maya
who live in towns surrounding Lake Atitlán.

Although a book-length collection of tales from the Lake
Atitlán region has not been published, Laughlin and Karasik
(1988) recently have published a book of dreams and folktales
from Zinacantán, Mexico. Their book includes different versions of two tales that I collected in Lake Atitlán—one a
widely distributed folktale in Mexico and Central America
about a man who turns into a buzzard from laziness and the
other a sexually graphic tale about an unfaithful woman who is
tricked by a spiteful husband into eating the cooked penis of
her lover. The details of the stories, however, vary consider-
ably, illustrating how each story has been adapted for each
specific environment with a style and flavor of its own, but not
giving any clue as to the ultimate origins of these apparently
pre-Columbian tales.

The *Zinacanteco* and *Joseño* versions of the folktale about
the cheating wife who eats her lover's penis have different

titles. "A Bellyful" is the name of the folktale from Zinacantán, where men go to the lowlands to prepare cornfields and hunt deer. "The Woman Who Loved Many Hombres and Died from Drinking a Lot of Water and a Piece of Sausage that She Had Eaten" is the title of the folktale from San José la Laguna, where big game such as deer are hard to find. The men farm some rented land on the southern coast in exchange for planting pasture for cattle, but they do most of their farming at home. Traveling merchants commonly go, however, to the southern coast to sell fruit (and other vegetables). In both stories, while the men are away, their wives are carrying on with other men. In both tales, the deceived husbands cut off the penises of their wives' lovers, but in the Mexican version of the tale, the woman is tricked into eating her lover's penis because it is mixed with the roasted penis of a deer. In contrast, the Guatemalan tale has the woman eating her lover's penis in *chirmol*, a popular sauce eaten with or without meat. The fact that the cheating wives die in different ways from drinking too much water—one's belly bursts but the other's doesn't—is most likely due to the varying imaginations of different storytellers or details getting distorted as they travel from mouth to mouth and mind to mind. Thus, differences in stories with common themes are accounted for both by the different environment in which they are told as well as the different memory and imagination of individual storytellers.

While the two versions of the folktale of the unfaithful woman eating her lover's penis appear to be pre-Columbian in origin, it is impossible to discern whether the tale originated in Chiapas, Mexico, and then diffused to Sololá, Guatemala, or the opposite. Likewise, it often is difficult to tell whether a given tale has Old World or New World roots. Identifying the Spanish or Mayan elements mixed in folktales is not as important as analyzing their present social and cultural content (Goosen 1974).

The existence of the same motifs in ancient tales in Chiapas, Mexico, and Sololá, Guatemala, also may be accounted for by people in diverse regions sharing and conserving an earlier common cultural region. As Laughlin and Karasik (1988:15) point out, however, clues to the antiquity of folktale elements found uniquely in one area such as Chiapas (or Sololá) are nearly nonexistent. Attempting to establish true, original versions of tales is difficult, if not futile, and " 'pure' tales are as rare as 'pure' cultures."

That scattered folktales have similar themes but vary in details even within the same region remains problematic. Cultures without a literary tradition rely on memory for the imparting of folktales, and no tale is likely to be retold in exactly the same manner even by the same storyteller. It's only natural for a teller of tales to fit common motifs into his or her own situation. Thus, when an Indian in a rather remote town is telling the story of four hapless persons who get into trouble because they don't know English, these persons are outside Indians from an even more isolated town, as exemplified in the tale "The Four Indians of Samayac." In more exposed and developed towns such as Panajachel that frequently deal with gringo tourists, the belittled characters who don't know Spanish are not Indians but gringos. In both cases, the main characters are from real towns which listeners can readily identify. Also, in both versions of the folktale, much is revealed about social and ethnic relations in a society stratified by class and race.

Tales are told under similar circumstances among the Guatemalan Maya as among the Mexican Maya (Laughlin and Karasik 1988:16). They are narrated to pass the time after a hard day's work away from home, to keep mourners awake at night during wakes, to exchange information with and entertain a guest or a host, to educate listeners about the values and beliefs of the culture, to commemorate specific historical events, and to entertain both children and adults. An illustration of this latter function comes from the life history of Ignacio Bizarro Ujpán, who is my main collaborator for the present book of folklore.

I met Ignacio when I first traveled to Guatemala in 1970 as part of a team of researchers studying culture change in the Lake Atitlán region.[1] Ignacio lived across a rocky, unpaved street from the house where I lived, and when I asked him to be my research assistant, to my delight he agreed. During my third season of field work, I asked Ignacio to write his autobiography and to begin keeping a diary. In 1981 we published *Son of Tecún Umán: A Maya Indian Tells His Life Story,* which I translated and edited. We published in 1985 a sequel, *Campesino: The Diary of a Guatemalan Indian.* In this latter book Ignacio relates how in March of 1980, he and several of his fellow townsmen were pressed into identifying the town's boundaries in the mountains and after a long, arduous day without finding any landmarks, he and his colleagues happily told *cuentos viejitos* [folktales] until late in the evening. "What kind of *cuentos viejitos,* did you tell, I asked him."

He said:

These are stories told by the old people, who mostly did not know Spanish. In the past there weren't many kinds of things like comics, but the old folks had their past times of telling stories that were fascinating to their grandchildren. They told stories like the one of the coyote and the rabbit, which is very long but amusing. Although the rabbit is smaller, he excels in all things and dominates the coyote, who is larger. What a pleasant story it is!

We still tell these stories. My aunt and my grandma have told them to me. When we do not have anything to do, these are stories we tell. Stories like the one of the jaguar-man who went to marry pigs in the forest and the

one of the idler who turned into a buzzard. There are a lot
of them, some very long. (Sexton 1985:155)

Since Ignacio was eager to work with me on a folklore
book and since he is an excellent storyteller, has a wide knowledge of his own culture, is well respected within his town, has
good rapport with the old folks who know traditional tales,
and knows a good number of modern and ancient tales himself, he was a natural choice to collaborate with me on a new
manuscript of folklore.[2] In all, Ignacio provided me thirty-four
folktales that I translated and edited.

These folktales are exceptionally rich in cultural content,
even in translation.[3] A preliminary thematic and cultural analysis of the stories reveals an insight into the sanctioning of
social obligations to participate in religious festivals and to
conduct *costumbres* in honor of *dios* [God], *dios del mundo* [god
of the world], *dios del mar* [god of the ocean], and various
dueños of sacred places by offering candles, incense, flowers,
and other precious items. They show a pantheistic view of the
supernatural which includes the gods of black, white, and red
beans and a Supreme, or Great God. Dreaming, especially, is
seen as an important vehicle for understanding the meaning of
life, and God may speak to people in dreams, as in the "Creation Myth." Evidenced in these tales is the belief that in earlier times people could turn into inanimate and animate objects
such as stones, tree stumps, cats, cows, coyotes, and snakes.

The tales also reflect the present world view that includes
brujos causing people misfortune such as illness or countering
the witchcraft of another *brujo*. Shamans and spiritualists divine and cure; humans change into their *nagual* forms, including winged creatures such as owls, eagles and hawks, and
quadrupeds such as mountain lions and jaguars. *Characoteles*
are persons who turn into *naguales* and act as spies. Men and
women may turn into coyotes and gather in packs to eat animals. Humans may also turn into *cadejos* [imaginary animals or

bad spirits similar to *characoteles* that lurk at night]. *Suerte* is a major determinant of fate, but there are good *suertes* and bad *suertes*, like the *suerte* of the *characoteles* that appear in "The Woman *Characotel*." *Secretos* are ritual acts to cure illness and to perform successful tasks such as hunting and farming. *Curanderos* [curers] are just as able as modern doctors for treating certain illnesses, but they drink a lot of alcohol and have pacts with the devil, as in "The Story of the Man [Devil] Who Was Put Inside a *Tecomate*."

These tales also provide an explanation for the origin and creation of the world and the plants and animals that populate it, including coyotes and rodents that once were people. In earlier times, tools worked by themselves in a Garden of Eden before woman and man, enticed by talking animals, partook of the forbidden fruit. God communicated with man and woman in dreams to teach them how to procreate. The first people were sinful and mistreated their tools; kettles, for example, were misused by burning their bottoms day and night over the *tenamastes* [three cooking stones]. The kettles in turn pleaded with the God of gods to make justice for being abused by humans.

These folktales reinforce cultural values and beliefs such as honesty, lest misfortune befall a person like the poor campesino in "The Hill of Chua Kapoj," who lost his daughter to the *dueño* of the hill for failing to keep his promise not to reveal the source of his daughter's magical dance costume. Misfortune also may befall a liar like the impersonator who pretended to be the young lad who killed the jaguar with his sling in "The Three Hombres Who Went to Look for Pacayas." Generally, however, instead of killing animals, people should be kind to them since they may either help a person, as they helped the man in the story "The Man Who Changed into a God," or trick a person, as they tricked the spiteful woman into cooking and eating her baby, as in the "Story of Sebastiana."

Industriousness is a virtue. Out of laziness a person could turn into a buzzard man, as in the tale "The Story of Mariano the Buzzard," or find fortune turn against him, as in the "Story of the Lazybones and the Perfect Intendant," in which indolent Baltazar, attempting to free a mule from the mud by pulling on his tail, instead pulls it off and gets a kick in the pants for his efforts. On the other hand, hard work will be rewarded with riches of the fruits of life. But a person should not be arrogant, pretentious, or exorbitant, lest he or she be deceived into marrying the devil as was the woman who wanted a special man and so married one with gold teeth; nor should one abuse power, for fear that God will take it away from the person wielding it.

Sharing is a virtue, especially the sharing of food with a pregnant woman so that she will not abort from craving. Envy, however, may bring problems, as in the case of the poor *compadre* who contrived to learn the *secreto* of his rich hunting companion in "The Story of the Hunter *Compadre*."

In the case of the "Tale of Two *Compadres*," we learn that fairness also is a virtue as well as justification for the old saying—what goes around comes around. The rich *compadre* always wanted to trick his poorer friend into being poor, and there is poetic justice in the rich *compadre's* suffering the same financial fate as he had intended for his poor *compadre* in advising the latter to try to sell the penis and testicles of his bull to the president of a foreign nation.

Cleverness can overcome great odds, as exemplified in the case of the rabbit who constantly tricks the coyote ("The Story of the Rabbit and His Uncle Coyote"). But a person should not be too clever since he may be able to trick others but not God, who punished the slyness of the rabbit by pulling his ears to make them long and by condemning him to hop on his butt forever.

Farming communities are by necessity in close touch with both wild and domesticated plants and animals in their surroundings. These tales also reveal much about the natural habitat of the Maya, especially with respect to the terrain and animals in it. In the Lake Atitlán region, when corn and beans run low, families often supplement their meals with wild greens such as *chipilín*. Likewise, when meat from domesticated animals is not available, men may hunt wild animals to put protein on their tables, although today most of the large game has disappeared from overhunting. In "The Story of the Hunter *Compadre*" a man turns himself into a jaguar to hunt deer, into a coyote to hunt spotted cavy (short-tailed, rough-haired South American rodents), and into a dog to hunt small animals like rabbits, raccoons, armadillos, and opossums. The belief that some people have the ability to turn into animals also is reflected in "The Story of the Red *Brujo* [Witch] of the Hill," in which flying *naguales* turn into owls, hawks, eagles, while other (nonflying) *naguales* convert into mountain lions, jaguars, dogs, and wild pigs.

In addition to these indigenous animals, we also find an array of other native creatures including: wild turkeys, monkeys, snakes, scorpions, rats, buzzards, pacas, wildcats, coati (a tropical American mammal related to the raccoon but with a longer body and tail and a long flexible snout), wolves, rabbits, *zompopos* [macrocephalic ants], birds, parrots, fish, sharks, crabs, *tepezucintle* [wild animal the size of a pup that looks like a wild dog], crickets, bees, and mice (who have their own shamans and fiestas with marimbas and who like men but detest women). Of these New World animals, only three were truly domesticated before contact: the dog, one variety of which was the short-legged, hairless edible type; the turkey; and the tiny, stingless bee, kept for honey and wax. In these folktales we also encounter truly domesticated animals introduced by the Spaniards: horses, donkeys, hogs, goats, bulls, and chickens (West and Augelli 1976).

In addition to wild greens and several varieties of indigenous corn and beans that the Indians eat as staples, we find in these stories other native plants that the Indians consume such as squash, avocados, pumpkins, chili, cacao, *pataxte* [or *pat ashte*, white chocolate]; *güisquiles* [a climbing plant whose gourd-like fruit is the size of an orange], *injertos* [soft brilliant green fruit], *güicoy* [medium-sized edible gourd], pineapples, yucca, sweet potatoes (South American origin), cucumbers, *jocotes* [yellow, plumblike fruit], and *pacayas* [palm fruit whose flowers also are edible]. In these folk stories we even learn of *chilacayotes* [large gourds fed to livestock] and of nonedible indigenous plants such as *petate* of *tule*, used to make mats. In addition to indigenous plants used by the Maya Indians, in these tales appear plants that were introduced by the Spaniards: bananas, plantains, watermelons, cauliflower, lettuce, onions, coriander, mangoes, apples, pears, and grapes. Wheat, which the Spaniards introduced and forced the Indians to grow because they thought corn was unhealthy, does not appear in these folktales. The Indians rejected wheat and preferred corn, which when eaten with beans and squash, provided better nutrition.

Not only are there real plants and animals, we also find imaginary or supernatural creatures, entities such as giants and dragons, and a magical golden ring. In the tale "The Story of the *Poder* [Power, Ability] of Persons When They Are Born," angels born in the flesh perform powerful acts such as rainmaking but keep their purity by abstinence from sex, alcohol, and tobacco. In the "Story of the Enchanted Hill, Tun Abaj" the *dueño* of the hill offers riches, but at the price of a never-ending, hellish cycling of one's soul in the form of a pig, which he eats.

Finally, an analysis of these tales reveals why they are often enjoyed in their own right as simple entertainment not only because of what they teach but also because of their humor. In a Tzutuhil version of the popular old tale the "Story of Don Chebo," the hero, a wealthy man, is always doing something comical such as trying to make a twenty-horsepower car by having carpenters build a big boxcar and putting twenty horses inside and trying to wire his son money by hanging it on a telegraph line. In "The Story of the Rabbit and His Uncle Coyote," the gullible coyote is constantly being duped by the mischievous rabbit. Even though the coyote is tarred and bruised, he stubbornly keeps coming back for more. An unfaithful wife in "The Woman and the Guardian" deceives her dense husband by dressing her lover like her mother and throwing the covers over him. When the suspicious husband throws back the covers, he believes he sees his mother-in-law and thanks her for coming to sleep with his wife while he's away working.

In addition to more subtle amusement, we discover earthy humor. In the "Story of Chema Tamales," Chema always makes money by betting and deceiving people. In one episode, he persuades a priest to give him money for a bird that he says is under his sombrero. When the priest sticks his hand under the sombrero to grab the bird, he grabs a handful of fresh human dung instead. In "The Story of the Man [Devil] Who Was Put Inside a *Tecomate* [Gourd]," the curer, in a pact with the devil, cures the king's butt ache by pouring water up his anus.

The risqué stories, collectively called *colorado* [obscene] tales, may be told only to adults. For example, in "The Two Lazy Men," two male drifters find a kind woman who gives them shelter and food for their work. But one of the vagabonds in the dark of night loses his way in the house and stuffs rice in milk in her butt, exclaiming to his friend how he has changed—now with a fat face and differently shaped mouth.

Lastly, priests who are supposed to uphold canon law but too often exhibit behavior less than angelic are the butt of many folktales. In "The Padre Pícaro," a lustful Spanish priest, who likes pretty, young, indigenous women, is tricked into mounting a bull all night instead of the young married lass he covets. In another story ridiculing priests, a priest living in an indigenous town desires *la riqueza* [the wealth, or sex] of a beautiful parishioner, but he is tricked into trying to seduce the woman's husband, who is dressed like a woman and who conceals a whip. Because of his lust, the roguish priest gets pain instead of pleasure.

FOLKTALES
AND
DANCE DRAMAS

The Hill of Chua Kapoj

This hill is located in the southeast-
ern part of our town. Chua Kapoj, or
Xe Kapoj, it is called in the Tzutuhil language. It is not known exactly in what year it
happened, but they say it is true because almost
all the people know and tell this story, which they
have learned from their ancestors.

In the past, two or three centuries ago, there was the
obligation of each *Joseño* inhabitant to participate in the dances
of the deer, *lebal* [Tzutuhil name of a dance],[4] monkeys, the
conquest, and the Moors. They say that the *alcalde*, or mayor,
made the dances obligatory, that each citizen had to be a
dancer, and that in each fiesta of the town the dances were
presented.[5]

The day for rehearsal was Easter Saturday, a day after
Good Friday. The mayor ordered that each family provide a
dancer for the dance of the conquest. The inhabitants said yes.
All were obliged because there were few townspeople. Even
the poorest families had to provide a dancer.

In this kind of dance there were two boys and two girls of
fifteen years of age who represented the great Quiché king.
Well, they looked for the four young people, but one of the
poorest parents didn't want his daughter to dance. Since it was
mandatory, however, he had to say yes so that he would not
spend time in jail.

The father counted each rehearsal with more pain because he didn't have money to rent the *traje* [suit] for the

dance. They say that this man was the poorest of the *Joseños*. His work was to fetch water for the people and to chop wood, but only once in a while did he sell some *reales* [money] worth of firewood. With these jobs he only earned money for food for his wife and child, but never was this man able to save any *reales*. He planned to save for the renting of the suit for his daughter, but he never was able.

Each day the fiesta drew closer. Half the month of June passed, and everyone went to Totonicapán and Santa Cruz del Quiché to rent a suit for the dance, and everyone traveled according to his means. The only one who didn't go was the father of the girl because he couldn't obtain the money.

When the rest of the dancers returned, they exploded *bombas* [fireworks shot from mortars] in the place called Chua Cruz, a place very respected by the Tzutuhiles, which in those times, they still took care of as a sacred place. When the father of the girl heard the sound of the *bombas*, he began to cry bitterly and cursed life. Each day he grew weaker from sadness, but he could do nothing to get money. The day before the beginning of the dance the father decided to flee the town so that he would not have to spend the fiesta in jail. In the early morning he made a *costumbre* [ritual] asking the *dios del mundo* [god of the world, or earth] to help them because it was certain that they found themselves in a precarious situation.

After doing the *costumbre*, the man said good-bye to his woman and daughter, who before he left gave him a few tortillas and salt for his food. He left his house very early so that no one would see him fleeing from the great imprisonment that awaited him. He left his house crying, and when he arrived in the place called Chua Cruz, he began to cry again, feeling shame and a lot of worry because he had left his woman and daughter who would suffer the drastic action of the *alcalde*.

After crying in Chua Cruz, he continued until he reached Cerro Cristalín, and there he began to cry again, despising himself for having been born so disgraceful, cursing his parents because they had been born so unfortunate and poor. When he quit crying, he began to eat a tortilla with salt. This he was doing when suddenly a young boy about twenty years of age arrived. He said: "Where are you going and what are you looking for? Do you feel a little sad?"

The man said: "I don't know where I'm going. I don't have any address. I'm fleeing from my house." The man told him all his feelings and about his poverty.

"Why are you sad? Don't you know that the fiesta of your town is very soon and you can return," the boy told him.

The man answered the young muchacho, "I am feeling sad, really sad. I have left my wife and my daughter. I'm feeling sad, and my wife and daughter will spend the fiesta in jail. I don't have money, I'm very poor. My work is to carry water to the people, to split firewood, and to sell some *reales* worth of firewood, and with this I earn the food for my wife and daughter. The mayor obliged my daughter to dance in the fiesta, and pity that when everyone went to get his *traje*, I didn't go because I didn't have money to rent the suit. Tomorrow begins the dance, and my daughter cannot dance. I'm sure that my daughter and wife will be put in jail because the *alcalde* is very wicked."

Then the young boy told him: "Don't cry anymore. It is I, the King and Lord of the Hills. Mine is all the gold and silver. I am powerful over everything, the visible and invisible. I have a lot of costumes for dancing. I'm the owner of all the invisible department stores. Mine are all the animals of the earth: the lions, jaguars, monkeys, and deer. I have a lot of game inside the hill. The pacas and the armadillos serve me as chairs and benches when I want to sit down. When an animal commits a fault, or when they do not respect me, my *latigos* [whips] are the snakes, hitting them. My policemen are the wolves, my *alguaciles* [runners] are the coyotes. When chickens do something wrong, they are for eating. I just order the coyotes to go to the town to steal and bring a number of chickens from the people. I have a lot of helpers to take care of the animals when I go on visits. Poor man, don't be sad. I'll give you what you need, but first I will warn you. Don't tell anyone about these things that you are seeing and hearing because if you do, you will suffer and die."

Only this the man heard. In a blink of an eye he was in an incomparable place, seeing much wealth in a spacious place but a place where one couldn't see the sun or the moon. One couldn't see the illumination, but it wasn't dark. The owner opened many doors, and they arrived where there were suits for the dance of the conquest. He said, "Look for a *traje* for your daughter to wear so that she can dance." The *trajes* began to talk and offered themselves as the finest *trajes*.

But a man very different from the *dueño* [owner] spoke with the poor man. "Señor, if you take a *traje*, you must look for an older suit because if you take a new suit your daughter will die and come to this hill." Obeying, the poor man began to look for an old suit.

The *dueño* of the hill, however, told the poor man he could take a new suit but to take care not to tell anyone. "If you tell anyone, your daughter will come here for sure. These things only you and I will know."

This is the way it was when the poor man entered inside and then left the hill. In a blink of an eye the father of the girl returned to the place where he was when he met the *dueño* of the hill.

It seemed that the man had been there only an hour, but he had been there a day and a night. He went back very happy because he had a suit.

When he arrived home, the dance had already started. His wife was in jail and his daughter was hiding because of the shame that she had not been able to go to dance.

The man ran to the house of the *alcalde* to ask for the liberty of his wife. His daughter was ready to dance, and the mayor set his wife free. Thus they arrived at two in the afternoon and visited their daughter. The wife admired the *traje* because it was incomparable.

Then the girl went to dance, but when she arrived to dance, the people admired her and inquired where she had obtained the money to rent a new suit, among other things. The suits of the other dancers were put to shame, and the same dancers weren't able to dance as the daughter of the poor man danced. The most unique dancer with the most unique *traje* was the poor man's daughter. On the main day of the fiesta of San Juan, 24 June, all the dancers were dancing in the atrium of the church. Then the parents of the dancers began to drink a lot of *chicha* [corn liquor] with the mayor.

Then there was a procession with the young girl in front. When they were in the middle of the procession, suddenly a very strong wind came and nearly carried away the young girl. The people were very scared. Suddenly another wind blew even stronger and picked the girl up some meters into the air, but she fell on the ground where the other dancers were. The people were frightened because these things were happening.

When they finished the procession and drank more *chicha*, because the dance was very pleasant, a man asked the father of the girl, "Amigo, when you were having difficulties and went to get your daughter's *traje*, you got the most unique one of all! It's the most beautiful and newest! Before we left at the same time to get our suits, you told me that you didn't have any money, but you brought back the most beautiful suit of all, which makes ours look bad. You brought back the best suit of the fiesta!"

Under the glow of *chicha*, the father of the youngster confessed that he didn't have any money and that it was a gift of the *dueño* of the hill of Qui'talin. "I wasn't able to pay for the renting of this *traje*, and he only lent it to me for the fiesta. Afterward I'm going to return it to the *dueño* of the hill. He told me not to tell anyone, but because I'm a little drunk, I'm telling you, my friend."

At this moment the youngster was dancing, and another strong wind came in the form of a hurricane, lifted her up, and turned her around many times above the church. The young girl was visible in the air, but the people were unable to do anything for her. The girl was in the air and the people were running behind after her, but they could do nothing to help her. They clearly saw the wind take her away in the sky to the hill. And from then on they called it Chua Kapoj, which is to say, the dwelling of the youngster.

When these things happened, the whole town was indignant and frightened because of all that had happened. At that moment they suspended the dance, and everyone was sad. And the father was repentant for having told his amigo.

Thus the young girl now lives in the hill, and her parents from pure grief died within twenty days. They were wrapped in palm mats because they were poor, and the two were put in the same tomb.

—Ignacio Bizarro Ujpán

The Story of
the Red *Brujo* [Witch] of the Hill

This is the story of the red witch of
the Quichés. When the king,[6] Tecún
Umán, died, his allies and Indian chiefs dis-
persed as did the fortune-tellers and *brujos*
[witches] of King Tecún. They saw that there
was nothing they could do to save his life. Each
one fled to the hills. In the hill Chua Cristalín there
came to live a red *brujo* who in Tzutuhil is called Ajitz Co'xol.

When Ajitz Co'xol lived in the hill, San José la Laguna
had a lot of wealth. Walking on foot in this hill, one found
many stones, and when a person picked up a stone, he found a
lot of gold. The Tzutuhiles of this town didn't know what
poverty was.

The witch lived then in the hill. But as he was Quiché, he
didn't take care of the Tzutuhiles well. This man had a red face
like a devil. The *brujo* ended up in a place called Paquixquil
and began to mistreat the Tzutuhiles. The *brujo* said that the
Tzutuhiles were not men. They just ate dead fish and dead
crabs. Each night he bothered them with the same maltreat-
ment, and finally the Tzutuhiles got mad at hearing the gibes
of Ajitz night after night. The *characoteles*,[7] [other] *brujos*, and
naguales [animal forms of persons, spirits] met in the middle of
the night and prepared to capture him in accordance with their
type of *nagual*, and they waited for the taunts of the Ajitz. The
flying *naguales* turned into owls, hawks, eagles, and the others,

while the other [nonflying] *naguales* converted into lions, jaguars, pigs, dogs, and goats. Each group was assigned its work, and the quadrupedal *naguales* waited in the place called Panatzam where there was a big stone weighing about four or five tons. Meanwhile the winged *naguales* got up off the ground, according to their species.

One night when Ajitz was being abusive, the hawks, owls, and the eagles arose into the air, went to capture him, and carried him in the direction of the stone where they let him fall where the four-legged *naguales* were waiting. The quadrupeds wounded him, but the *brujo* was a very strong man, and they were unable to kill him. Again, he went to the hill.

This happened many times, but they weren't able to kill the *brujo*. Finally because of all the blows and wounds Ajitz received, one night he repented, but he cursed the people of San José with poverty by appealing to the *dueño* of the hill. This is why San José is poor. Ajitz took all the wealth to Santa Clara and that is why they are rich and San José is poor.

—Ignacio Bizarro Ujpán

The Story of
the Daughter of a King
Who Was Carried Away
by a Poor Person

This story is more than 100 years old, and it was told by the grandparents and parents of Don Miguel Gonzáles Mendoza. That is to say, this story was told by the already deceased Flavio Gonzáles, Miguel's father.[8]

They say that there had been a daughter of a king, the only one who was pretty among all the other daughters of the king and all the other women of the pueblo. She wanted to marry a poor person. But her father told her she had to marry a man who was well-off. But the girl was more inclined to join the poorest man in the town. Finally, the girl left with her groom without advising her parents.

Then the man and woman went looking for work, passing through many towns. Finally, they arrived in a town and obtained a house. The man looked for work with the people, and the girl prepared the meals at home, but at times the woman was regretful about the poor life they were suffering because in the house of the king, nothing had been lacking.

One day the man said to his woman, "I'm going to go to the mountain."

His wife said, "Go to the mountain, but be very careful. Don't worry about our poverty."

The man went to the mountain, a little happy and a little sad, because he could be persecuted by the father of the woman. He was walking to the mountain when he saw a house and approached it, but the house was locked and no one lived there. Then the man walked a little more ahead when he saw a beautiful plantation of plantains, pineapples, yucca, watermelons, and oranges. Since the man saw that there was no owner, he began to pick the plantains and the other fruit. He carried a load home. When he arrived home, his wife forgot about their poverty, seeing that the fruit was the best.

On the third day the man went again to the mountain to bring more fruit, and all went well. When he arrived home, the woman was very happy and said, "We're going to sell this fruit, and with this we will make our living." Then the woman went to the houses selling plantains, pineapples, yucca, and watermelons.

In three days the man went again to get the same thing. Then the woman said to her husband, "I want to know the mountain where you get all the fruit. I also want to carry a little."

"With much pleasure. I will take you to the mountain where there is a lot of fruit that is not owned by anyone. It is true that there is a house but no owner lives in it.

"Well, let's go."

The two left for the mountain, and when they arrived they picked the most beautiful plantains and pineapples and filled their sacks. They were ready to load them when suddenly a black-colored man[9] came out of the house and said, "Today is when I find you! You are the thieves who have always been coming to pick my fruit!"

The man said, "Forgive me and my wife. We will not come back."

The Negro answered, "I'm going to pardon you. I'm not going to kill anyone. You can return, and you can take the fruit that you have picked. The one who's not going to return is the woman. She is going to stay with me. I'm alone here, and I need a woman."

The woman was locked in the house of the Negro. The poor man returned very sad and distressed, and he did not bring his plantains. When he arrived home, he began to cry in front of the people, saying that his woman was taken by a Negro, owner of the plantation. The people lamented what had happened.

The man cried day and night for his woman. He was unable to eat or work, much less sleep. The people of the town told him to go to the mountain again to see if he could get his wife, but the man didn't return because he saw that the Negro was stronger.

They say that in these much earlier times, the animals such as the jaguar, the lion, the coyote, the monkey, and other animals spoke to men. They met with the man who had lost his woman. The man told the lion, "Look, Brother Lion, you are the strongest. You can fight with the Negro and free my wife." The man said this crying.

The lion understood the suffering of the man. He said, "Poor fellow, you cry for a woman. I am seeing your weaknesses. Well, I'm going to fight so that the man will set your wife free. Come and show me the house." Then the two of them left.

The lion told the man, "Now, I see the house. Stay here."

The lion went to knock on the door, and then the Negro came out. "What do you want?"

The lion answered, "I want you to give me the woman of the poor man."

The Negro didn't talk much. He grabbed his shotgun, and he shot the lion in the face. The poor lion returned with his face bloodied and told the man, "I can't do anything for you. The man is very strong, and there is nothing we can do. Look at me, how my face is!"

The lion told the man, "I'm going to give you some advice. Go deeper into the mountain and look for the jaguar. He is stronger than I."

The man went to the mountain, saying, "Brother Jaguar, I'm looking for you. I want a miracle from you."

The jaguar appeared and said, "What do you want, you puny man? Now you see that you need me a lot."

The man said, "You are my big brother. I need you to do me a favor. I went to get fruit without knowing the plantation belonged to a Negro, and when we went there for the fourth time, the Negro kept my wife. I would like you to go to ask the Negro who has my woman."

"Weak man, it doesn't take much effort for me to fight with a little Negro."

The jaguar went to the house of the Negro and knocked at the door. Then the man opened the door and said, "What do you want?"

"I want you to give me the woman of the man."

"Go away. I don't want to talk anymore."

"Give me the woman for good or worse!"

When the Negro heard that the jaguar was very ferocious, he grabbed his shotgun and shot him twice in the face. The poor jaguar returned and told the man, "I wasn't able to do anything for your woman. The man is very astute. Look at my face. He wounded me with bullets."

The jaguar went to the mountain and the poor man remained crying. Later he went to look for the monkey, but the monkey told him, "I don't want to have problems with you men."

Then he talked with a snake, and he told him of his situation. The snake told him, "Why are you men very much enemies of the snakes? We never live in peace with you. Now you see that you need me a lot. Well, I indeed can take your woman out of the hands of the Negro. Wait for me, and you will see."

The snake entered into the house of the Negro and put his tail in the nose of the Negro, thinking he would die if he could not breathe. But the Negro woke up and the snake left running. The Negro nearly killed him with a machete. When he reached the man he said, "I can't do anything. The situation is very precarious. I'm going to give you a better idea. You can talk to the rabbit because he is a good defender[10] and can do a lot for you. But you need to look for him at once."

"Yes," said the man, and he went looking in the plains, always crying for his woman. When he met the rabbit, he said, "Señor Rabbit, *buenos días*."

The rabbit answered, "*Buenos días*."

Then the man crying told the rabbit of his situation.

The rabbit said, "Now you call me 'señor' and even say 'Good morning.' It's because you want something from me. But I know man as being cowardly and violent because when we rabbits eat some leaves of your bean plants, you then run to kill us. Now I know your weakness. I'm going to do you a favor, but to earn the freedom of your woman, you will have to work a lot. But the work we are going to do in the night so that the Negro will not know what we are doing."

The rabbit said, "We're going to use science. We are going to get your wife out as soon as possible. We're going to dig a hole below the ground, not deep and in the form of a tunnel. When it's ready, we are going to make twelve entrances and exits, and at each exit we are going to leave orange branches that have a lot of spines."

The man did everything that his defender said. He prepared the passage with twelve entrances. Then he told the rabbit, "Señor Rabbit, everything is ready."

"Let's go," said the rabbit. When he arrived at the door, he called the Negro. The Negro came out furious and said, "What do you want?"

"I want you to give me the woman of the poor man."

The Negro ran behind the rabbit with a machete, and the rabbit ran into one of the entrances to the hole, and the Negro saw where the rabbit had entered. But the rabbit was quite clever, and he came out of another hole and grabbed an orange branch to hit the Negro. When the Negro turned around to see, the rabbit ran into another hole and came out of another. It was a hard fight. The Negro got tired and ran behind the rabbit, but the rabbit just went back into the same place. He just entered one exit and came out another until finally the Negro fell on the ground from the great aches that he had received from the orange branches.

When the Negro fell down, he told the rabbit, "No more blows, now. Kill me once and for all. My body aches. Take my keys and get my shotgun and kill me once and for all."

Then the rabbit went to fetch the shotgun, and he killed the Negro with one shot. Only then was he able to free the woman, who had been chained in the house. Then the rabbit gave the woman to her husband, and for that reason, they called him *"el abogado,"* the defender.

—Miguel Gonzáles Mendoza,
Recorded by Ignacio Bizarro Ujpán

The Man Who
Changed into a God

This is an old story that was told by
the grandparents and parents of Don
Miguel Gonzáles Mendoza. That is to say,
this story was told by the already deceased
Flavio Gonzáles, Miguel's father.[11]

They say that in a pueblo lived a man, but he
was not happy in his town. So he said, "I'm going to
leave my town to find my fortune." He sold his home and *sitio*
[homesite], grabbed his suitcase, and left.

When he passed some men, he asked them, "What are
you doing?"

They answered, "We're killing some ants."

The man said, "Have some compassion for them. Don't
kill them. I'll pay you for them."

"Yes," they said, and they took the money and now they
did not kill the ants.

He arrived at another place, and asked some men what
they were doing.

They answered, "We're digging around for some *zompos*
[short for *zompopos*, or macrocephalic ants] to burn them because they are finishing off the milpa."

"Please don't burn them," said the man, "They are children of God. I'll pay for the milpa."

"Yes," said the men. They took the money, and now they
did not burn the *zompopos*.

When he came to another place, all the animals were in crises — they were hungry and thirsty and being persecuted. The man asked them what was happening to them. The animals answered, "Señor, we're going to die. We don't have food, and when we want to steal some ears of corn, pumpkins, watermelons, and other things, the people kill us. We are very thirsty and when we approach the river, the people have a certain hostility toward us. They don't want us to drink water of the river; they kill us."

"I'm going to do something for you," said the man. Then he went to the town to buy two baskets of ears of corn, *güisquiles*, pumpkins, cucumbers, all that is food for the animals.

The man had to pay a *mozo* [helper] to carry two large vats of water to quench the thirst of the animals. When he arrived where the animals were he said, "Eat and drink until you are full."

"Yes," said the animals, very happily. And they ate until they were full. When they finished eating, the baskets were still full of food and the vats full of water [as if by some strange power], and the man told them to save it for tomorrow, and they could eat more.

The man continued on his way, and ahead he met a group of hunters who had a deer to kill. The man said, "Please don't kill him. Set him free. I'll leave you money so that you can buy meat." And the hunters released the deer.

A little more ahead, the man met a señor with blond hair who said, "My son, where are you going?"

He told the señor, "I'm going in search of my fortune."

The señor with the blond hair gave him a golden ring. "This is a ring of gold. It'll help you and save you from death."

On the road, the man with the golden ring met another friend, and the two came to a town where they asked for work in the palace of the king. Thus they worked, one just as much as the other. But the king took a preference for one of the *mozos,* whom he wanted for a son-in-law. His daughter, however, loved the other one more. Thus, there was a certain problem. Finally, the woman married the man who had the golden ring. But the other *mozo* despised him.

The contemptuous one looked for a lie. He told the king, "Your Majesty, King and Lord of this town, I don't want your son-in-law to ridicule you. Your kingdom is great. Your son-in-law is going around saying that he can build a house in one night, much better than your palace."

The king became very angry and he sent to call his son-in-law. And he said, "It's being observed that you are going around criticizing and saying that in one night you can build a house better than my palace. If by morning you have not built the house, you will be beheaded and burned."

He left sad and went to his wife and told her what his father-in-law, the king, had ordered. Then he remembered that he had a golden ring. He took it out and talked to the ring. It told the man, "Tonight you and your wife are going to sleep. Don't worry, you and your wife will sleep. If you hear some noise, don't leave. I am your *suerte* [luck, fortune, destiny, fate]. The king is not going to kill you. I'm going to call all the animals that you earlier helped. They are going to save you from death."

The golden ring talked to the animals, large and small, even the insects, so that in just one night they finished constructing the house. The animals began the construction, some carrying adobe, others wood, others water, yet others were masons. And in one night they finished building the house. And it was better than the palace of the king.

When the king got up in the morning, he saw the house and now he did not behead his son-in-law because he had fulfilled the order of the king.

Again the scornful one went before the king with another false accusation against his son-in-law. The man said, "Great

King, your throne and your crown is belittled by your son-in-law. King, your son-in-law is going around saying that he is more powerful than you. He claims he can plant milpa in the morning and in the afternoon he can harvest it."

The king was very angry. He sent for his son-in-law and said, "You're making fun of me, going around saying that you can plant milpa in the morning and harvest it by the afternoon. If by tomorrow you don't bring the harvest, you will be hung upside down."

The man told his woman. "My dear husband," said his wife, "I have certain *secretos* [magical or sacred rites]. Tomorrow I will give you one. Let's sleep, don't think about death."

The next day, the man got up very sad. The woman told him, "Go to plant corn on a piece of land this morning. For the *secreto*, carry some locks of my hair, and when you arrive at the land, put a little of my hair locks on each corner where you are going to plant the little corn. Then sink a hatchet in a piece of timber and then look for some shade and sleep peacefully."

The man planted a little maize, put the pieces of hair in the corners, sunk the hatchet into a large log locking it in the wood, and looked for some shade to sleep. He did everything that the woman told him to do.

He slept a lot. When he got up from his sleep, he saw all around a great plantation of milpa. He began to pick the ears of corn, and he carried them to the king to show him that he could plant and harvest in one day. The king congratulated his son-in-law.

Then another enemy went to the king to make another false declaration. He said, "King and Lord, your kingdom is very respected by all of us. But your son-in-law is lacking respect for Your Majesty by saying that if he wants, tomorrow he and his wife can give birth to a baby, and they will give him your name. How can a person have a son in one night?"

The king was madder than before and sent for his daughter and son-in-law. He said, "You damned son-in-law, you're going around saying that tomorrow you are going to have a son and give it my name. You have scarcely been married a week, and you think you are going to have a son. If tomorrow your son is not born, you will be burned in front of the whole town so that you won't claim you are greater than I."

The son-in-law left very sad with his woman, and he told her, "Your father doesn't like me. Tomorrow he's going to burn me in front of the people."

His wife replied, "Don't be sad, I'll give you a *secreto*. It's easy. My father won't be able to do anything. The *secreto* is for you to go right now to the shore of the ocean and wait until a big wave comes and leaves a fish, catch it, and come running."

The man was on the shore of the ocean when a big wave left a fish, and the man ran to catch it. He returned running to the house and told his wife, "Here's the fish."

When they went to sleep, they placed the fish between them. When midnight came, the fish turned into a beautiful baby and began to cry. When the husband woke up, the woman was already giving her breast to the baby. The man thanked God.

Then he went to wake the king so that he could come see the baby. The king did not believe it, but he got up to see whether it was true. When the king received the baby, it already had its teeth and was smiling a lot. The king admired these things. He said, "It's certain that you have been saved from death. The child is going to have my name." Thus it was when the man was spared from death because his wife had *secretos*.

The woman told the man, "Many are your enemies who are accusing you falsely before my father. They are envious because I didn't want to marry them. It's better that we go to the coast to look for another life before my father kills you."

The daughter of the king and her husband left during the night. When dawn broke, the wife of the king went to see her daughter, but now she was not there. Then she began to cry and mistreat her husband, the king, for everything he had done to them.

They say that when the couple passed through the towns, no one would give them shelter because they knew she was the daughter of the king. Finally, they arrived at a town that was on the shore of the ocean. There they gave them shelter because it was said that in this town there was a big problem that no one had been able to solve. From the ocean came a dragon[12] to eat the people. He devoured both the small and the big. Then the *jefes* [chiefs] of the town ordered that each family give a boy or girl to leave on the sand, and when the dragon came out of the ocean, he ate them. Another day, another child. Thus it happened that each family took its turn feeding the dragon.

In the house where a family gave shelter to the king's daughter and her husband, it was this family's turn to provide a child for the food of the dragon. The parents began to cry because it was the hour when they were to put their son on the sand. But they cried a lot because it was their last son. All their other children had been eaten by the dragon. The man told the parents of the boy, "You're not going to put your son on the sand. Today I'm going to the shore of the ocean to see what we can do."

"But, señor, then the people of the pueblo will kill us because the dragon is going to enter the town if his food is not on the sand."

"My wife and I have *secretos*. There's nothing to worry about."

But the parents were very worried.

"I'm going to the beach to kill the dragon," the man told his wife.

On the road he met two little dogs, and he told them, "Little dogs, we're going to work hard, but afterward you are going to eat better."

The little dogs replied, "Señor, we are going to work as you command."

When they arrived at the beach, the man told the dogs, "You're going to be put on the sand so that you will be swallowed by the dragon, but you are not going to die. When you feel that you are in the belly of the animal, you are going to destroy the guts, liver, and everything that is the intestine of this animal."

The dogs said, "We're going to obey you, but we'll give you the signal—you'll see the water tinged with blood. And if there isn't this sign, then we are already dead."

The little dogs were on the beach awhile, and then came the dragon. He saw that there was no child placed on the sand. From hunger he swallowed the two little dogs. When the dogs reached the stomach of the animal, they began to destroy the liver, the guts, and everything in the intestine of the animal. The man saw that the water was tinted with blood, and he was assured that the dogs had been able to work well. In an hour the dragon came out of the water and onto the beach and threw up the dogs, and in this same place he died. Thus the people were liberated.

The man returned to the town to tell the parents of the child that there would be no more children for the dragon. "Now he's dead."

The parents of this child were filled with happiness and went to advise the *jefe* of the town. The *jefe* sent soldiers to see if the animal was dead. The soldiers returned to say that it was true that they found the dragon dead on the beach.

Then the *jefe* called together the whole town to tell them that in the town a god had arrived who had freed them of the dragon. The people brought candles, incense, and copal to worship this man. All the people said that the man was a god. He and his wife didn't go to work. They gave a good house and good food to him and his wife every day, as well as to the dogs, because they and the dogs had liberated this town.

The Story of the Rabbit
and His Uncle Coyote:
A Tzutuhil Story

They say that because he is small, the rabbit calls the coyote uncle, and that he is the *compadre* of the buzzard.

In a church, a priest said mass everyday, but not many people came. Also, food was very scarce. He just ate avocados every day. Thus, the father prepared a garden where he planted a good selection of vegetables—lettuce, cucumbers, pumpkins, watermelons, cauliflower, and others. The father blessed his garden and left for the convent.

In eight days he went to look at the garden. The cultivation had all come up. He blessed it again and went to mass, asking God to give him a harvest later on, because he needed to eat a little better.

First the cucumbers began to give fruit. But also, the rabbit needed to eat the cucumbers, and when he realized that there had been a garden planted, he seized the cucumbers. When they were half ripe, he said, "I'm going to eat my cucumbers." And he ate them all up. The father had not realized what had happened in his garden. He thought that the cucumbers were good and ready to eat.

When he arrived there wasn't a single cucumber. The father said, "My goodness, who came to steal them?" He said,

"I'm going to have patience. I have hope for the watermelons." And he returned again to his convent.

But the rabbit saw that the melons were ready to eat. He began to eat watermelons until he finished them off.

When the father arrived to get watermelons, there weren't any. The father knelt down on his knees saying, "My goodness. All of my fruit perished. Who could the thief be? Well, I'm going to have patience with the pumpkins." And he went back again to his convent.

But the rabbit realized after he had finished off the watermelons that there were pumpkins, and he said, "My goodness, I have *suerte* [luck]. I've everything to eat without suffering much. There are some who plant, work very hard, and even kneel down praying to God, but they never have the luck as I."

One morning, the padre very happily went to the garden to get his pumpkins, but when he arrived there was not a single pumpkin. "Who's the devil who's betraying me? I'm unable to eat a little better. All the fruit has been stolen. But I'm going to have patience. My hope is that I will still have my lettuce and cauliflower. And so that a thief will not enter, I'm going to put a guardian in the entrance."

Then the reverend made a dummy of black wax in the form of a little boy, and he put it in the entrance. He told the dummy, "You're going to guard here to see who the thief is." The father blew on the face of the dummy as a *secreto* and blessed him.

A little later the rabbit wanted to enter, but he had problems because in the entrance was a dummy of wax. And he said, "Negro, get out of my way." But he never spoke. The rabbit was angry, and he said, "Now, I'm going to hit you." And then the rabbit hit him with his left paw, but his paw stuck to the wax. He said, "Let go of my paw!" But the wax did not respond.

The rabbit said, "If I hit you with my right paw, I'm

going to kill you." When he hit it with his right paw, his other paw became stuck in the wax [because when wax is warm it's sticky]. The rabbit became more angry and said to the little Negro, "You want to equalize your force with me. I still have two paws. If I hit you with my other paw, little Negro, you are going to die." But the little Negro did not answer.

The rabbit hit the Negro with his other paw, and the same thing happened to it—the paw got stuck in the wax.

The rabbit said, "You have grabbed three of my paws, and if you don't release me, I'll kill you. I still have free my strongest paw."

And he hit him with his other paw, and the same thing happened—his four paws were now entangled. He said, "Little Negro, you have seized my four paws, but with my head, I'm going to kill you." The wax didn't answer.

The rabbit said, "This time there's really no forgiveness. I'm going to kill you." And he hit him with his head. The same thing happened. The rabbit remained completely entangled in the wax.

Then the priest in the morning thought about going to see the dummy. When he arrived at the vegetable garden, he found the rabbit stuck in the wax dummy. The father ran to advise the sacristan. The two carried a chain and tied up the rabbit with it. The padre said, "Damned rabbit. Because of you I'm suffering a lot. You have done me a lot of damage. You have left my garden without any fruit. Your sentence is that we are going to pour boiling water on you and put a hot *asador* [roasting rod, spit] up your anus. You're going to die tortured."

The father obliged the sacristan to boil the water and heat the roasting iron until it sparked. He obeyed and made the fire in the patio.

The poor rabbit was very sad waiting for his torture, but he could do nothing. Suddenly the coyote passed, very mannerly and of good humor, taking a walk. He saw the rabbit in the distance and approached him, "Nephew Rabbit, what are you doing here?"

The rabbit said that he felt a great relief when the coyote arrived. He said, "Uncle Coyote, here I am waiting for lunch. They invited me to eat meat, but I'm very small and I don't eat much."

"You're my nephew. You can give me a little meat. I'm hungry," said the coyote.

The rabbit answered, "Uncle Coyote, if you would like to take my place, when the hour comes for lunch, to you they will give all the meat. I don't like meat. I like vegetables more."

The coyote replied, "Thanks, nephew, I'm very grateful. The truth is that I'm very hungry." The same coyote asked, "Why do you have the chain around your neck?"

The rabbit, who was very clever, told him, "It's because they appreciate me very much. The señor doesn't want me to go, and, for that reason, I'm with this chain. But it's easy, uncle, to take the chain off me," said the rabbit.

The coyote took off the chain and freed him. The rabbit said to the coyote, "Uncle, allow me to put the chain on your neck so that they will give you a lot of meat, and the owner of the house will be very happy with you."

"Yes," said the coyote, and he was tied up with the same chain.

The rabbit was very happy to be set free, and he went to do more damage in the garden.

Then the hour arrived for the sentence of the rabbit, and the father and the sacristan went to see if the water was boiling. But when they came and there was no longer a rabbit, the father said, "See how clever this animal is. In the morning there was a rabbit; now there is a coyote. But we're going to see what is going to happen to him." Then the coyote was frightened, but there was nothing he could do.

The father and the sacristan carried the coyote for the torture. They poured hot water on him, stuck a hot roasting rod up his anus, and said he was paying for what he had done, not leaving any fruit in the garden. The poor coyote was howling from the great heat of the boiling water and much pain in his body from the roasting iron. The father told him, "This is just a punishment. If you return again you are going to die."

The poor coyote left crying because of his suffering. His whole body was blistered, and he had a burned anus.

Little by little, he was recuperating. "One day," he thought, "I'm going to go looking for the rabbit, and if I find him, I'm going to kill him and eat him."

The rabbit was very happy in an *injertal* [*injerto* tree, grove], eating ripe *injertos* [soft, brilliant green fruit]. The coyote was passing through the *injertal* looking for the rabbit.

The rabbit said, "Uncle, where are you going? Because you are so thin and so ugly, you walk like a sick person."

When the coyote realized that the rabbit was there, he said, "You damned rabbit! Because of your deceit, I suffered a lot. Remember when you said that you had an invitation? It was a deception. Now come down from the tree. Today, I'm going to kill you."

The rabbit said, "No, uncle, it wasn't I. It was probably one of my brothers. We are twelve brothers and we all seem alike."

"You're not going to lie to me anymore. I know you," said the coyote.

"Honest, uncle, it wasn't I."

The coyote said, "All's forgiven, give me a ripe *injerto.*"

"Very well, uncle," said the rabbit. "Open your mouth. Here comes your *injerto.*" When the ripe *injerto* fell into the mouth of the coyote, Uncle Coyote liked it.

"It tasted good, throw me another one," said the coyote.

The rabbit looked for a big green one and said, "Uncle, open your mouth. Here comes the ripe *injerto.*"

The coyote opened his mouth to receive the *injerto.* Since the fruit was green, it stuck in the coyote's mouth, and the coyote fell to the ground rolling over trying to get it out but he was unable. He remained three days in the *injerto* grove before he was able to get it out.

The rabbit went away very happy, because he was able to deceive the coyote again. When the coyote recovered, he went looking again for the rabbit to kill him.

The rabbit, however, had a foreboding that the coyote was going to kill him. He looked for a big clay kettle and filled it with wasps. Then he ate dinner. He was there when the coyote arrived and said, "Little wretched rabbit, you tricked me again, and because of what you have done to me, you are going to pay with your life. Now, I won't forgive you. I still feel sick from the *injerto* that you left stuck in my mouth."

When the rabbit heard these words, he began to dance. And the coyote said, "Good, you're dancing because of all the bad things you have done."

"Coyote," said the rabbit, "I'm dancing because of happiness. Look there; there's a kettle full of tamales. Today is my birthday. We are going to eat the tamales when my little brother comes, but on the condition that you have to dance until my brother arrives."

The coyote said, "Rabbit, have a little respect, because you are tricking your uncle."

"Look, uncle," said the rabbit, "I've never behaved poorly with you. It was probably my big brother. He is more mischievous. There are twelve of us brothers. Uncle, forget all that has happened with my brother. Later we can eat the tamales. Dance, uncle, dance! Today is my birthday," said the rabbit.

"Yes," said the coyote. He danced and danced until he got tired.

"Well," said the coyote, "I'm just dancing, and the rabbit is not coming. It's better that I rest awhile."

The rabbit didn't arrive. The coyote was waiting and waiting. Finally, he said, "Now, the rabbit is not coming. He fled in fear. This time I'm really going to eat all the tamales," and he opened the kettle that was full of wasps.

The wasps were very angry, and when they came out of the kettle, they began to sting the coyote all over his body. He shouted a lot because of the ache of the stings. Because of the pain, he began to run, but the wasps followed him. Finally, the coyote freed himself from the wasps, but his whole body was swollen.

"My goodness," said the coyote. "This time he deceived me like an ignoramus, but with the forgiveness of God, I'm going to look for the rabbit and his life will be over. I'm going to eat him."

He left in search of the rabbit without realizing that the rabbit was walking behind him. The rabbit said, "I'm going to trick him again." He placed himself again as if he were supporting a rock with his back.

When the coyote saw him he said, "Damned rabbit, because of you the wasps nearly killed me."

The rabbit didn't answer.

"Rabbit, I'm talking to you."

"Uncle, right now we're going to die," said the rabbit, acting as if he were supporting the rock with his back. "Now is the final judgment. The world is going to end."

"Right now I'm going to eat you," said the coyote.

"No, uncle, if I leave here, it's sure that the final justice is coming. Help me, uncle, you are much stronger than I. Look here, your back can sustain the rock, because if you don't help me the world is going to end."

"Yes," said the coyote, exerting a lot of effort supporting the big rock.

"Uncle, use more force; don't let go. I'm going to look for big sticks to fix the world."

The coyote said, "Run to look for sticks for support before we die."

The coyote remained, spending his effort, and the rabbit

went away content, and now didn't return. The coyote howled and howled until finally he used up his strength and said, "My goodness, I'm going to die," and he quit below the rock. And the rock did not move. Then the coyote cried over his unfortunate luck and said, "I'm suffering much deceit from this damned rabbit. Now is the time to look for and kill him once and for all so that he won't trick me again."

The coyote went in search of the rabbit, and when he found him, the rabbit was seated on the edge of a spring of crystal clear water. In this spring one could see the moon well, and when the coyote came near he said, "Rabbit, this time now your life is really mine. Now I'm going to kill you."

The rabbit, seeing the moon inside the spring did not want to answer. And the coyote again said, "Damned rabbit, your life is over."

"Uncle, what are you saying?" said the rabbit. "I've never talked with you. If something bad has happened, it was done by my brother, not me. It's that we are twelve brothers, it was probably my little brother."

"No, I know that you always have tricked me, and now I'm going to get revenge," said the coyote.

The rabbit continued to just look at the brilliance of the moon in the spring, looking under the water. And he said, "Uncle Coyote, here I have a problem. I brought meat for you, but it fell inside the water. Here I want to give you this meat, but I'm unable to get it out of the water. Try, uncle, perhaps you can get it out."

"No, I can't," said the coyote.

"But it's certain that inside the water you can see the meat," said the rabbit.

"Yes, I see it," said the coyote. But it wasn't meat; it was just the reflection of the moon that was seen in the water.

"Uncle," said the rabbit, "I want you to come get the meat out of the water."

"Yes," said the coyote, "I'm hungry."

"Stay here guarding it while I go to get a *botecito* [small jar] to take out all the water, and then it will be easy to get the meat out," said the rabbit.

"Very well, nephew, run because I'm very hungry," said the coyote.

The coyote was guarding and looking into the spring, wagging his tail a little, licking his chops a little, saying, "I want to eat meat." He was waiting and waiting, but the rabbit did not return again. The poor coyote was trembling with cold, and he didn't gain anything.

"Well, this is another deceit. We're going to see," said the coyote. "The rabbit is going to be my food. I'm going to look for him until I'm able to kill him. I'm an animal a lot bigger than he, and he's tricking me. I've suffered a lot." And the coyote took off in search of the rabbit.

One afternoon the rabbit was very happy. He made a hammock of lianas and placed it over a *barranca* [ravine] and began to swing happily when suddenly the coyote arrived and said, "Rabbit, come down out of the hammock. Today's your day; I'm going to eat you."

The rabbit continued to swing in the hammock, very content, and the coyote again said, "Get out of the hammock."

"Uncle, here it's very pleasant. Come with me. Let's have a good time. The two of us can amuse ourselves."

"No," said the coyote. "I have suffered a lot because of your deceit."

"It wasn't I. Perhaps it was some of my brothers. We are twelve and are the same color. Uncle, come to the hammock. Two are more fun."

Finally, the coyote climbed up in the hammock. Then the two began to have fun. And the rabbit asked, "How do you feel?"

"Very happy," said the coyote. And that's the way they were for a while.

Suddenly the rabbit said to the coyote, "Uncle, stay here in the hammock while I go to get us a refreshment."

"Very well, nephew," said the coyote.

When the rabbit arrived at the edge of the ravine, where he had tied the hammock, he cut the liana. The poor coyote fell to the bottom of the ravine. He broke six ribs and knocked out his four fangs and broke his tail. The poor coyote did not eat for a month.

The rabbit went on very happily obtaining food in the plains.

When the coyote recovered his health, he just kept talking saying, "My goodness, I'm suffering a lot in this world. My goodness, I'm forsaken. What is my fault? Can it be because I'm the most sinful among all the animals? Or is it that my luck doesn't help me. A smaller animal has done me a lot of damage. This time I really know that as an ignoramus I have suffered a lot. From now on I'm going to use my head," said the coyote.

One day the rabbit was on some land where there was a lot of dry grass. Where he was walking, it had just been cleaned by a campesino. Suddenly the coyote arrived and said, "Why talk a lot? Now, I'm going to eat this rabbit."

When the coyote tried to catch the rabbit, he couldn't. The rabbit said, "Already you have seen that I'm clever. When you want to catch me, you can't. It is because I'm innocent. God helps me a lot. Uncle, forget all that has happened. It isn't I. You can stay here. They have told me that today they are going to celebrate a fiesta. I have to sweep and prepare a place in the center of this land so that all around there will be dry grass and no one will see us and kill us."

"When are they going to have the fiesta?" said the coyote.

"Tonight," said the rabbit.

"Who's going to have a fiesta?" said the coyote.

"Uncle, my eleven brothers are going to come. They're

going to bring many lights, light many firecrackers, and explode many *bombas* [fireworks shot from mortars]."

"What are you going to eat?"

"We're going to eat chickens. Uncle, stay with me to prepare this place. Help me sweep the center where we are going to be, and put all around us the dry grass so that no one will see us."

"Good," said the coyote, and he began to sweep the center of the land and cover it all around with dry grass.

When it was all ready, the rabbit told the coyote, "We are going to wait till night comes."

"Very well," said the coyote.

"Uncle, your hair is too ugly, not like mine, which is fine. Uncle, if you like, I have a remedy so that your hair will be finer than mine."

"Thanks, nephew," said the coyote, "give me this remedy so that my hair will be fine."

"Very well," said the rabbit. He poured tar all over the body of the coyote. "Uncle, your hair is going to come out very fine."

"Thanks," said the coyote.

When night came, the coyote asked, "What time is the fiesta going to begin?"

"Be patient, uncle, the night is long," said the rabbit.

"Uncle," said the rabbit, "it's better that I go to call my brothers. Already it's late, and they haven't come. Stay here and guard this place. You can't go with me because you have tar on your body. We're going to come with a lot of light, and when we are close, we're going to light firecrackers and explode *bombas* as a signal. Uncle, please, so that the fiesta will be more gay, you have to dance and jump with joy."

"Good, very well," said the coyote, and he stayed in the place cleaning.

Then the rabbit left and lit a fire around all the grass that surrounded the coyote, and the rabbit ran off and sat down on top of a tree trunk to see what was happening with the coyote. When the fire caught strongly, the rabbit sat on the trunk and said, "Uncle, now we have come, begin to dance."

"Yes," said the coyote, and he began to dance, but without realizing that he was not able to leave because he was surrounded by the fire. When he realized it was a fire, he began to shout and cry. Finally, he took off running and he passed through the flames. But as he had tar all over his body, when he went through the flames, the tar caught fire. The coyote saw that he was on fire, and he threw himself into the spring of water. Only then did he put out the fire. But when he left the water, he had neither hair nor whiskers.

He spent a lot of time sick, and when he regained his health, he went to God to accuse the rabbit. He said, "My Lord, I want justice. The rabbit has played tricks on me and lied to me. I was at the point of losing my life, and for that reason, I want justice."

God told him, "With much pleasure I will do justice, but you have to present proof."

The coyote said, "Well, there isn't much proof, but no one is able to deceive God."

"Yes, but here we need proof," said God.

"Look how I have a body full of blisters without hair. Touch me. I have six broken ribs; I don't have four fangs. Feel my tail! It's broken!"

"It's true," said God. He sent to call for the rabbit, and when the rabbit arrived God said, "You're a small animal, but I see what you have done to your uncle. It is a mortal sin."

The rabbit didn't answer.

"Now I am sending you to hell," said God.

The rabbit answered God, "Lord, I know that you pardon sinners. You have pardoned thieves, adulterers, and murderers. I know that you are going to forgive me."

God told him, "I'm going to forgive you but you have to do a job. You have three days beginning tomorrow to look for two shark eyes. If you don't bring the eyes of a shark, I will send you to hell."

"Very well," said the rabbit, and he went away a little sad and a little content. He thought, "What am I going to do to get the eyes of a shark?" He went many places looking until he arrived at the ocean. He saw woodcutters working, and he sat down looking at the men sawing wood. Then lunchtime arrived, and the workers took their lunch and went to sit down in the shade of a tree to eat. But they forgot their shotgun.

The rabbit, seeing that the men began to eat, little by little went to steal the shotgun. And then he went again to the beach to see if a shark was there. In a while, a shark of the ocean appeared. The rabbit, very confident in his astuteness, grabbed the shotgun and hit a shot in the face of the shark. But he didn't die. He went again into the ocean.

The rabbit remained thinking, and he saw a buzzard and said, "*Compadre*, come with me." And the buzzard alighted on the sand.

"*Compadre*, what do you want?" said the buzzard.

"Please carry me to the other side of the ocean. I'm looking for a shark, and I only need his two eyes."

"Very well," said the buzzard, "get on."

The rabbit sat down on the buzzard until they reached the other side of the ocean. "*Compadre*," said the rabbit, "if you're able to kill the shark, you can eat all of the meat. I just want the two eyes. But with one condition, you have to carry me to the other side of the ocean."

"With much pleasure, *compadre*," said the buzzard.

The rabbit buried the shotgun in the sand, and he began to dance. Suddenly the shark came out of the ocean, and he said to the rabbit, "Muchacho, you are dancing."

"Yes, sir," said the rabbit.

The shark said to the rabbit, "Muchacho, I had bad luck on the other side of the ocean. Without realizing, I wanted to sun myself a little on the sand when a man shot me in the face.

Thanks to God that my face is like bronze, and the lead didn't penetrate, but if this man shoots me in the tail, this time I would be dead," said the shark.

"Then you sharks carry your life in your tail," said the rabbit.

"Yes," said the shark.

The rabbit said, "This time with confidence you really can be on the beach. I'll guard you so that no one will be able get near you."

"Please watch over me. I want to sleep a little while on the beach to enjoy the sun."

"Don't worry, sleep. I'm a little animal, but honorable."

"Thanks," said the shark, and he went to sleep on the sand.

When the rabbit saw that the shark was fast asleep, he went to take out the shotgun and he discharged a shot in his tail. The shark did not move anymore. The rabbit was very happy, and with his claws he removed the eyes. Then he told the buzzard, "Now, you have meat to eat."

"Thanks," said the buzzard, "I'm going to eat a little so that I will have strength to fly over the ocean." Then the buzzard carried the rabbit to the other side.

"Thanks, *compadre*, go back. All the meat is yours."

When the rabbit presented himself before God with the two shark eyes, God was amazed at the cleverness of the rabbit and said, "Rabbit, today I believe that you are a damned animal. And you will remain little forever. You won't get any bigger. You will also always move around with your butt on the ground. Your ears are going to get very large." And God pulled his two ears. For that reason, the rabbit has two big ears, and each time he hops, he always lands on his ass.

And God told the coyote, "For your stupidity you broke your ribs and your canine teeth. Your punishment is that all your life you will go around looking down toward the ground, and as you broke your tail bone, you will go around always with your tail hanging down. And for having had your hair poured with tar, your hair won't grow any longer. It will be short. And for the last punishment you will keep eating green *injertos* and sleep on the rocks because if you were a little more clever, I would give you a better place. This is a remembrance of the justice of God."

•

The Story of the Man [Devil] Who Was Put Inside a *Tecomate*

The old folks use this story as an example to educate. It is a story of a woman who was pretentious, exorbitant, and arrogant.

This woman lived with her parents. She was neither very pretty nor very ugly. Many men of the town were in love with her, but her pretention was to have a husband with gold teeth. Her father said, "Do you want to marry?"

"Yes," she said, "but when I find a man who has gold teeth." The woman was already thirty years of age, and she wasn't able to choose a husband with gold teeth.

One day the woman went to wash clothing in the river below a bridge. The devil thought about deceiving this woman, seeing all her exaggerations. When the woman was happily washing clothing in the river, the devil took the form of a man with gold teeth, and he placed himself on the bridge with his face looking down at the woman. When the woman looked up, seeing the man with gold teeth, she said, "Only now am I having any luck." And she told the man, "Come down here with me. You are my husband. I've wanted a man with gold teeth for so long! How happy I am now that I have one!"

The man came down with her to the river and said, "You are my woman. I'm the man who will make you happy. Look at my gold teeth!"

The woman said, "Many wanted me, but none of them had gold teeth. Now let's go to my house." And the two went to her house. When they arrived the woman told her parents that she had found the man that suited her.

Her parents gave them a house to live in. The father of the woman told the man, "Son-in-law, now we're going to the campo to cultivate the land because this is my work."

The son-in-law answered, "We'll do it tomorrow."

The next day the father-in-law said, "Let's go to work."

He answered, "Today, I don't want to work. I have to continue my practices."

"What are your practices?"

"My practices are different," he said.

This man got inside a glass of water and disappeared. Then he got inside a kettle and disappeared. At times he got into a fire and disappeared. The mother of the woman cried and told the man, "Behave yourself! Don't do devilish things." But the man just smiled and smiled, and did nothing in the way of work.

For advice, the woman who had wanted a man with gold teeth went to a shaman to ask what to do about her husband, who was a devil. The shaman told her, "To conquer the devil is easy. Look for a *tecomate* [gourd jar], neither large nor small with a plug. Then tell your husband to get inside the jar, as he can do anything. And when he is inside the jar, cork it well and take it and throw it in the garbage. From there he will not get out."

When the woman arrived home, she looked for a jar, and she told the man, "If you are so clever, get inside this jar."

"Yes," said the man, and when he was inside the jar, the woman closed the opening with a plug, and she went to throw it in the trash. From there he did not get out again. The man looked at those who were outside the jar, but there was nothing he could do to get out. He spent many days in the trash.

Suddenly a man arrived at the garbage to urinate, but this man was shaking from a hangover. He didn't have money to buy a drink. This man was named Pedro.

The man inside the jar was saying, "Pedro, Pedro, help me! I'm here!"

But Pedro didn't see anyone, and he continued urinating. Then he said again, "Pedro, help me!"

Then Pedro went toward the jar and said, "Who is it?"

The jar moved, and the man said, "Please open this jar. I want to leave."

"Why are you there?"

"The woman told me to get inside, and when I did, she closed the opening and she brought me and left me in this trash. I'm the devil, but I'm unable to leave. I need help."

But Pedro was clever and said, "I'm going to open the jar, but if I let you out, I'm going to need a drink because of my hangover."

"Don't worry, I'm going to give you more *tragos* [drinks]." Then Pedro opened the jar, and the devil came out and thanked him.

Then he said, "Pedro, I don't have money to give you for a drink, but tomorrow you will have a lot of money. You have helped me a lot. But now it is I who has to work for you," said the devil. "Prepare a small bottle of plain water and a spoon. You're going to be a *curandero* [curer] and I the sickness. Right now I'm going to put myself in the teeth of the king. He has a lot of money and can pay you well. I'm going to be in the teeth of the king, and he will begin to have a severe toothache. Not a single doctor will be able to cure it. When the doctors examine the teeth of the king, I will put myself in his stomach, and he will have a severe stomachache. When they examine his stomach, I will go to his anus. Then I will go back again to his teeth. I'm going to torment the king with aches. The doctors won't be able to do anything. You have to knock on the door and say that you are a *curandero*. They will have to accept you," said the devil. "When you go to the king, give him a spoonful of water, and then I will leave his teeth and go to his stomach. Then he will shout with a stomachache. Give him another spoonful of water; it will calm his stomachache. Then I'll go to his ass, and his pain will be even worse. Then have him lay down on his bed, spread his cheeks, and pour a spoonful of water in his anus, and he will be cured."

"Very well," said Pedro.

Then the devil left to place himself in the molars of the king, and the king began to ache very intensely. He called all his doctors, and none was able to cure him. When they examined his molars, there was nothing wrong with them. Then his stomach began to ache, and when they examined his stomach, they found nothing wrong. Then his anus began to ache, and when they examined it, they found no illness. It was a big problem—no doctor could cure him.

Pedro arrived looking very tidy. He arrived at the hall door, and a maid came out and asked him, "What do you want?"

"I had a notice that the king is very ill, and I bring medicine for him."

The maid went running to tell the king.

The king said, "He can't tell any better than the doctors what I have here." The maid returned to tell Pedro no. And the king still had his intense pain.

Then Pedro called again at the hall door and said, "I want to cure the king!" The maid went again to see who it was.

Pedro told her, "I bring a remedy for the king," and the maid went again to tell the king.

The king said, "I'm dying with pain. This man can enter but on the condition that if his remedy doesn't work, he will be shot."

Then the maid went to call Pedro at the door. When Pedro went into the house of the king, he said, "King, you are very sick, and here I bring a remedy for you."

"Give me this medicine," said the king.

Pedro gave him a spoonful of water, and his toothache stopped. But he still had a stomachache. Pedro gave him another spoonful of water, and his stomachache went away. But the king still had an ass ache, and he was shouting in pain. And Pedro said to the servants, "Put him face down on the bed with his cheeks spread." And Pedro poured a spoonful of water in his asshole, and in that instance the king was cured.

The king was very happy and grateful. As a reward, he gave Pedro two *arrobas* [twenty-five pounds each, or fifty pounds] of money. Pedro went away very happy. Outside, in the street, Pedro met the devil again who said, "Amigo, now you can end your hangover; you can drink more. You freed me from the gourd jar, and thus we'll be friends forever." And they shook hands.

Then the people say that the *curanderos* are sometimes more proficient than doctors, but what happens is that they drink a lot, and they are very good friends with the devil, and nothing happens to them.

Story of Sebastiana

They say that in our towns a long
time ago lived a woman named Sebastiana.[13] But they say that she was very lazy
since childhood. She was so because her parents
never counseled her so that she would learn to
work. Sebastiana grew up, however, and had to
marry a husband named Xcuc. When the woman married her husband, her life was much worse because it took a
lot of effort to take care of Xcuc.

Xcuc was a working man because he planted a lot of corn
and beans and other things, but the woman didn't want to do
anything. She only wanted to sleep every day. She didn't want
to grind corn or cook beans or bring water from the lake. For
her each day was more difficult than the other. She said that it
was better to die than to be suffering in this world that was
only full of work and pain because one has to work to eat. She
neither wanted to bathe nor wash the clothing of her husband.

Xcuc suffered a lot because of the laziness of his woman.
Xcuc's consolation was his little dog. He told his problems to
the little dog, and the animal wagged her tail and moved her
ears as a sign that she also understood the suffering of the man
because of the idleness of the woman. When the female dog
went near the door to see if the woman would give her a
tortilla instead of a tortilla she gave her blows. The animal left
with tears in her eyes and to herself said, "Why did God give
hands and feet to the arrogant who don't know how to appreciate the value of life? When we animals want to work we

can't because God didn't give us the speech or hands to work or feet to walk. Yes, we have our feelings, but we can't do anything about being unable to work.

"The ungrateful woman doesn't give me a tortilla, but I'm not being arrogant if I am unable to work. Someday I'll be able to work to get revenge from the woman," said the dog. But the animal was very hungry, and approached the door again to see whether Sebastiana would give her a tortilla. The woman, however, began to mistreat the dog saying, "Damned dog, you always want a tortilla. It takes a lot out of me to make the tortillas and make meals for my husband. You don't see my suffering or help me grind corn and make tortillas. Happy is the life that you only spend sleeping or once in a while going to the field with my husband."

Sebastiana again told the dog, "My life is one of suffering because most of the time I work without rest." The dog acted as if she understood the pleas of the woman, moving her ears.

Between laziness and more laziness, Sebastiana gave birth to a boy, but that made the situation worse because with children her hardships multiplied. Xcuc, however, went to work very happily because his desire was to have a son, and he told Sebastiana to prepare the meal on time. Then Sebastiana washed the *nixtamal* [corn cooked in lime or ash water] and began to grind corn to make the tortillas. When she finished making tortillas, she realized that she didn't have any water, and she put her baby in the hammock, but very angrily because she also saw that she had a lot of dirty clothing. Then she told the dog, "I'm going to the lake to wash clothes and bring water back when I return. Stay sleeping here in the door of the house to guard my son."

Then Sebastiana went to wash clothing. When she went to the lake, however, Xbalbay, *dueño* [owner or god] of evil, gave the dog the power to do something bad to the woman as fruit for her laziness. Then Xbalbay told the dog, "With my power, you are going to have feet and hands and a mouth to do what I tell you." At that instance, the dog spoke to Xbalbay. Then Xbalbay said, "Make the fire."

"Yes," answered the dog. She made the fire.

"Put the big, clay kettle on the fire, and take the baby out of hammock," said Xbalbay.

"Very well," said the dog, taking the baby out of the hammock.

"Put him in the kettle."

"Very well," said the dog, putting the baby inside.

"Prepare onions, tomatoes, and coriander."

"Very well," said the animal, doing what the *dueño* of evil commanded.

"When this is cooked we will prove that Sebastiana is very miserable with you, but it is a day that we're going to take advantage of my power. Let's eat."

And they began to eat, part of which was the cooked baby. When they finished eating, Xbalbay told the dog, "Put a small grinding stone in the hammock in place of the baby so that the mother will not realize that her son is what is cooked."

"Very well," said the dog, putting inside the hammock a small grinding stone. Then the *dueño* of evil told the dog, "I'm going to disappear, but I will always be at your side. When the woman comes, tell her to have a good lunch and that you are leaving to buy meat and tell her that her baby is swinging in the hammock."

"Very well," said the animal.

Xbalbay disappeared, and the dog remained, swinging the milling stone in the hammock.

When Sebastiana arrived the dog spoke, saying, "My dear owner, be happy with me now that I'm working for you. Now I have prepared your lunch. It's a tasty stew. What I want to do is take a rest from rocking your son in the hammock. I'm going to the pueblo to buy meat."

"Very well, that's what I want," said the woman. "So that you will help me, I'm never going to hit you again," she said.

Then the woman began to swing the baby in the hammock, thinking that her baby still was sleeping. She did not realize that she was swinging a stone. The woman said to the dog, "If you see more cats and dogs, they can come with you to help me so that I will not suffer more in this life. You already understand my hardships."

The dog didn't answer. She changed back again to not speaking, being the same as she had been before.

When Xcuc arrived from work, Sebastiana told him that they should eat because the food was hot. "Very well," said Xcuc, and he approached the fire where they always ate. But when the woman began to finish the food, she noticed the hands and the head of the baby, which frightened her a lot. Worse was the fright of Xcuc, who stopped eating. When they went to open the hammock, they saw that in place of the baby a stone had been left. They had already eaten the lunch, and the animal had disappeared with the *dueño* of evil forever. When the people heard these things, all the women were forbidden to speak to or hit the animals.[14]

—Elena Cholotío Meza,
　　Recorded by Ignacio Bizarro Ujpán

The Story of
the Mouse and the Man

This story is very old and it was told to us by my grandmother when she was alive. It goes like this.

The rat is a very good friend of man, although man doesn't imagine it. The rat thanks God for the life of man because man gives food to the rats. When there is a pregnant woman in the family, the rats are very preoccupied to see if a baby is born. When the hour of birth arrives, the rats get beneath the bed to see the birth. If a boy is born, they rejoice and make *costumbres* [rituals]. Among themselves are shamans who ask God for the life of the newborn, and they have a big party with a marimba and drinking a lot from happiness.

But if a girl is born into the family, the rats become sad and very distressed because the newborn is an enemy of the rats since the woman is the one who guards the corn, beans, chili, and other things of the house. Then the rats aren't able to eat because the woman is the caretaker of the house and guardian of all the things. But the rats are enemies of the woman and the best friends of the man because when he plants his seed, the rats are always able to eat it. When the man harvests his corn or other cultivations, there is always some grain that isn't picked and is left [on the ground], which greatly serves the rats for food. Also, when the man eats lunch in the field he leaves pieces of tortillas thrown about, which also serves to feed the rats. For that reason, the man is the more highly esteemed by the rats.

When a man gets sick, the rats become very sad because if the man dies, they remain abandoned, and there isn't anyone to give them food. The rats have to change houses since they don't want to live there anymore because of the death of the one they loved more. But when a woman dies, the rats gather and have a big party and drink a lot with glee that there was a death of an enemy. The rats become very content because there isn't anyone to take care of the house and they have the liberty to eat whatever they want, and they can feel more peacefulness since the things are abandoned.

This story is also told by the old folks of today.

—Ignacio Bizarro Ujpán

Story of the Priest When He Was Invited to a Birthday Party

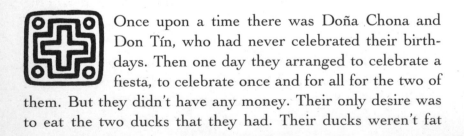

Once upon a time there was Doña Chona and Don Tín, who had never celebrated their birthdays. Then one day they arranged to celebrate a fiesta, to celebrate once and for all for the two of them. But they didn't have any money. Their only desire was to eat the two ducks that they had. Their ducks weren't fat because they were not giving them food to eat. Then the two of them decided that the party they were going to have would be at lunchtime.

Don Tín told Doña Chona to prepare the two ducks in something special. And thus Doña did so, roasting the ducks and preparing the tortillas. Very happily Don Tín said, "But if only we two are going to eat, we won't be able to finish it all. We need to invite someone to come to lunch with us."

Doña Chona replied, "Better to invite the neighbors."

Don Tín answered, "Don't you know that our neighbors are our enemies? They can't come into our house."

Doña Chona said, "Then better that we go to invite the mayor."

"No, because the mayor is my enemy. Last time he fined me. He can't come to our house."

Then Doña Chona replied, "Let's invite our *comadre* [co-mother]."

Don Tín answered, "That's not possible because her god-son no longer lives with us. She can't come to this house. Our son is dead, and she never came to visit us when we were very sad. More for that reason, she can't come in the house."

Then Doña Chona retorted, "Then it is better that we invite the lawyer because one day he may help us with a problem at a cheaper price."

Don Tín was even more resentful, saying, "The lawyer can't be invited because the last time I had problems with you, this lawyer told me to get rid of you once and for all and throw you out of the house. So the lawyer doesn't have the right to come into our house."

Then Doña Chona, a little angry, said, "The last suggestion I'm going to make is that we should invite Father Andrés to come have lunch with us because someday we are going to get married and the father won't charge us for the cost of the mass."

Don Tín was convinced and jumped with joy. "That indeed is very good!"

The father lived far away from where the birthday people lived, but that was unimportant to Don Tín.

"Although it seems distant, I'm going to call on him," said the man. And he left for his town.

But when he went walking to the town, Doña Chona was careless and didn't see when the dog went into the kitchen and carried off a whole duck. When she realized what happened she exclaimed, "What am I going to do? Only one duck is left for lunch!"

Since Doña Chona enjoyed the fast life, in a little while Don Chema arrived, taking advantage of the absence of Don Tín. Don Chema was the lover of Doña Chona, and after enjoying sex with her, he felt hungry and ran to the kitchen and ate the other duck, leaving only the frying pan in which the duck was cooked. After having lunch, Don Chema left very satisfied because he was content with sexual pleasure and in addition he had eaten the lunch of the birthday people.

Doña Chona was worried because now she had nothing for lunch for Don Tín and the priest. But she was very clever. "I have deceived my lover and to deceive the padre is simple," she said.

When Don Tín arrived with Father Andrés, very happily they entered the house. The father entered praying, and then he greeted Doña Chona. The reverend was thinking he was going to have a good lunch in this house.

Doña Chona with her astuteness arranged for the father to be seated near the pot covered with a table napkin. The father asked, "What are we having for lunch?"

"Roast duck," replied Doña Chona.

"I like roast duck," said Father Andrés.

But Doña Chona was looking for a lie to deceive him and Don Tín, and she told Don Tín, "The knife is dull; you need to sharpen it because it will be easier to carve the ducks."

"Yes," answered Don Tín, and he grabbed a file and began to sharpen the knife.

While Don Tín was sharpening the knife, Doña Chona went to the padre to tell him, "Father, you have reached the most difficult part of your life; you're going to die because my husband is sharpening the butcher knife. He says he is going to cut off your testicles."

The father, very frightened, said, "How could this be? Your husband invited me to lunch."

"That's a lie, Father, he is thinking wickedness against your life. Leave before he cuts off your *huevos* [eggs, balls]."

"Thanks, Chona, thanks," said Father Andrés, and he took off running without saying good-bye to Don Tín.

When Don Tín realized what was happening, the priest was already far away, and he asked his woman, "Why did the father take off running?"

Clever Doña Chona said, "Remember, you went to call this reverend. He took the roasted ducks. All that remains is the frying pan. Come here and see," she said.

Without hearing more, Don Tín went running after the father with the butcher knife in his hand shouting, "Father give me them," speaking of the two ducks, but the reverend was thinking that he was asking for his *huevos*. And the father ran even harder, and Don Tín after him, and he said, "I only want one." But Don Tín meant that he wanted the father to leave him a duck and keep one for himself, because the woman said he had stolen the two and that's the reason he said to leave him one.

But the father thought that he wanted a testicle because the woman had told him he wanted to cut off his *huevos* and he saw that Don Tín carried a knife in his hand. But the knife was only to carve the two ducks, not to cut off the *huevos* of the father. But since the clever woman had told him that Don Tín was going to take his testicles and he had a knife, he was scared. For that reason they say that one has to be careful because it is easy for the women to trick the men because in this world there are all kinds of women. But also there are women who are very sacred to their husbands.

—Ignacio Bizarro Ujpán

The Story of the *Poder* [Power, Ability] of Persons When They Are Born

 According to this story, in past times corn, beans, and all that man grows were in abundance. It was because here on earth men had been born who were dedicated to making rain over the land. Mainly for that reason it rained very consistently, and thus the crops turned out better.

When a person was born in charge of making rain, God gave him the luck at birth. At birth he brought a very small *tecomate* full of water and a small green cape on his back. Then the midwife and a member of the family took the *tecomate* from the hand of the baby and the cape from his back and put them in a place so that no one would look at them. They didn't tell the rest of the members of the family. Just the midwife, the mother, and a member of the family were the ones in charge of looking after the luck of the baby.

On the eighth day they bathed the baby. On this day the

midwife had to do a *costumbre* to give thanks to God that a new man was born who had come ready to work for many others.

From this time the luck remained guarded until the boy was fifteen or sixteen years of age, a young boy. Then his parents told him that he was born with the luck to make rain and looked for the best shaman to make *costumbres* in the hills, asking for protection of the youngster, who now was preparing to begin his work making rain.

According to this tale, in each town, there had been two or three persons with the ability to make rain but these individuals had been born directly for the service of God, in the form of angels but born in the flesh; that is to say, they had been born of woman. But during their lifetimes on earth they could never touch nor get near a woman. During their lives, they kept their purity. They neither drank nor smoked tobacco.

Those born in *tierra fría* [cold country, above 2,000 meters] were those who went to make rain on the coast, and those born on the coast were those who came to make rain in the *tierra fría*. In the air and in the clouds they made the changes, and it was communicated to them how many hours of rain they were going to make.

When they left their houses, they never advised anyone. They only said that they were going to work in the campo and took their hoes, machetes, and the other things that a man takes when he goes to work. Many times they left at night, and then this was when it rained at night.

In each town there had been a *dueño* or *jefe* [chief], and it's he who arrived first in the hill where there was a clothing store that had special clothes that they used to make the rain. The *jefe* or *dueño* was the one who arrived inside[15] the hill and talked to the *dueño* of the store, saying, "Open the door and windows of the store because now the men are going to arrive and put on the clothes. The men of the clouds are ready to make rain over the earth."

Then the *jefe* [chief] of the men put on his clothes for his work, and then he was hurled among the clouds to make thunder for the first storms, which was like a signal for the rest of the hombres. When they heard the first storms, they ran to the same hill. Then they left their hoes and machetes hanging on the branches of the trees and went to the store to put on their clothing. They too were hurled into the air, disappearing among the clouds to make more storms and heavier rain.

The men of these parts went to the coast to make rain, and when they finished their work, they selected the best plantains and pineapples and other coastal fruits. When they returned, they descended on the same hill to leave the clothing in the store and happily went to their houses with their fruit that they had brought from the coast for their parents.

In the enchanted hills there was a lot of clothing for those who worked making rain. To make rain for two or three hours, green clothing was used; to make rain with a hurricane, red clothing was used; and to make rain for many days, black clothing was used, which indicated mortality. That was when the rivers flooded, the hills had landslides, and the cultivations of the people were swept away by the strong currents of water, and people died because of a lot of rain. But when these things happened, it was because they had received an order from God to punish the earth. When these things happened, it was because the people had committed a lot of sins and never agreed to ask forgiveness. When God was tired of seeing a lot of sin, He gave the order to these men of rain to clean the earth.

One time, so the story goes, in San José there had been three men who were true sons of God in charge of making rain, and the place where they found the clothing they used for their sacred work was in the area called "Patzalú," also called the window of the sacred world. In this place, always the men of the clouds arrived to choose their clothing to make rain.

One of these men had a brother who was very curious to

know where his elder brother got his fruit. One day he told him, "My dear brother, where do you get such beautiful plantains and pineapples? I want to get some too."

His brother answered, telling him a lie to shut him up so that he would not have to reveal the truth, "These fruits that I bring home I get from a señor who brings them from the coast and sells them to me in the afternoon, and for that reason, I'm always carrying fruits in the afternoons."

But the younger brother didn't remain quiet or accept the answer.

One day the two brothers left together to work in the campo. In the afternoon, when they finished work, they heard the thunder of a tempest. Then the older brother told his brother, "You can go on ahead to our house. Meanwhile, I'm going to look for a little firewood for our mother to be able to cook our food." But this was a lie because he knew that this afternoon they were calling him to make rain.

The younger brother said, "Very well," and acted as if he were going home. But farther ahead he hid to see if it were true that his brother was going to gather firewood, because he had always stayed but never brought firewood for the house. Then the older brother went toward the Hill of Patzalú, and the younger brother followed him a long way to see what was going to happen, finally arriving at the place of the clothing store, which was used to make rain. When the elder brother arrived, he knelt, put on green-colored clothing and a cape of the same color, and disappeared among the clouds. And a light rain began. The younger brother was very frightened and amazed at what he had seen his brother do. But in a little while two other men arrived and did the same thing. They too were flung in the air and went among the clouds, and a strong rain began.

The boy was scared even more, but little by little, the storm went away. Moving away, the tempest was heard until it reached the coast. Only then did the boy think about what he had been seeing. He looked in the front where the doors and the windows of the store were open. The boy approached, gradually, with much fear, and he succeeded in reaching the door. When he went inside the store, however, the clothing began to talk to the boy. The new clothing began to smile and offered to have the boy put on this better clothing. The boy went farther inside, but the store was immense. The sun could not be clearly seen, but it wasn't dark. One could see well but couldn't see the source of the light.

A new piece of clothing told the muchacho, "Please put me on. I'm a new piece of clothing that the men of rain have never worn. Now I want to go with you, and we will go among the clouds." The color of the clothing was black, but it glistened from its beauty.

The muchacho was curious. "Yes," he said, and he put on the clothing of the color black. Upon putting on the clothing, the boy now didn't sense when he was elevated among the clouds. The same clothing lifted him up, and it began to rain harder, and there was a stronger tempest, incomparable to what the real men of rain had done. But the men of rain didn't realize what was happening. When they finished their work, each went down to the hill to leave his clothing and go to his house. But during the night, the rain was harder, and a strong hurricane uprooted trees, blew away the *ranchos* [rustic dwellings], and carried off the animals. There was a lot of damage.

At dawn, each of the men of rain went to meet in the hill to see which of them was making so much rain. God hadn't given an order to make justice. They put on their clothing and disappeared among the clouds and communicated with those of the coast, who were also preoccupied with what was happening. Neither those of the *tierra fría* nor those of the coast were making rain. All of them were waiting for orders from their *dueños*. Then all of them met to investigate who it was that was being a bother. All of them cast themselves among the clouds in groups to capture whoever was making strong rain and a severe hurricane. But when these men went among the clouds, the rain got harder because when they were among the clouds, it provoked more and harder rain. Never were they able to find the boy that was dressed in the new clothing of the color black. They spent many days looking for him.

Finally, one of them, the strongest, succeeded in seeing that among the clouds there was a muchacho swept along by a strong hurricane. He called each of them to tell them to each bring a long lasso.

"Yes," they said, and they all ran to the hill where they had gotten their clothing because everything was there. Each one of them brought a very long lasso.

Together they disappeared among the clouds and formed a great circle of 100 kilometers, but when they got near, they weren't able to capture him because the muchacho carried a tremendous force, and no one was able to stop him. They went until they reached the ocean. Then the hombres prepared more and struggled a lot, and finally among all of them, they lassoed the boy, but they weren't able to stop him. Then they said, "If we can't stop this hombre, the world is finished." They all said, "Now is the time of judgment." But they kept struggling, until they were able to take him back. They put a lasso around his neck, another around his waist, one on his feet, and yet another around his arms. Together they carried him tied to the hill where he had gotten the clothing. Not until they descended on the hill did they realize that he was the brother of one of their companions. And only then did the rain calm. But because of this boy, a lot of people suffered. They lost their cultivations, many animals, horses, and sheep. From that point many remained very poor; many houses were lost. Because of this rain that lasted several days, many *barrancas* [ravines] were formed, and, for that reason, there are many rocks because the good earth was washed away by the rain.

When the boy took off the clothing, each man of rain gave him and his brother twenty lashes, and in this same place the men told the boys that they were going to die within a few days. The two boys went to tell their parents what had happened and what they had done. In a few days they fell sick with a fever and a severe headache, and in twenty days, at the same hour on the same day, they died. They were buried in the church.

From that time, God took away this power from the men. Now, on earth, these persons aren't born as before. The rain has to be made by angels, real spirits, and only God has the right to make rain over the earth. This is because the men had behaved very badly and abused His power.

—Elena Cholotío Meza,
Recorded by Ignacio Bizarro Ujpán

Story of the Dance of the Deer

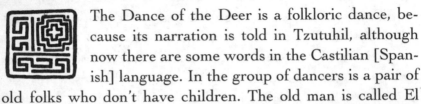 The Dance of the Deer is a folkloric dance, because its narration is told in Tzutuhil, although now there are some words in the Castilian [Spanish] language. In the group of dancers is a pair of old folks who don't have children. The old man is called El Anciano Cazador [The Old Man, The Hunter], or Rij Achii Pamazat in Tzutuhil. The old woman is called Catarina, or Rijlaj Catal in Tzutuhil. With them dance two *pastorcitos* [dear little pastors] who are called shepherd boys, who are like

mozos [helpers or servants]. With the pair of the old folks dance two children about ten years of age. In the dance they are called the *perritos* [little dogs]. They have names, one called Apik' and the other Amoss.

In the beginning of the dance the old folks enter to dance. With them dance the two *perritos*. The old man treats the little dogs as children and comments on his sadness at not having sons. Also, the old woman relates her sadness at not having children, that she only has two little dogs. She tells them that she doesn't have a child because when she was a young lady, they bewitched her just because she married a deer hunter. She comments that she is in agreement with her luck of not having children and it's better to have her two little dogs.

The old man tells his woman to take good care of the two little dogs because these little dogs are deer hunters; with them they can earn good pesos and good *reales*. The old lady answers not to worry, that she is being careful with the little dogs.

The old gentleman relates his sadness of not having children, that he wishes to have children but it's a pity that they had died because his woman had been bewitched. Also because of her *suerte* [luck, fate], their children had died because she had been born on the very day that the hunters of deer and other animals of the mountains had been born. The old fellow says that he did a lot of *costumbres* but all were futile and didn't work.

In each story that they tell, they always dance to the older tunes, the old man with his cane in his right hand and a small *chichín* [maraca] in his left hand. The old woman is a man who dances and acts like a woman. Each time they rehearse the dance, the two are men, but one acts as if he is the real man and the other behaves like a woman.

This kind of dance is very curious and makes a lot of people gather. Men arrive near to hear what the two old folks say. But the women don't approach. They remain somewhat distant because the old man behaves very abusively with the women — he gropes their breasts and inserts his cane between their legs, and more for that reason, the women don't get near this kind of dance.

After the old persons dance a lot, also the jaguars, deer, monkeys, large and small, dance, acting as if they were in the mountain, dancing separately. And the old folks, little dogs, and little shepherd boys dance separately. The jaguars and monkeys mix among the people, dancing, but they don't talk. They just ask for fruit and money by means of gestures, and the people give them fruit and their centavos but with the condition that they have to dance in front of whoever gives them the gift.

The most humorous ones of this kind of dance are the old folks and the dogs. After dancing another tune, the old man tells his woman, "My beloved Catarina, now that we're dancing to this tune, I'm going to the mountains to hunt deer or whatever other animal I find with my two mutts. When I return with the animals, we are going to sell the meat."

Catarina answers, "I don't want you to go to the mountains. It's very dangerous. There are many jaguars, lions, and monkeys. You can lose your life, and if you perish in the mountains, who will I have? You know that we don't have children. Who will take care of me?" Then the old woman begins to cry.

The old man responds, "My dear wife, don't worry. Nothing will happen to me. Now that I have my two dogs, it's they who will protect me when I'm in the mountains."

The old lady answers, "I don't want you to go to look for deer because if in the mountains the animals eat you and the two little dogs, I will be distressed from sadness, and I will die. I will die too! It's better for us to keep dancing." Then the two begin to dance.

After dancing to the tune, the old fellow tells his woman,

"I'm going to the mountains to look for animals because my *suerte* [luck, fate] demands that I go to the hunt."

"Why do you want deer meat if there aren't many in our family?" she implores.

"It's that we are going to sell the meat to earn some good pesos and some good *reales*. Then we will have what we want when we're very old, because when we are really old, we won't be able to work." Then the old lady is convinced that her husband has to leave to hunt.

Then the old gentleman says to his dogs, "Now the day has arrived that we have to leave to look for the good animals to get good meat."

Then the dogs speak, "Yes, we want to kill animals," and the two dogs begin to bark as if they were hunting.

Then the old woman tells the dogs, "Take care of my husband so that nothing will happen to him in the mountains."

Now the dogs don't speak; they only answer, "Guau, guau, guau."

Then the two position themselves in front of the marimba to make a *costumbre* so that the god of the hills will grant permission and so that nothing bad will happen on the hunt. Then the old woman places the candles and the myrrh on the table and the embers inside the incensory. While the old lady is preparing the things for the *costumbre*, the old gentleman does his commentaries. When everything is ready, the old hombre begins to burn candles and the myrrh and begins to call the names of the *dueños* [gods] of hills and places that he knows. But when he begins to say these things, he becomes serious. At this moment it seems comical. The old man bows to call the *dueños* of the hills and says the following:

God, *dueño* of the Santo Mundo [Sacred World, Earth], I'm your son who is a poor hunter. Here I am calling the *naguales* [animal forms] for all the gods; here also I'm calling all the spirits of all the dead of our fathers

62

and grandfathers, and I'm doing it so that with all these spirits nothing will happen to me in this dance. It's certain that it's a game to please our brothers and friends who are watching so that it isn't I who is persecuted by the spirits of the dead. Here, Santo Mundo, *dueño* of Pachico, *dueño* of Pakap, *dueño* of Paquixquil, *dueño* of Pacoral, *dueño* of Subantaa, *dueño* of Xe Cay Laj, *dueño* of Panucuy, *dueño* and lord of Caká Siguan, *dueño* and guardian lord of the pastor *semanero* [weekly pastor] Xe Cristalín and Pa Cristalín, lord and guardian of the animals of the sacred hill, Paraxaj, *dueño* of the window of the sacred world, where you keep the spirits of the invisible ones, where you keep the spirits of all the ancient shamans who were here on earth. I am calling all of them. Now I'm the son of all of you; I'm speaking with all of you so that the spirits of everyone will be present in this *costumbre* that isn't mine but yours; so that the spirits of all those that I've just finished calling be with me. I'm offering this sacred sacrifice as a fine and present. I call your names because I am part of the sacred world. This dance, which comes from our parents and grandparents, is an ancient dance.

When the old man says these things, he pours *aguardiente* [sugar cane liquor, or firewater] around the table and begins to say the names of the dead shamans that he knew, drinks his drink, and gives a drink to his woman.

When he is finished doing the *costumbre*, the two enter to dance the better tune. When they are dancing, the rest of the dancers, that is to say, the jaguars, lions, and monkeys disappear among the people. The old man then says good-bye, kissing the old woman, and begins to make big whistles, calling the two little dogs. To the cane he ties a *pita* [a string made from the agave plant], making more sure so that it won't be thrown away. He ties his *caites* [traditional sandals], slings his knapsack or satchel, and then begins the big shouts, acting as if he were in the mountains and mixing among the people, stating that he is in the places that he had mentioned when he was doing the *costumbre*, shouting and saying that he is running behind the deer and that he is seeing many jaguars, lions, and monkeys, every little while kneeling down entrusting himself to the *dueño* of the hills and to the *dueño* of the window of the sacred world. In truth, the old man mentions all the names of the places and mountains that he knows. Or he mentions all the names that he was saying when he was burning the candles; every little while he says that he is in such a mountain and he says that he now killed a jaguar, now the lions, running a lot with his two little dogs and acting as if he were suffering a lot.

First he kills the lions, jaguars, and monkeys. When he kills the first animals, he carries them as cargo on his back to where he finds the old woman, and there he puts them on the ground. Then the old woman comes and burns a lot of incense, as if she were giving thanks to the *dueños* of the mountains. She says the same things as her husband said.

Then the old man says, "Catarina, now see that indeed we have a lot of meat. Now I'm going to kill the animals that are better known as the deer." Then the old fellow enters again to kill the deer, and he mixes again among all the people, looking for concealed deer. When the old man finds one, he follows it and rushes it and encourages the little dogs, who struggle a lot until reaching the deer. When the deer are tied, the jaguars are in charge, carrying them *cargados* [on their backs as cargo].

When they approach where the old woman is, the little dogs go out ahead, and when the old woman sees that dogs have arrived, she gets up and grabs the incensory. She burns a lot of myrrh, or incense, to meet the old man when he comes loaded with the deer.

When the old man reaches the place where they are dancing, he begins another *costumbre* to give thanks to God, because during the hunt in the mountains nothing happened to his little dogs. He behaves as if he were skinning the deer. After taking off the skin of the deer, they place on the neck of the old woman a cape that the deer dancers use. Then the two old people enter to dance some other tunes, telling the people they are sunning the hide [or skin] of the deer that he had killed in the mountains. The old woman appears with the cape tied to her neck, which the old man is holding up from behind; the dogs dance in a column with them, saying a lot of funny things to get a lot of laughs from the aficionados.

There is one thing—when the old man goes to look for the animals among the people, the women hide or retreat and shout a lot when the old man approaches them because the old fellow is very naughty. He puts his cane between the skirts of the women, feels the breasts of the señoritas, looks for the good-looking young girls and kisses them, and says that he is going to separate from Catarina because he has another better than her. And when he wants, a very pretty girl is carried *cargado* to where he had left his woman and tells her that now there are two and not to get angry because life is that way. But the woman that they carry *cargado* is made to feel very ashamed because all the people are laughing at her. And the old man tells more jokes about the women, all that he knows and all they have told him about the women of San José. The only thing is that he doesn't tell their names. After making these commentaries, they continue dancing and dancing until they get tired.[16]

—Ignacio Bizarro Ujpán

Creation Myth

The world was made 500 million
years ago. But earlier, no one can imagine how it was before these 500 million
years. And at the beginning of these 500 million
years, the world began to form. Before these 500
million years, there were mountains, only mountains. There were no people, no animals, not any kind
of animals. People were formed, and then there were animals.
But before this, there were no animals, only mountains and no
forms of life. And then when God started to reign and to form
the world, that's when the volcanoes, water, rivers, waves, and
everything were made.

After all this God made man and woman, then the world,
and the peoples, because the first man was the seed of the race
—only one. At the same time, the man and the woman were
the same thing: the same heart, the same flesh. From this, man
and woman resulted. After this the man had a son. A son and
then a daughter, and then it was the world.

Then the world was formed. Every son made a house; the
father in his house made the son. And this son ended up with a
family also. And this is how a little village was formed. But
before this first man and woman it was only one body.

Now the first man started to work, but he didn't have to
work with much strength. He just went to put his ax or his
machete with a stick, and there it was—all alone the ax went
into the stick and cut it. The stick was cut and felled, and then
the man took the stick. Then he went to another stick, and that

was all he had to do. Then the same, and another stick was cut. And then the stick fell and the machete fell. And so in this way he continued to cut the wood. The sticks fell and the machete fell.

And to clear the land there was only one tool, which was not like a regular hoe. He just put the point of the tool into the ground and it did the work by itself. And the land was all cleared.

At this time only God spoke with the man. The man didn't have a father or a mother, only himself, only one person. And the woman was the same and there were no other people. He was the whole world. He was the first one. And then, when all the land was cleared, God spoke to the man in his dreams. God said, "Here is the seed at the door of your house. Take this seed and plant it. Only plant one seed. And then a meter of seed. From that one, plant another." This was like corn and beans. And this is how he dreamed that God had spoken to him in his dreams.

The next day when he got up he went out the door and said, "I dreamed that there were some seeds at the door of my house because that is what God said in my dream. I'm going to look for them." And he found them. He found corn and beans for sowing. And these were planted on the land that had been cleared, where he had first worked.

When he changed his work is when woman sinned. It happened that the woman listened to the word of an animal because at this time all of the animals spoke and understood. God said in the dream of the husband of the woman, "Your wife should stay in the home. Only you will go to the campo to clear and work the land and plant, and the woman will stay in the house. She will stay and take care of the house and make lunch. But at the same time she is responsible for the animals, because the animals need food."

So the woman stayed at home and the man went to work. And that woman took care of all the animals. The time came when all of the animals had arrived. She gave all of the food to the animals because the animals knew that she was their patron. The woman was the *dueña* [owner] of the house, and the animals knew that it was she who had to feed them.

Then afterward, because the animals could talk, they spoke to the woman. "Why are you a woman, and why are you alone? Only you live in this house. Why don't you have a man?"

And the woman said, "Yes, I have a man. I have a husband. My husband went to work in the campo. That's why I am alone. Why do you ask?"

"I ask because I wish to ask."

"Why do you wish to ask?" said the woman to the animal.

"Because I feel like it. I like chatting with you."

"Why do you feel like it; why do you like talking to me?"

"Because I wish to and also I want to try your food because our food is different. I don't know what your food is like, but I want to eat your food. And if you like our food, that is to say, the food that we animals eat, then we are equal," said the animal.

"I can't," the woman said, "because my husband told me that we can't eat this food, this animal food. Animals have one kind of food, and we have another, because God left food for us and God left food for you who are animals."

"But it's the same because we talk to you and you speak to us. It's all the same."

"You say that it doesn't matter, but it does. If I eat that food—your food—then I, too, am an animal. And if you eat our food, then you are not an animal—you are a person."

"Oh no, you don't have to think about that very much. You eat some of our food and that is that."

And then the animal grabbed some fruit, the food of the animals, and said, "Why don't you taste this? Why don't you try its flavor, the flavor of our food?"

Then the animal split open a fruit and gave it to the

woman. He did this by force and pushed it into her mouth. The woman felt the flavor of the fruit, the food of the animals. And so the woman said, "But this food is delicious. Why don't we eat this? Why does my husband say that it is forbidden, the animals' food? He says that one would die. He says that he knows that you can't eat the animals' food. And now I'm not going to die. I'm alive, and I ate the fruit. I received the food of the animals. I already tried it, and it tastes good. And I'm alive. I'm going to go advise my husband of this. Well, good-bye, animals."

The woman left to go to her husband. The woman never went to her husband in the campo, but this day she went to him and she said, *"Buenas tardes."*

"Buenas tardes," said her husband, "and what are you looking for?"

"I came because something happened to me at home. I gave food to the animals and one of them, the kind that talks, forced me to eat their food. I ate it, and I thought it was very good food. I told him that you had told me that it was forbidden to eat the food of the animals, that you told me a person would die if she ate that food, but I ate it and I'm not dead. Now, please, you try it. It's really tasty."

"We'll see," said the man. He took the food from the woman's hand and ate it. And that is when all of the tools broke and fell—all of them—and they didn't work anymore. That was when the sin happened, because that's when the woman ate the food of the animals. That, then, is when she sinned. And when the man ate the food of the animals, that is when all of the tools fell down and quit working by themselves. The man looked at his wife, who was naked, who wasn't wearing clothes, and the woman looked at her husband, who didn't have clothes either. At this time there were no clothes. They didn't know whether it was necessary or not to wear clothing.

When the woman sinned with the animal, God said, "At

that same time there was a sin among you, because the woman accepted the food of the animals. I told you not to take this food. Now what has happened is a sin. The woman sinned and the man sinned, too, because they received the food of the animals. Now the man has to work with pure force. He has to sweat; water must come from his body. He has to earn his own food by his own effort. He has to move his whole body; his whole body will have to move. All of his five senses and those of the woman will have to work. The woman too will always have to work and suffer. If the man doesn't make enough, the woman will have to put up with it. She may or may not have clothing, but she'll have to work and she'll have to suffer because the two sinned."

And God said, "And now the king of the animals must be found. Where is the king of the animals? I want him to present himself to me." He called the king of the animals.

And the king of the animals presented himself before God. And God said, "You are an animal. Why did you offer your food to my daughter, to the woman Evarial?"

The animal didn't speak.

"Why did you force her to accept the food?" And the animal didn't speak.

The woman repeated, "I ate the animals' food because the king of the animals made me. It's not my fault. The king of the animals is the one because he forced me. I didn't want to, but he forced me to do it, and I had to accept it. He pushed it into my mouth with his hand."

"And now the animals can't just eat their food," said God. "They have to work, they have to look for their food. They will have to go to the rocks, the stones, to search for their food because the king of the animals sinned, and the king of the people sinned also. But first, these animals will have to go to the rocks. They will have to go there to look for their food. Their food will be a fruit that has to be thrashed that is found in the mountains. They will no longer come into the house to

live. And the king of the animals will go into the volcano. And
if he doesn't find food he will have to eat dirt. And now he
can't talk. Before he talked, but now he can't speak because
his speech is taken away from him. I had given him a little
voice, but now that he has sinned this voice will be taken away
from him—his speech will be gone. And his hands and feet
will be taken away; only his body will remain. He'll have to
walk dragging his body. This is his punishment forever, and he
won't have the right to enter the house of my son. His speech
is also gone. Only his hearing and his eyes remain. He has to
walk on the ground pulling his body himself. Food will be
scarce; there won't be very much for him. Like this he will be
all of the time.

"Now my children have to work. The woman has to have
a son, a son and a daughter. Some men and women have to be
born. They'll have to make their own clothing. For now, they'll
have to sew leaves together." Then the man and the woman
started.

Now, first the hands, feet, and speech were taken from
the animals and only the animals' hearing and sight, only these
two things remained. And afterward God said, "Go on, animal! Go to the volcano in the mountains! You don't have any
right to stay in my son's house. You are to go to the pasture.
But be careful because that is my son," said God, "and God is
always in heaven so he has good luck. You don't have any
right to bother my son. He works there in the mountains, but
you don't bother him."

God said: "And now my son you are a man."

Man: "But why don't the tools work by themselves anymore?"

God: "You have to work by your own force now."

Man: "What is the cause for that?"

"Because of the animal," said God.

"Because of the animal? Because the animal offered food
to my wife and we fell into sin?"

"Yes, that is correct, my son. Now, my son, you are a guardian. You will work in the campo and in the mountains also. If you should encounter this animal in the mountains while you are working, take out your machete and cut his head. Never cut him in the middle or behind. Only in the head —there you have a right to, my son. Cut here," said God. "The animals have no right to kill my son. But you, my son, you are a guardian. If you think a lot, and if you think only about your work and your food and don't think about my name, then the animal has the right to bite you. The animal also has rights so you have to be careful. You only have to call my name, call my name all of the time. Because these animals have to be working."

Then to the animals, "When my son is thinking a lot and doesn't think of my name, it is your name he is glorifying. Then you have the right to bite my son. This is the law. Now everything is arranged. Now you, my son, guardian, have to work forever. And you are going to have children—men and women. And what are you going to do when your strength runs out? This strength is going to end within six months or within six years. You will have to wait one day at home because you will tire and will have to rest, like a sick person. Your bones and your flesh and your blood will grow tired. You will have to rest a few days. But after this if you don't have the courage or the strength to continue working, because your strength is gone, what will you do to keep your strength as it had been before?"

The man said, "I don't know."

"Well, you don't know. You are my son and now I will leave you a *costumbre* to do. When you don't have any more strength, look for this: the seed, the sowing seed. And this will have to be burned. Then the flavor of this seed will come up to heaven where I am. I will receive the smoke of the seeds, and then this will be food for you. If you do this custom now— burn the seeds—then the next day you will have lots of strength. Then you will feel like the man of before. And so now then, if you just go to work, nothing will happen. Go to work with your tools, and work happily, content with everything, happy. If you go singing to work, then your wife, too, will keep singing. She will grind the corn and do all of her other work singing, happy, and content. When your strength runs out, you will have to do another *costumbre*. And this is how you will live until the time when you will rest with me. But for now it will be how I tell you. Be careful not to have two wives. Later you will see another woman, but don't think anything, only one, only one wife. And for you, woman, only one husband. Because if you, my son, are going to have two wives, you are just like the animals. And if you, my daughter, woman, are going to have two men, then you, too, are like an animal. Then you will be punished and you won't be worth anything here in the world. If you follow my law, everything will be happy. That's what has to be done. Just follow the *costumbres*," said God.

All of the animals went to the mountains, to the volcanoes, to the rocks—all of them. The woman stayed at home alone to fix lunch, to fix food for her husband. The man went to work in the campo. He was there working, and he thought, "Ay, I had better go home. Because I'm very happy and content and so is my wife. She is singing now. I'd better go to her and sing with her, too. We will both sing because we are both happy at this time. What God said was true. But I want to look at the animal because God said I would find the animal here where I work. But where can I find this animal? I haven't found him. Oh well, it's not worth worrying about. I'll keep working," he said. But just then, when he had thought about the animal, there it was only about a yard away. The animal appeared. "Ah, this is the animal," the man said.

The man spoke with the animal, but the animal didn't speak anymore as he had before. He only did his head like this [Sajón moving his head and sticking out his tongue]. Then the man said, "Ah, the animal is hungry now. But what does he eat? God knows, but I don't know." The animal just listened and looked, but now he couldn't speak and he didn't have hands or feet. He just listened, like this [Sahon being still].

The animal heard the man say, "The animal is hungry, but I don't know what kind of food he eats; only he knows."

Then the animal started to eat dirt. The man watched the animal, and when the animal was eating the dirt, the man said, "Oh, that's his food. That's easy then. He just eats dirt," said the man. When the man said this, he thought, "They are right because he is to blame. We can't eat the soil. Or maybe we can also," said the man. The man sinned because he thought that he, too, could eat dirt. When the man thought this, that is when he felt that he didn't have any strength. "Now I'm so tired." He lay down in the shade, and now had no strength because he thought, "I, too, can eat soil." God said that it was for the animals when they can't find the fruits of the mountains. It is like that with us now. When we don't have bread, it's all right. When we still have bread, we think, "Now we'll have a cup of hot chocolate, milk, or coffee." When we have bread, we take the bread; we have milk with bread, or coffee with bread, or chocolate with bread.

And so, that is how things were then. When the animal didn't find the fruit, he ate dirt. And when the man saw that the animal was eating the dirt, he thought, "I, too, can eat the dirt." That is when he sinned. That was a sin. That is why he didn't have any more strength. He fell down and was overcome by tiredness. When this happened, he fell asleep.

When sleep came to him, God spoke to him in his dream. God said to the man, "Be very careful. Why do you want to eat the soil? If you eat dirt, you will return to the soil. You will turn back into an animal. The soil is not for you. That's why I left food for you. Why are you thinking of eating the soil? Be careful, my son. That is why I left the *costumbre*. You still need to follow that *costumbre* because now all of your strength is gone. Why do you want to eat dirt? Now I need a *costumbre* from you. A *costumbre* must be made."

And so the man asked God, "Señor God, what kind of *costumbre* am I going to do?"

"You will follow the same *costumbre*, the *costumbre* of burning seeds: the seeds of the fruit, the sowing seeds. Burn 2 pounds the first time; the second time, 4 pounds; the third time, 5 pounds; and the fourth time, 6 pounds. Up to 100 pounds can be burned. That will be later. Not now, because now is the first time. It's new; you are new. Now what you are going to do is burn 2 pounds. Burn 2 pounds of seeds, and the smoke from these seeds will rise up in the air to the heavens and that's where I will be. I am looking at you right now to see what you are doing in the world. There is always this *costumbre*. Now you have your strength, but don't think anymore about eating the soil. Don't think about anything like that. Think only about the one God and continue working. You have to have good children—men and women. And teach all of your children the *costumbres*, all of the children of your family. They will learn this and when they are grown, they, too, will follow the customs. You are doing this now for when you are old. You are doing part of the custom for yourself and part of it for your children. Each of your children is part of the custom." So said God to the guardian in his dreams.

And so when he returned to his work after awakening, he said, "I was sleeping. But why did I fall asleep? There is a reason, because God said when one works very hard he tires very quickly. I have worked very hard, and when I saw the animal eating dirt, I thought that I could eat it also. And after that I sinned. That made this dream—and this dream was very important. I think it's best that I go home now to my wife and tell her what has happened."

He arrived home to his wife and said, "I worked. I worked very hard but I ran into the animal, just as God had said—that I would find the animal there where I work. It's true because I did find the animal. But he started to eat the dirt, and I thought I could eat it too. This is what I thought, and then I fell asleep. Then, when I was sleeping, God spoke to me in my dream. Now I know everything. Now there is no pain [trouble]. He said that we are going to have children — both sons and daughters. He also said that we must follow our *costumbres*. This very day we are going to do it; we're going to follow the *costumbre* because God told us to burn the seeds. It's nothing! It's only 2 pounds that we have to burn today. And after that he said 4 pounds, then 5 pounds, then 6 pounds, and on up to 100, then up to 200, 400, and 600 pounds. This is for strength and enjoyment and happiness, and it is really very good. There's no problem. Now I'm able to carry out the custom. That is how God spoke to me already."

"And what did you do so that God talked to you?"

"God spoke to me while I was working. This was because the animal started to eat the soil, and I thought I could too. I was also wondering where I was going to find this animal because God said that I would see him at my place of work. I was thinking about the animal, and then I met him. He was the same animal — the king of the animals — that was right here in our house that had hands and feet. But now he doesn't have hands and feet, and he couldn't talk. He didn't speak to me, he just moved his head like this [Sahon moving his head]. God had said that when the animal couldn't find food that he had to eat dirt. That was what I thought, and that is exactly how it was. Right then, right in front of me, he started eating dirt. Then I knew what God had said was true because the animal had to eat dirt. So I thought that maybe I could eat it too. But as soon as I did I fell asleep. I fell down right there and slept. After I slept a little God spoke to me in my dream. And that is why we have to carry out the *costumbre*, starting this same day. So today I won't go to work. Let's just get on with the *costumbre*. We'll eat first and then start."

"All right, fine. Now I'm happy. But when you came

home today I felt a little sad in my heart. I don't know why."

"It's because this *costumbre* is necessary. So we are going to do it today. We're going to continue to live here in the house and be happy. That's all we're going to do. There is no other way, no other work, only that. And in this way we can live very well. We're going to have many children. We'll see what kind of children we have, how their faces will be. Yes, we'll see if the children we have are good-looking."

"Oh yes, we'll have children. That's no problem. Then I will be happy."

They started to eat, and after they had finished the meal they went to sleep. The woman dreamed that now she needed a *costumbre*. God told her in the dream that she had to carry out the *costumbre*. "Because if you don't do as I ask, you will die, and then you won't finish your time here on earth. I don't want you to die. And I don't want you to eat the soil. I don't like the idea that you would eat filth, mud, or dirt. I don't like that," said God. "You are my children. You must eat good things. Look for good things to eat because I already have a garden. In this garden there are many fruits. These are for you. There, in this garden, no animals will exist. They are in the mountains and the volcanoes. Now there is nothing here. Right now I'm going to show you where the garden is—where there are oranges, limes, apples, peaches, and many others, hundreds of others, that are good for you. But I like your work. This garden, this farm, must be cleared. I'll give you fertilizer, and every single year you will have to put fertilizer in the soil. It will bear good fruit for you. The seeds must be dried and every three months burned. That is to be your ritual." That was all that the wife of the guardian dreamed. And so when she awakened she said, "I was sleeping. I fell asleep."

"I did too. The same thing happened to both of us. But tell me what you dreamed. Tell me what God said to you while you slept."

"Now, I am very happy, very content," said the woman, "because God said in my dream that we are going to have a garden. And this garden will have many fruits—oranges, limes, apples, peaches, many different kinds. We'll have to go see it. And because of this we will need fertilizer. Every year we'll have to put fertilizer in the soil. All of the fruit is for us and the juice, the water, all for us. And the seeds that we find inside will serve for our offering. He says that every three months we will have to burn seeds. And we will do it because it is good to do so. That is all of the dream. And your dream?"

"I, too, dreamed that God talked to me," said the man. "God said in my dream that we are going to have children. And these children that we will have will be both male and female. And when we need clothes for our children, we will ask God for them. God will give us clothing for our children. This will be very pleasant. I have a great desire to see my children now. But the *costumbre* must be continued. That is what God told me while I slept. Well now, let's go see this garden."

The two of them, the man and the woman, went to look for the garden, and sure enough they found it. They only walked a short way, something like ten meters or so. And there was this garden, and there were many fruits there. The fruits that were there were already ripe and ready to eat. When they arrived there, they picked some of the fruit and tasted it. It was very tasty.

Then the woman said, "Now it's not necessary to prepare food at home because we will get full just by eating all of this fruit."

"But, no!" replied the man, "because God said that you have to make our food. Yes, we will eat this fruit, but it will be a help to us—that's all. When we go out for a walk, we'll be able to come here and eat the fruit. Because if it isn't this way it wouldn't be right. Because you know that in the past I worked in the campo without effort. When I got to the campo,

I just sat down and only the tools worked all by themselves. But now I'll have to work. This is a garden. It needs lots of work. I'll have to clear it all. You won't be able to help me very much, maybe to pick some of the fruit. I'll have to look for fertilizer. What are we going to do? Well, we'll at least have this land. It is very pretty. When we have children, they will come with us here to eat fruit. Now we are very content. And today we will have our ceremony. We'll burn two pounds of seed because that is the way the ritual is."

Before there weren't any candles or drinking water. They went through with the ritual of burning the seeds. Then God said, "That isn't the correct way to do it. You need water. First, you eat and then drink the water. Burn the seeds first, then throw water onto them." According to the dream, that is what they had to do. They had to have the juice of the fruits for the ceremony. Then they threw orange juice on the offering, and then apple juice. And still something was missing. God told them what else had to be done with other kinds of fruits.

So it went that they were there living in that place and taking their fruits into their home. And they were very happy. They continued with the *costumbre* of having the offering. And this man and woman ended up having about twenty children. They had many children and all of them lived—all of the men and all of the women. One of the women was named María, another Juana, another Teresa, and so on. Of the men, one was Martín, one Juan, one Andrés, another Zac, and another Pedro. Each of the children had a different name. And out of all of these children there was one who was very jealous, very mischievous, very offensive.

The first son made an offering and the smoke from this offering rose up toward heaven. The second son also did the *costumbre*, but the smoke from his offering stayed here on earth —it didn't rise. It just stayed here on the earth. For the third son the smoke rose up, but very little. For the fourth son, once again the smoke rose a little. There were five sons in all. When the first four burned their offerings, the first son's smoke went to heaven, the second son's smoke stayed close to the earth, and the same with the fourth son's smoke, rising but not very high. Then the fifth son's smoke rose all the way to heaven. All of the other brothers said, "He is very small. Why did his offering go to heaven and ours didn't? Because we're much bigger and we're the first sons. Why, if he's so small, did the smoke from his offering go to heaven? What are we going to do about this?"

Then the oldest, the first, since he had made an offering from which the smoke went up to heaven said, "It was our own fault. Because to properly carry out the ceremony one must go down on his knees like this. And you didn't kneel down. You just did this [Sajón standing up]. You didn't get with God."

"Ah, yes, that must be what was lacking, of course."

"When we do it again, we must take care that it is done properly," said the big man, the oldest son.

"Oh, that's good."

So when they did the ritual again the oldest son knelt down and made his offering, and the smoke went up to heaven.

Then the next son said, "I'm going to make my offering here." The second son knelt down and made his offering. "Now my smoke will go to heaven." The smoke rose up but very little. It only went up about two or three meters but not to heaven. The third son also did the same thing. For the fourth son, the same thing happened. The fifth son, the very smallest son, then offered his sacrifice. And the smoke from his offering went up to heaven. This was the same that happened with the oldest son. The smallest son's smoke rose up to heaven. Then the other three said, "Why doesn't the smoke go up to heaven?" Then to the oldest son they said, "We can understand that your offering would go to heaven because you are the oldest. But him! He's so small! He's the youngest of all of us. And we're bigger. Why doesn't our smoke rise up?"

"It is because you three are lacking something," said the oldest.

"No, we lack nothing. Because you told us that we had to kneel down, and I knelt down. All three of us knelt down."

"I don't know. I told you that something was missing. Something must have been missing."

"No, nothing was wrong. That can't be."

"Something was missing."

"We will call our father. He knows." And after they had called their father he arrived, and the oldest son said to him, "We did the *costumbre*. When I did it the smoke from my offering went up to heaven and the littlest one's smoke went up to heaven. But the smoke from the offerings of the other three would not rise up."

"What words did you say as you were doing the offering?"

"I thought, 'We'll see,' as I was making my offering," said the other son.

"Oh! That's why your smoke didn't rise. You can't say that. You can't say, 'We'll see.' This must be done with the whole heart. And you, what did you say?" he asked the other.

"I thought, 'We'll see if He gives us land because I am hungry.' This is what I thought when I started to work on the offering."

"Ah, that's the reason that the smoke didn't go up to heaven. And you, what did you think?"

"I thought, 'This offering isn't worth anything. I'm not doing this very well.' That's what I thought."

"That's why the smoke didn't go up. And what did you think?"

"I thought, 'This *costumbre* is very good; that is, good luck.' That's what I said, and then I started my offering."

"Ah ha, that's why your smoke went up to heaven. And you, my little one, what did you think when you made your offering?"

"I said, 'I am much smaller. But if you will pardon me, God, I will make an offering.' "

"That's why your smoke went to heaven. You three are different. You didn't carry out the ceremony with all of your hearts. And you all said words that were not very good. Because of this your smoke didn't make it to heaven. Now I'm going to tell you what must be done, how the custom must be put into effect, like this way or that way."

"Oh good. Now we'll know."

And after this they did the *costumbre* again, but the same thing happened. These three thought, "Now we're going to do it again. We'll see whether or not the smoke goes up." They thought the same thing, and for this reason, the smoke still didn't go up to God. That of the oldest son and of the youngest did go up to heaven again.

The other three said, "No, no, no! It's just that God doesn't help us. We're big. Why doesn't the smoke go anywhere? It seems that God doesn't love us and it's because of this. It must be because God won't help us. Maybe it would be better if we just killed this little boy. We'll kill him."

These three got together and said, "We won't say anything to the older brother because for him it was right that the smoke went up, because he is grown. We can't command him, but the little one we can. Why did his offering get accepted and ours didn't? That's what we're going to do—we're going to kill our little brother. But how are we going to kill him? With a machete, or catch and behead him? What we'll do is take off his head. The three of us will grab him and behead him. We'll go to some secluded place and grab him and do it."

And so when the time came they said to the little muchacho, the youngest, "Would you do us the favor of accompanying us for a walk? There is a very pleasant place, and that is where we are going." And so the young son went with the other three brothers. They went to some place like a mountain. When they were there they grabbed him and cut off his head. They killed him! They killed the little boy, the youngest son! And so the little boy was dead. They returned home.

The father asked, "And your brother, where is he, because he went with you?"

"He's coming; he's coming."

But the whole day passed by, and he didn't come home. And so the father said, "Well then, your oldest brother will come with me, and we'll go look for the little one. You stay here."

So they left and went to the mountain. There they heard the little boy screaming. The head was in one place, and the body was very far away from it, about ten or fifteen meters separated from the body. And then the father heard what the little boy was shouting. "Mother, father, mom, dad!" The head was saying, "Father," and the body was saying, "Mother." The body and the head were talking when they arrived.

"My son is dead." They picked him up. And when they did, his head didn't move. He had died once and for all. Then they went to get the body because they wanted to take that with them, too. It didn't move. It didn't do anything. The head didn't talk anymore, and the body didn't talk anymore.

"Now I'm going to punish them," said the father. "Now I'm going to hit them. Because this is a very serious crime, I will punish them. I'm going to think about what punishment I'm going to give them. If I kill them, that wouldn't be good either, because I'm not God," said the father. "We'll see what God says."

They took the whole body to the house. When they got

there, there were the three brothers. These three that killed
the brother fell down. One was left without a hand, another
without a foot, and the other without an eye. That's how it
turned out. They were no longer complete. They were still
alive, but one didn't have a hand, one didn't have a foot, and
one didn't have an eye. One of his eyes was closed; another
didn't have a hand; and the other didn't have a foot.

Then the father fell asleep. God said to him in his dream,
"It is not your fault, because you didn't notice it. But I saw it,
and that's how it was. I saw it. I saw them kill my son. And
now my little son is with me." He called him the little one. He
said the little one had come. "The little one, the youngest son,
is here with me. Don't feel bad. You are my son. You are a
guardian. Here he is. This little one's brothers killed him, but
he is not dead. He is here with me. He has a good place. He
has a good home, because he was not at fault. He made an
offering in my name, and because he did it in my name, I
received the offering. But the others are in danger. They did a
very bad thing, and this is their punishment. They cannot
make up for what they have done. They will always be the
same. When they finish their time on earth, they will come
here, but they will be the same always; one without a hand,
one without a foot, and the other without an eye. That's that.
That is the punishment I give. Care must be taken. When a
ritual takes place, it must be done with the whole heart. If the
person does not do it with all his heart, the offering is not
worth anything."

And that is the way that it was. The ceremonies had to be
carried out with all of one's heart. The person making the
offering had to talk a lot to God. The little boy was not dead.
He was with God. Because God said to the man in his dream,
"Don't feel bad, because the little boy is here. The oldest son,
the first son, is good. He will carry out my law. The little one
carried out my law, but the others wanted to kill him. They
killed the person here on earth, but he is here with me. Don't

worry because he is here with me. He has a good place, a good house, and good clothes. It is very good here. And now everyone must think about doing the *costumbre* very well." This is what God said to the man in his dream. And that is all.

This is the story of the world.

—Juan Sajón Martín

Story of the Lazybones and the Perfect Intendant[17]

 This story is very popular among the native people, mainly the old folks. Also, they use it as a means of giving examples to their children and grandchildren.

They say that earlier a pair of persons lived in these pueblos, but they were very lazy; they didn't want to bathe, work, or wash their clothing. The story says that for them work was an enemy. From idleness they suffered a lot of poverty; it cost them to obtain their daily food. The man was called Baltazar and the woman Manuela.

One day they set to talking about their life—that only they were suffering the most in the town. The rest of the people had their money, land, and their *chompipes* [common turkeys], but they didn't. Then they began to discuss it. Baltazar said to his woman, "I want us to have a change in life. I want to work with the people to earn our corn and our money, but each morning you get up very late. When I go to ask for work with the people, the women tell me that their husbands have already gone to work, and others tell me that our *mozos* [helpers] go very early to work. Well, this poverty is your own fault because each day you get up very late, and for that reason, the people don't give me work."

Manuela answered her husband and told him, "My dear husband, it's certain what you tell me, that I get up very late. It's because I don't have firewood with which to make a fire; I don't have coffee to make nor do I have *nixtamal* [corn cooked in lime or ash water] to grind. Otherwise, with much pleasure I would get up earlier."

"It's true what you say. We are much to blame, and for that reason we are very poor."

"Now we are going to struggle," the two said.

When night fell, they slept because they thought they would have to get up very early the next day. All night long they slept very contentedly. When it was dawn, that is to say, at the hour of getting up, Manuela told Baltazar, "I'm getting up to make a fire and make some tortillas so that you can go look for your work with the people."

Baltazar said, "Don't get up yet. It's very early and cold, and you can get sick, and we don't have money to buy you a remedy."

"Fine," said Manuela, and she continued sleeping very peacefully. And the two of them continued sleeping.

A little later Baltazar woke up and told his woman, "I'm going to get up to split the firewood so that you can make a fire and cook tortillas."

Manuela told her husband, "Don't get up. It's very early and you can make a mistake with the ax; I'm just one woman, and I can't do anything to cure you."

"Fine," said Baltazar, and he slept more.

When they got up, it was already seven in the morning. Then the two began to maltreat one another.

"Well," said Baltazar, "we have done nothing for this day. Better that I go to the coast to earn a living."

"Very well," said Manuela. "I will make some tortillas and some onions for your food."

The story says that Baltazar prepared his bundle, crying and cursing poverty. He passed through Pazilín very sad. When he passed through Pachichaj, he was bitten by a dog, but he did not give any importance to the bite. On the road he met a man who had a mule stuck in a muddy place. The owner asked Baltazar to help him get the mule out of the quagmire.

"Yes," said Baltazar, putting down his bundle. He thought the man was going to pay. Then he began to get the mule out, but such bad luck had Baltazar that he grabbed the tail of the mule and was heaving a lot to get him out. The mule, however, was well planted in the mud. In the end of it all, Baltazar was pulling and pulling the tail of the mule and suddenly the tail of the mule came off. The owner of the animal became very angry that Baltazar had torn off the tail of the mule, and he struck him with a good kick. Poor, unfortunate Baltazar in place of earning a few centavos was given a blow.

The story says that he continued walking, and he passed through Paxob. There he forgot about the blow and felt hungry, but since the tortillas were very cold, he didn't eat. He continued walking until San Rafael Panán. There he asked permission from a señora to heat up his tortillas and roast the two onions. The owner of the house was pregnant, but Baltazar didn't give any importance to the señora being pregnant. After warming the tortillas and roasting the onion, he began to eat. The story says the woman was salivating because she had much desire to eat roasted onions, but since this family also was lazy, there was nothing in the kitchen, and it made her much ashamed to ask him for a little of the onions. But Baltazar, as if nothing had happened, upon finishing eating was in the town looking for work. But the señora, since she was pregnant, felt bad that she wasn't given a little onion, and finally, in the end, the señora aborted. The baby died because she only carried it five months.

When the husband arrived, she told him what had happened. "The abortion was caused because a certain Baltazar was eating in the house and didn't give me a little roasted onion, and that was only thing that caused the abortion."

The husband became furious, more than just angry, and ran to the justice of the peace to demand that this man be held responsible for the abortion, that is to say, for burying the dead baby and the cure of the woman, the mother. A commission ran throughout the whole town to find and capture Baltazar.

When they found him, they took him to jail without knowing what his crime was. In place of looking for work, he wound up in jail. The next day they took him out of the jail and to the presence of the intendant of the town where there the plaintiff, the husband of the woman, appeared to accuse Baltazar because the husband wanted money for himself, since he, too, was a lazybones.

They asked the husband what sentence he wanted against Baltazar, and he asked that they shoot him once and for all if he didn't recognize the damage that he had caused his woman. But Baltazar didn't have the means to pay the husband. Baltazar answered with these words, "Señor Intendant, I left my pueblo to come here to look for work. I have left my woman. We are very poor. We just have a *ranchito* [small, rustic house] where we live."

The intendant asked him, "What happened in the house of such a woman?"

He answered, "Nothing has happened. Only I asked the favor of the woman of this señor to warm my tortillas and roast my two onions; the señora gave me permission. I heated my tortillas and roasted the two onions and ate peacefully."

The intendant asked him, "Why didn't you give a piece of onion to the woman of the house?"

"Señor Intendant," Baltazar answered, "I didn't have more than two little onions and some tortillas. I didn't have anything to give to this woman."

The intendant said to the husband, "It wasn't this man who has caused the abortion; the blame is yours. Every man ought to have something in his house, at least onions. Then your woman aborted because she wanted to eat something but you didn't have anything in the house."

Then the intendant declared, "There is pardon for Baltazar because it wasn't he who committed the abortion."

But the husband became angry and was crying because he had lost his first son at the time of pregnancy. The intendant wanted to thus set aside this case, but the husband of the woman was insistent and asked for money or death for Baltazar, but Baltazar had nothing. The intendant made justice thusly: "Affected husband, you want to ask him for money, but he has nothing because he is going around looking for work. However, there is one thing that he can do in order for you to gain something."

Again the intendant spoke to Baltazar. "Miserable hombre you are since you didn't give an onion to this woman and for that reason she aborted." Then the intendant sent for the woman. When the woman arrived, she appealed anew, explaining what had happened.

Then the intendant was very final. "Baltazar, ingrate and miserable person; it is because of you this woman lost her baby. Husband, idler, you don't have even an onion in your house and neither do you want to pardon this man that you say has caused the abortion of your woman. Woman, you have suffered from an abortion and lost your child who might have been a virtuous person on earth." The intendant sentenced Baltazar thusly, saying, "Baltazar, the husband doesn't want to pardon you; he wants for you a sentence. Well, I'm going to sentence you thusly. You will take the woman to your house, then impregnate her, and give her a lot of onions so that she won't abort again. And after nine months, return her to her husband but pregnant. And if you don't comply, then I am going to order you to spend ten years in jail. Thus you will learn not to eat things in front of pregnant women because it is much more sinful to eat in front of a woman."

The story says that the husband was regretful, but once and for all he wanted the intendant to comply with sentencing Baltazar. Instead of bringing money home for his woman, who was waiting for him, Baltazar brought home another woman. For that reason, the people say when one is an idler everything turns out bad. He finds no peace. And even now, a person who meets a pregnant woman can't eat in front of her because for sure it will cause an abortion. If a person eats before a pregnant woman, he has to give her a little of what he is eating to avoid problems like the one that happened to Baltazar.

—Elena Cholotío Meza, San José,
Recorded by Ignacio Bizarro Ujpán

Story of
the Gods of Corn

The story says that formerly white corn was very abundant. Yellow and black corn weren't sown by the *cuerda* [.178 acre], just behind the *ranchos* [rustic dwellings]. The same was with beans; they were just planted behind the *ranchos*, and with the little that was planted much was realized, with very good harvests. The people said that they had sufficient corn even to the point of wasting it. Also beans were abundant to the point of being wasted—the white bean, colorado [red] bean, and the black bean.

The people at that time didn't respect the corn or the beans; nor were they in accordance with giving thanks to God. Also, the people committed many sins. Then God wanted to finish off everything that was in the world, and He planned to make the justice, or the end of the world. He said, "I'm the God who made man and woman. I have given them all the things that there are in the world, but they don't respect me. I have given them corn, beans, tomatoes, chili, pumpkins, *güisquiles* [a climbing plant with fruit the size of an orange], *guicoy* [edible gourd, pumpkin, medium-sized with big grooves on its surface], *chilacayotes* [very large gourd fed to livestock], sweet potatoes, yucca, cacao [chocolate], *pataxte* [or *patashte*, white chocolate]; moreover, I have given them all kinds of herbs, such as *chipilín* and the *quilete* [mulberry herb, a slightly bitter wild plant that is eaten cooked]." Then God was now ready to make justice.

But the story says that there were three gods of maize: the god of white maize, the god of black maize, and the god of yellow maize. These three gods realized that the real God was ready to make justice. Then the god of black corn spoke with the gods of beans to tell them that now He was going to end the world. Then the gods of beans were very happy when they heard that justice was going to be dealt, and they said, "If only God would do justice sooner because our lives are full of torment. They burn us a lot in the fire; day and night we are put over the *tenamastes* [cooking stones, or three-stone hearth]. Never do we feel relief because when they take us from the fire, they grind us for tortillas and bean burritos, throw a lot of chili on us, chew us, and turn us into *caca* [excrement]." The story says he who was the most tormented was the black bean.

The god of black corn and the god of black beans came to an agreement to tell the real God to make justice soon, or to make the world come to an end soon. They said, "We are the gods of black maize and black beans. We have come to talk to you and know that you are a greater God than we are." First the black corn god knelt and said, "My Lord, how I wish that you would make justice sooner. I am the god of black corn and I am suffering a lot on earth. I'm the most despised by the people of the world because of my black color.[18] They don't want to eat me. The people despise and maltreat me. The women throw me like trash in the patio of their *ranchos* [rustic houses]causing me to suffer from the great heat of the sun, and when it rains I'm washed with currents of water. Neither the chickens nor the young goats want to eat me, and for this mistreatment, I ask you make justice so that I not suffer more in this world."

"Very well," said the real God. "Soon I'm going to make justice to end all the things of the world."

Then immediately the god of black beans said, "I know

that you are a more powerful God than I, and for that reason, I ask you to soon make justice to finish off all the people and us because, in this world, I'm more tormented than the white bean and the red bean. All the people torment me daily. They cook me in the morning; they cook me at noon; and they cook me at night. All the time I'm over the fire, and I don't feel relief."

And the story says that the poor kettles and the *tenamastes* said, "We are witnesses. Our suffering is equal, and, for that reason, we ask you to do justice so that we will have a rest from our lives."

"Very well," said God. "Well, I'm going to make justice, but first I have to call the witnesses."

Then he spoke to the witnesses. He talked to the *tenamastes*, the *tituntes* [the small rocks that keep the kettles from falling when placed on the *tenamastes*], and the kettles, who all presented themselves before God and said, "God of all the gods, have compassion with us. We are the most tormented on the fire by the people of the world."

The story says that first they asked for justice. The *tenamastes* said, "Look at our faces. They are burned, burned day and night."

"It's true," said the *tituntes*, "look at our noses. They are burned. Every little while we are inside the fire."

Immediately the kettles said, "God, look at our *culos* [butts] that are burned by the people of the world, all the time that they have us over the fire; at dawn over the fire, at noon on the fire, in the afternoon over the fire, at night over the fire. Our asses day and night are burning over the fire. Our suffering is equal to that of the black bean, and, for that reason, we ask you to make the final justice for our bodies to finally feel some relief."

"Very well," said God, "I'm going to make the final justice, but first the others must come to say why they approve if I'm going to make justice."

The story goes that the real God sent to bring the gods of white corn, of yellow corn, of white beans, and of red beans. When they arrived, He asked them if they wanted justice, or for it to be the end of the world.

"Fine, we indeed approve the final justice of the world," said the gods of white and of yellow corn. "We are the most punished by the people, day and night they have us over the fire. They make lime to peel our faces. Then the women grind us with their grinding stones. Then they burn us in the *comal* [earthenware dish for baking maize tortillas], and they take us out as tortillas or wrap us between leaves and again put us in the fire and take us out as little tamales. Then they chew us with their teeth. For us it's the most cruel punishment, to the point we can't go on. And for that reason, we ask for justice for ourselves so that we will come to feel eternal rest."

When the God heard these things, He said that He was going to make the final justice. But He said it was better to talk to everyone to see if they were in agreement that He would make all the things in the world disappear. The story says that God sent to call the god of tomatoes and chili, and He asked them if they were asking for justice to end everything that was in the world.

The god of tomatoes and chili said, "My life is in your hands. You know of the dishonor of the men and the women. Well, you can make justice. But there is one thing—in the world there are good and bad hombres and good and bad women. Isn't it possible that the good will suffer because of the bad?" The story says that this is what the god of tomatoes and chili said.

"Very well," said the Great God.

He sent to call the god of the pumpkins, *güisquiles*, and *güicoy*, and he asked him, "Do you ask for justice to finish with everything that exists on earth?"

Then the god of the pumpkins, *güisiquiles*, and *güicoys* said, "It's certain that I am a god, but inferior to you, but indeed I'm able to express my sentiments. The gods of corn and beans ask for justice, but they are the biggest liars of all. It's that they are very envious of me. The poor hombres and the *mujeres* [women] plant more pumpkins, more *güisquiles*, and more *güicoys*. They take care of them well, and when the first pumpkins, *güisquiles*, and *güicoys* are ready, before picking them, the men and women kneel and give thanks to the god of pumpkins, *güisquiles*, and *güicoys*. What happens is that I receive the first appreciations of the men and the women, because in a short time comes the harvest of the pumpkin, *güisquiles*, and *güicoys*, and the harvest of corn is ready much later [very late]. More for that reason, much later than me, the gods of corn receive homage. That is the envy of the gods of corn and beans. I'm not in agreement with the justice because the men and women are respectful. They have respect for the gods of corn, but what happens is that the gods of corn are more arrogant, and for that reason, they ask for the justice." This is what the god of pumpkins, *güisquiles*, and *güicoys* said.

When the god of sweet potatoes and yucca was called and appeared before God, he said the same things that the god of pumpkins, *güisquiles*, and *güicoys* said.

The Great God called the god of chocolate beans and *pataxte* to give his opinion. But the god of brown chocolate beans and *pataxte* was a very good friend of the gods of corn, who also obliged the big God to make the final justice, to finish off all the people of the world. Finally, God was convinced to make justice, without taking into account what the god of pumpkins, *güisquiles*, and *güicoys* and the god of sweet potatoes and yucca had said.

Then the god of *chipilín* and *quilete* realized that it was going to be the end of the world, that the big God was now ready to make the justice. Then he presented himself before the big God to protest the justice. He said, "Great God, I'm not in agreement with the end of the world [justice]. The gods of corn and beans are more deceitful. The people of the world are well obedient. The men and the women are always in accordance with you, Great God. And they respect me a lot. Each time that the poor men and women arrive in the campo before picking the species of herbs, they first give thanks to the god of *chipilín* and the *quilete*, and they kneel and kiss each kind of herb that they find, because the poor people only eat corn and herbs. For that reason, I'm not in agreement with the justice."

The people of the world, however, were all confused and couldn't find out what to do, because according to the god of herbs, the Great God was ready to make the final justice. Thus, many people began to adore the god of the herbs because they came to know that the god of herbs was able to have calmed the ire of the Great God so that He would not make the justice.

The gods of corn and beans felt very offended. On earth, however, there had been the respectful people and disobedient people, and the obedient began to give thanks to the god of pumpkins, *güisquiles*, and *güicoys*; the god of sweet potatoes and yucca; and the god of *chipilín* and *quilete*. In contrast, the disobedient and cowardly people became loco. Many took their women and children and went to the caves to escape. Others dug tunnels below the earth to hide from justice.

Then the gods were in agreement with the good and respectful people, but they had great anger against those who went to the caves and those who hid below the earth. The gods of corn, and the gods of beans, and the god of cacao and *pataxte* again presented themselves before the real God to tell Him about the bad behavior of those who went to the caves and who went in the tunnels and to tell Him to make justice.

Then God made justice by talking to the caves and obliging them to turn women into male coyotes and men into female coyotes. He did the same thing with their children. And it remained commanded that they stay in the caves and big rocks where they will beget sons and daughters until the end of time and that in the caves and in the rocks they will experience hunger and thirst for their disobedience.

Also, for the men, women, and children who had hidden under the earth, it remained commanded that the earth convert into female *taltuzas* [rodents who dig long tunnels in the earth] those who were men and male *taltuzas* those who were women, the same thing with their children. And the earth complied in doing what God had ordered it to do. Since then, the *taltuzas* remained living below the earth where they make their living for all of their lives. Since this time, the *taltuzas* remained the enemy of the obedient men and women, and the enemy of maize and all the cultivations because through them they received eternal punishment. Coyotes also are enemies of the people because they steal their chickens, their *coches* [pigs], *chompipes* [common turkeys], and they persecute the people for revenge.

—Ignacio Bizarro Ujpán

Story of
the Dance of the Conquest

The Dance of the Conquest is a
dance deserving respect of the indigenous people, mainly of the southwest
Cakchiqueles, Quichés, and Tzutuhiles. This
dance is presented in the fiestas of the town, that
is to say, in the titular fiesta of each town.

I'm going to tell and write what it is like in my
town, San José. The person who organizes this dance, or say
the one who is in charge of looking for the dancers, is named
the *tutor* [the guardian, or person in charge] of the dance. The
tutor is the one who spends a lot of money and is very devoted
to the patron saint of the town. Before looking for the dancers,
the *tutor* goes with a shaman to tell him to make a *costumbre* to
begin the rehearsal of the dance of the conquest. Then the
instructor and the shaman indicate the day and hour to do the
costumbre, either in the house of the *tutor* or in some hill. Thus
when the day arrives, the *tutor* prepares the candles, incense,
myrrh, sugar, beers, and *aguardiente* [firewater].

When the hour arrives to begin the *costumbre*, the *tutor*
tells the shaman the names of the persons that he wants to
come as leaders of the dancers, like the king Tecún Umán;
Don Pedro de Alvarado; King Quiché; Witch (Ajitz); and the
Lacandón. These are the important dancers. Without these, it
is not possible to begin the rehearsal. Then the shaman mentions the names of the persons who they are going to audition

to occupy these positions. The shaman, who ordered the candles and incense, drinking the *tragos* [shots] of *aguardiente* with the tutor, says under oath that in this moment will be met the spirits of the dead conquerors in the war, and the two of them say, "May the rehearsals of the dance be done with safety in this *sitio* [homesite]." Also they mention the names of the Spaniards. First just the shaman does this, then the two of them do it.

The names of the dancers are in this order:

The shaman thus mentions the following names and calls their spirits.

Dead Caciques

INDIANS	SPANIARDS
King Tecún Umán	Don Pedro de Alvarado
Huitzitzil Tzunún	Don Francisco Carrillo
Caal Aleján Chávez	Don Juan de León y Cardona
King Tepepul (Tepe)	Don Pedro Portocarrera
Ixcot	Don Lorenson Moreno
Saquimox	Don Francisco Calderon
Ajcot	Don Crijalba (Crijol)
The Witch and his Son	

The Lacandón or the Lacandones. (When there are enough people there are two Lacandones, when not, there is just one.)

Separately they mention the King Quiché, his two sons, princes, and two daughters, princesses, also called Malinches.[19] In the hour when the shaman is making the *costumbre*, he calls the spirits two by two, an Indian and a Spaniard until finishing with all of them, but never a Spaniard first.

The shaman begins with these words, "My Lord, God of

the World, here your son kneels before you to ask your forgiveness in my name and [the name of the *tutor*], your servant." He also says the name of the saint of the town and calls
the spirit of this saint and continues saying, "O King Tecún
Achii, O King Tecún Alaa, present your spirit here in this
house. O King Tecún, I ask you in this moment to leave for
awhile the hill, Chui Pach, where your spirit always resides
and remains. We need you here, O Tecún, Man of Nagual,
who walks among the clouds and in the air. O King Tecún,
who for us, your sons, you lost your life, your blessed blood
spilled on the plains of Xelaju [Quezaltenango], we call you so
that in this moment you will be present with us. Appear in this
house, now that the *tutor*, your son, wants to be responsible for
presenting the dance of Tecún [the conquest] so that in these
times your children and your grandchildren will always remember how you lost your life and so that people from other
towns may see how it was with you. O King Tecún, man of
men, bless this house and give corn, beans, and all that is
necessary to the *tutor* for the dance. O King Tecún, present
your spirit here; we ask you that our enemies will not be able
to do anything against us, that all will turn out well—that
there won't be any blows, that there won't be any injuries
among the dancers, that you will be with them at the hour of
the presenting of this dance; that you will be dancing with
your son who is going to represent you here, Your Holy
Spirit."

The shaman takes a good drink of *aguardiente* and gives it
to the *tutor*. Then he pours a glass of *aguardiente* around where
they are burning candles. He pours a glass on the main door of
the house, a glass on each corner of the *sitio*, and a glass on the
center of the *sitio*. At this moment when he is pouring the
aguardiente, he says, "O King Tecún, here in this holy place
sounds the drum and *chirimía* [indigenous oboe]. Here are going to be your children who are to represent the story of your
life. O King Tecún, you have to be in this *sitio* to protect them

from their enemies. Don't allow the devil to do something against them." All the time the shaman is spraying incense in the whole *sitio*. Preferably this *costumbre* was done during the night so that no one could see it. Indeed, if they do this kind of *costumbre* in the hill, they always come to finish it in the house when they return. The shaman says thusly, "Don Pedro de Alvarado, man of Spain, man of Rome, your Holy Spirit be here with us. Here I, your servant, call you because your Holy Body was here previously on these lands, and, for that reason, we want your Holy Spirit to be here with us in this moment. Don Pedro de Alvarado, who for a moment and a little while, crossed the ocean to bless this house for us and for each one of those who is going to be a dancer, so that he gives a good response to the *tutor*. Speak in the minds of each person so that all will turn out well. Don Pedro de Alvarado, strong man of Spain, man of a blond beard, man of boots and gaiters, don't allow us to lose. Protect us because you also have power on the earth."

When the shaman says these things he drinks and pours *tragos*, as always, and he smokes a lot of cigars [or cigarettes]. Then he begins to dance inside the house, acting as if he's dancing as Don Pedro in the dance. When he is finished with this *costumbre*, the shaman and the *tutor* give their hands to each other [the *tutor* kisses the hand of the shaman and the shaman in turn kisses the hand of the *tutor*] as a sign of commitment that once and for all they will declare the name of the person who is going to teach the dancers. This person is very clever. He has the story, and, moreover, he knows the dance and the movements of each one. All of these things they do through the drinks. The following day the *tutor*, a little drunk, goes to look for his helper, and the two go together to the houses of the other persons to convince them to be dancers in the dance of the conquest. This they do in the same order as the order of the names agreed upon in the earlier *costumbre*.[20]

The *tutor* and the assistant always carry *aguardiente* and cigars in a pocket of their jacket to each house they go.

When they arrive at the house of a person, they chat and convince him through the warmth of *tragos*. When the person visited is a little drunk, he then commits himself as a dancer. Then the *tutor* and the dancer fix the date for the first rehearsal.

In order that all the dancers will gather in the house of the *tutor*, they go to all of them and convince them by means of *tragos*. The problem is that when the glow of liquor passes, many are regretful. This becomes a big bother for the *tutor*, because to become a dancer costs a lot of money and takes a lot of time. The *tutor* has to struggle a lot to find new persons but always with the *tragos* and cigars. If the owner of the house knows that they want him to get drunk, he doesn't accept the *tragos*, and he looks for pretexts, saying that he is feeling ill or he has to leave for work. Then this hombre doesn't want to be a dancer and he does not accept the cigars. The *tutor* and his helper go to other houses until completing the number of twenty-three persons, a minimum of twenty.

The days and the time pass; the *tutor* goes again to the shaman to tell him that all is ready, and they indicate the day for another *costumbre*. Then the *tutor* and his helper go again to the other towns to look for the musicians of the drum and *chirimía*, and the special person, *maestro*, who is going to teach the dance.[21]

The *tutor* is well prepared to wait for the shaman, the same with the musicians and the teacher, generally at night. Then they introduce one another, and the *tutor* gives each a drink and food to eat. Then they make the commitment to begin and finish obligations of the dance. The *tutor* says, "Señor musicians of the drum and flute [oboe], now we are here in this *sitio* and this house together with the teachers. I ask you and I plead with you that we begin and finish. I don't want you to abandon me nor I you. With the señor of the white hair and white beard, señor of incense, of myrrh and copal,[22] now we join with you." And they all kiss each other's hands. This *costumbre* is in the house of the *tutor*.

Then the rest of the dancers arrive. The shaman begins the *costumbre*, calling the names of the persons in accordance with the list that the *tutor* has and the positions of each dancer. Then the shaman begins to call the spirits of the dead, who fell in the war, in the presence of the persons committed to dance, who are all there. Next the shaman calls the person who is going to be Tecún, who in turn kneels and calls the spirit of Tecún. And the players play the drum and the *chirimía* in correspondence to this dancer. Then he calls the one who will represent Pedro de Alvarado, who kneels. The musicians again play. And they do this with all of them until they are finished.

When the inhabitants of the town hear sounds of the drum and *chirimía*, they know that in this house they are going to rehearse the dance of the conquest. The townspeople go to offer their help, but not in money, only in *aguardiente* and cigars.

Formerly the rehearsals were Holy Saturdays, or say, a day after Holy Friday. In those days those who were going to go out as dancers had to arrive. The first day of the rehearsal in the morning, the musicians begin to work very early, and the pair of them are seated with the teacher of the dance beside them [they are all seated in a row], but before they give their *tragos* of *aguardiente*, they pour a *copa* [drink] on the hides of the drum and one over the *chirimía*. It is a *secreto* [ritual] so that the instruments will sound better and reach the ears of the people and give them the sentiment to help the *tutor*. That is to say, that the drum and the *chirimía* call the attention of many people.

In this same manner the *tutor* and the assistant go to the houses of the ones who are going to turn out to be the King

Quiché, King Tecún, Don Pedro de Alvarado, and Huitzitzil Tzunún. They do the same thing with all of them. When they are all ready, the shaman leaves first with an incensory in his hand, burning incense and myrrh, and behind go those who are going to turn out to be dancers. The shaman and the teacher position each one in his place spraying each dancer with incense and saying these words, "You are going to turn out to be King Tecún and the spirit of our father be with you so that nothing will happen to you." They do the same thing to all of the other dancers. Then the shaman pours a glass of *aguardiente* on the patio of the house as a toast to the spirits of the dead as an opening act, and the musicians begin. Next the teacher is ready to begin.

The musicians are on the corridor of the house. King Quiché and his children are in the center, in front of the musicians, on one side the Indians, and on the other the Spaniards, forming approximately a square.

The first who enters to dance is the Lacandón, a member of an ethnic group who is the agile servant of Tecún. The Lacandón, who runs a lot in the dance, turns around many times and shouts a lot. Then the King Quiché enters together with his children; they dance the whole square. Then he leaves his children, and he enters dancing to get the King Tecún. They make a whole turn around the *sitio* and cross diagonally to get another dancer to form a file, and they continue to do this with all the caciques. Then in a file, dancing in step, that is, a foot in front and a foot behind, with Tecún at the head of the file, they continue until they arrive at the center, forming a circle in the form of a *caracol* [snail, curl] with King Quiché dancing peacefully in the center, and all the Indians surrounding him. This they do for some minutes. Then they undo the curl and dance in a file a whole *cuadra* [turn] and leaving each dancer one by one until finishing in their former places. Each time they make a turn, they leave a dancer in his position. To say it more clearly, the King Quiché dances one *cuadra*, a dancer enters, and he does the same with the next dancer, taking more than an hour.

King Quiché then stops in front of the dancers and begins to dance, looking in the direction of his children. When the children see that their father is close, they enter dancing to rendezvous with him. Right in the middle of the *sitio* they pay reverence, and together they arrive at their posts. Then the two daughters leave, positioning themselves face to face in front of their father and beginning to sing, which gives a lot of feeling, in a very sad tone, singing of his youth and his old age and his great Quiché kingdom. When his daughters finish singing, the King Quiché says, "Now, don't sing more, my daughters, I feel very sad; my heart is very oppressed because the arrival of the Spaniards is very near." And he says that he has received notice from the Great King Montezuma of Mexico that in Chal Chuapa they are lying in ambush to kill the Indian people. King Quiché says he needs the help of the gods in this sad situation. And he does. He says that the war is about to begin but that he doesn't want war with the Spaniards, that it's better to accept the baptism that they come offering in the name of Jesús.

Tecún speaks in front of the people, declaring the war, in a very strong voice. Then Huitzitzil Tzunún dances the *cuadra*, making turns on the corners until reaching Tecún. Tzunún gives reverences and speaks to the King, offering to give his life in the struggle and offering the number of fighters that Tecún needs for the battle. King Tecún thanks Huitzitzil Tzunún. Then Tzunún returns to his position, and another dancer enters, until they all finish.

All of the Indians enter with Tecún at the head of the file, dancing the *cuadra*. They make a diagonal cross in both directions, making an "X," until they arrive at their posts where the caciques continue to dance. King Tecún remains seated in a chair, acting as if he were sleeping with his head down.

King Quiché speaks with his two sons to go on a commission to Xelaju to tell King Tecún that the former had a dream that Tecún soon was going to lose the war and that it would be better to make plans to fight the war and prepare his people. The princes answered, "Father, Great King Quiché, we will make the trip. Nothing will happen to us because we are two young persons. Soon we will give the advice to the great King Tecún."

Tecún continues sleeping in the chair, the caciques dance in their position to signal an alert. Then the two princes enter dancing, paring off face to face, back to back, face to face, and so on, dancing the *cuadra*, entering by a diagonal cross[23] until arriving at the place where they find Tecún. The princes show reverence, but Tecún continues sleeping. The princes wake him up, saying these words, "Tecún, Tecún, get up because you are sleeping. You don't realize that each day your enemies are getting closer. You don't know that your enemies are near."

Tecún, however, acts as if he is having a profound dream. Then Tecún stops and touches his face and acts as if he were waking up from a dream, and says, "Don't be frightened, dear princes. I don't know whether what I'm hearing or dreaming is true, beloved princes. I've been dreaming that a dove incarnate was flying over my head, telling me that my enemies each day are getting closer, looking for a way to kill our people of the Quiché kingdom, that in the hill of Chui Pach they are ready for their ambushes. Dear princes, from now on we will go to the great King Quichétun[24] so that he will give us permission to begin the battle." Speaking to everyone, Tecún declares, "Huitzitzil Tzunún and faithful friends, I ask, in the name of our race, that all of us go together to the palace of the great King Quiché."

All the caciques speak, saying, "King Tecún, our lord, all of us are ready to travel." Then for security, the two princes go in front as a vanguard, and Tecún immediately goes with all the caciques dancing in a file, making many turns in the *sitio*, acting as if they were traveling a long distance. Then they go into the center to where King Quiché is dancing.

All the Indians kneel. Tecún speaks, "O King Quiché, all of us Quichés, Cakchiqueles, and Tzutuhiles have come to be in your palace so that you can declare war against the Spaniards so that our people will not be allowed to die."

King Quiché, beginning with Tecún, grabs the hand of each one in order and tells him to rise. Then King Quiché begins to talk to Tecún. In a break, the daughters of the king sing to Tecún. After the conversation, King Quiché gives his banner to Tecún as a signal that Tecún now has the authority over all. Tecún gives his scepter to King Quiché as a commitment that he has to remain loyal and tells him to declare war. With war declared the two embrace. Tecún makes the commitment that he is a valiant warrior and that he will fight until death. The Indians kneel again to receive the blessing of the great King Quiché, then they separate and leave dancing until reaching their places. The Indians continue to dance in their posts.

At 11 A.M., or a little later, is the hour that the Spaniards enter, lead by Don Pedro de Alvarado. Then the one-who plays the drum acts as if he is playing a side drum, and he who is playing the *chirimía* acts as if he is sounding the bugle of war.

When the people hear the side drum and the bugle, they run to see if the Spaniards are coming. Then Don Pedro de Alvarado begins to speak, declaring war and saying that all the Indians will die and that the Spaniards will live. When Don Pedro speaks in front of his Spaniards, Tecún doesn't leave peacefully. At first Don Pedro avoids Tecún, but Tecún harasses the line of soldiers. They pair off, and Tecún pushes him and doesn't let him speak. But Don Pedro also enters *bravo* [becomes pushy] and doesn't permit him to speak or bother his soldiers. The two are very angry and strong.

After talking, the Spaniards enter one by one dancing the *cuadra* until finishing with everything. When they arrive in front of Don Pedro, they offer help and their force to win the war. When everyone is finished dancing, all of the Spaniards leave dancing in a file led by Don Pedro de Alvarado, acting as if they have been walking very, very far, showing fatigue and passing near the Indians, but the Indians act very *bravo* and taunt them with their bows and arrows.

After dancing, Don Pedro then sends two of his soldiers on a reconnaissance as messengers to tell Tecún, so that there will be no bloodletting, to accept the baptism that Pedro de Alvarado comes offering in the name of God, so that all the Indians recognize a living God. Then the Spaniards Francisco Carrillo and Juan de León y Cardona enter dancing, the two acting as if they are traveling a distance. On a corner they encounter him, or better said, they encounter the king, Tepepul. To him they say that the two of them have come to fulfill a mission on behalf of Don Pedro de Alvarado and that they need to talk with Tecún Umán. But Tepepul tells them that it is he who guards the frontiers and no one is able to enter without the permission of the king. Then Tepepul leaves the two Spaniards in this same place, and then he goes dancing very rapidly to where the King Tecún is positioned. Tecún answers that he is not able to see anyone and that he doesn't want to speak to a single Spaniard, that it's better that these Spaniards leave so that they don't lose their lives. Tepe returns dancing with much agility to where he had left the two Spaniards, and he tells them that they had better return to where they have come so as not to lose their lives.

The two Spaniards return dancing and dancing and suddenly they run into the *brujo* [witch.] The witch first divines with his green and transparent stones with which he deals with these two men, and makes many signs, speaking in mimicry with the two stones. The two Spaniards say that they are carrying out an order of Don Pedro de Alvarado and that they need to speak with Tecún Umán. The witch remains frightened, his whole body trembling with fear. One of the two Spaniards hits the witch, and then the witch becomes angry and he asks them again what it is they want. They repeat that they want to talk with Tecún Umán. Then the witch enters dancing and shouting with his son [also a witch] to tell Tecún that two foreign men, sons of the sun, need to speak with him.

Tecún answers that these two Spaniards can come but as prisoners with their eyes blindfolded and without arms, being that he is the king of Quezaltenango and no one is able to see his palace. The *brujo* returns dancing until he reaches the place where he had left the two Spaniards.

The Spaniards had been left as prisoners under the guard of the Lacandón. When the *brujo* arrives, he begins to punish them, saying that these are two demons, two animals with great big ears. The Spaniards are very maltreated and very tortured by the witches. Then the *brujo* ties them up with a chain, covers their eyes with rags, ties them, and takes away their swords. While the two Spaniards are being punished, the witch, seated in a chair, places his green stones and jade again, burns incense, and makes a *costumbre* so that on the road no one will be able to do any harm. After doing this ritual, he then ties a lasso on the belt of each Spaniard, and carries them in tow while his son and the Lacandón shove them and oblige the Spaniards to dance, but they are unable because they are very much made to suffer. In this manner they take them to where they find Tecún Umán.

The Spaniards would like to talk to Tecún, but the *brujo* and the Lacandón continue to taunt them and don't allow them to talk. When Tecún scolds the Spaniards, the witch becomes very content. The Spaniards are treated like prisoners of war and taken anew to the place of the witch, where they take the rags off their eyes, untie their hands, take off the lasso from their belts, and give them their swords.

Then the Spaniards leave in liberty and head in the direction from whence they came, dancing until they reach the place of Pedro, to tell him what they have suffered. Don Pedro becomes furious and declares war, proclaiming that all the Indians will die and that all the Spaniards will live. Tecún does the same thing, declaring that all the Spaniards will die and that the Indians will never be conquered.

The two lines, Spanish and Indian, prepare for the battle. Tecún encourages his Indians, and also Don Pedro de Alvarado runs in front of his soldiers. Then they begin to fight; they clash forward in two lines, Indians and Spaniards, and they don't permit one another to pass to occupy the positions where they always have been dancing. They clash many times, and finally they interchange, Indians and Spaniards occupying the side that each group pursued; that is to say, struggling for the possession of turf. And they continue fighting.

Then Tecún acts as if he pierces a lance in a leg of Don Pedro, and Don Pedro falls to the ground. He is helped by the two Spaniards, picking him up little by little, walking very slowly. Don Pedro acts as if he had recuperated from his wounded leg. Later he says that Tecún had broken his leg with a lance and that he has lost his horse in the battle. Then he gives a burst of laughter, acting as if nothing has happened, and goes in the direction of Don Pedro Portocarrera, saying, "Lend me your lance, Pedro Portocarrera. Today I have to finish killing off these insolent, Indian swine."

Then they begin the battle again, Tecún encouraging his allies to all fight against the Spaniards and saying to Don Pedro de Alvarado these words: "It isn't necessary to borrow a lance to finish the battle. If you are a valiant man, with your arms and my arms we are going to fight, man to man, to see who is stronger [without weapons]."

Don Pedro de Alvarado bursts out laughing, saying that he has 500 men and two small canons to finish off all the Indians. Then the Spaniards remain stopped in their positions in file, as also are the Indians. Tecún goes out with the witch following to protect him. Pedro de Alvarado goes out with a Spaniard called Grijalba following behind to protect him.

Thus they begin to fight again with much force, Don Pedro with a lance and the same with Tecún. The two go from one side to another. When Tecún feels very exhausted, he hides behind his caciques. While he recuperates, Don Pedro de Alvarado, also exhausted, hides behind his soldiers.

While Tecún pursues Don Pedro, the witch burns much incense and myrrh, running a lot with his incensory in his hand, acting as if he is doing a *costumbre* to conquer the Spaniards. Meanwhile, Tecún and Don Pedro are in full battle, the two changing positions many times. This fight between the two of them lasts about a half-hour.

When Tecún feels very tired and is unable to run much, Don Pedro puts out a total effort to lance him and acts as if he pierces his lance in the chest of Tecún.[25] Then Tecún falls on the ground [earth], making out as if he were dying. The *caciques* [chiefs] go out to help him, but all is useless. Tecún says good-bye to his allies, and acts as if he were dead, not speaking anymore.

Thus goes the rehearsal. Some days before the fiesta, all the dancers go to San Cristóbal Totonicapán, Santa Cruz del Quiché, or Chichicastenango to rent the clothing for the dance. When they return, they light *bombas* in Chua Cruz, about halfway from Cristalinas. Then the families and friends go out to meet them. The *bombas* are the signal that the clothing of the dancers has come. Each dancer takes care of his clothing in his house but with much respect. When 21 June arrives, each dancer carries his clothing to the house of the *tutor* of the dance. When all the dancers are there, the shaman is ready together with the musicians of the drum and the *chirimía*, and also the teacher. At eight at night they march to the hill to make a *costumbre* of much importance and much worth for the dancers. All of them go to the hills with the clothing and masks. Each dancer carries four or five candles that last through a night of burning, and they also carry small candles, *bombas*, and a lot of *aguardiente*.

When they are all in the hill, they first begin to adorn the holy place where they are doing the *costumbre*. They adorn it with pine needles and flowers, and they pour *aguardiente* so that evil will not enter at the hour of doing the sacrifice. When everything is ready, King Quiché kneels with his sons. The shaman gets up, lights the candles, passes them over the bodies of the dancers one at a time, and puts them in their places, corresponding to their dance positions. This, however, is on a rock in the middle of the mountains. Then the shaman gives them a *trago* of firewater, and also the shaman drinks his first drink. King Quiché gets up, and Tecún Umán and Don Pedro come, and they all kneel with candles in their hands. The shaman begins his work, calling all the names of the gods, *dueños* of the hills, asking that nothing will happen to these men who are going to be Tecún and Don Pedro, that the owners of the hills take care of them and protect them on the main day of the fiesta and no witch or *characotel* [a person who turns into a *baguate*] or evil spirits be able to harm those who head the dance. The shaman calls the spirits of the dead that are in the cemeteries, the spirits of those who have died by falling in a *barranca* [ravine]or by drowning, and the spirits of the ancient deceased shamans. He calls the spirits of King Quiché, Tecún, Don Pedro, and others so that on 24 June all will be well protected. He also calls the spirit of the patron saint of the town and other saints that the shaman knows. When he finishes these prayers, the two get up who are kneeling and give their *tragos* while the musicians execute the drum and *chirimía* in the way that they play for these two dancers and light a *bomba* for each one.

The shaman has to do the same with all the dancers. This *costumbre* does not come to a conclusion until three in the morning. When everything is finished, the shaman says, "Yes, it all turned out well, so there will be no problems during the fiesta." He says whether some dancer has lost his way in his life or is going to fail in the dance.

The dancers have carried from their houses tortillas or little tamales with meat or eggs, and when midnight comes, they invite the shaman to eat in this same place. The shaman suspends his work while he accepts the food.

When he has finished burning the candles, that is to say, when all is consumed by the fire, each dancer carries his clothing and returns. From the place called Chi Cua, one can see all the Spaniards and Indians, always in two files, in the form of a procession. Then the musicians begin with the drum and *chirimía*, and they enter the pueblo, dancing in the early morning, about 4:30 A.M. to 5 A.M. until they reach the front of the church. They make a whole turn, enter the church, all kneel down, embrace, and bow to the patron saint as a vow to celebrate his fiesta.

Upon leaving the church, they head dancing to the house of the *tutor*, where they rest for a moment. Then they go to their houses to rest all day.

On this day all the dancers buy plenty of bread and chocolate. At ten at night on 21 June, the musicians of the drum and *chirimía* leave to go to each house of each dancer. There they play their instruments for fifteen to twenty minutes. Upon finishing they are given chocolate and bread, but as there are a lot of dancers, the musicians just take the bread and keep it in a sheet. The musicians have to take two helpers to take care of the bread.

On this night the *brujo* and the Lacandón go out dancing, and they also are given bread. These two dancers have to go accompanied by their brothers and other kin to take care of their bread because they have to dance in each *sitio* of the dancers, until the twenty-second dawns. The twenty-third and the twenty-fourth of June dawn the same way—the musicians, *brujo*, and Lacandón collect plenty of bread.

The main day, 24 June, the dancers go to the house of the

tutor and then in a procession to the front of the church. When the procession of the patron saint leaves, the dancers go out in front of it. King Quiché forms a barrier in front of the musicians. The Indians are in one file and the Spaniards in another. The Indians dance during the procession; the Spaniards just walk accompanying them. They don't dance. And they go to their houses.

Only when the procession ends does the story begin. On this main day of the fiesta, when the hour arrives to bring the Spaniards, they all come mounted on their horses, but first they have to make a lap through the whole town. Then the witch and the Lacandón pursue them. They aren't allowed to enter in front of where the Indians are dancing, the Lacandón on one side and the *brujo* on the other.

What affects the Spaniards is that the witch carries an incensory, but instead of burning incense, he burns chili to ward off the Spaniards. Also the Spaniards run with their horses because they can't bear the odor of chili. Not until the witch finishes burning the chili that he carries in his handbag are the Spaniards able to advance in front of the church. Then the horses are removed by their families and they begin the story.

At the hour of the war, the horses appear again. Then the Spaniards mount again to begin the war, but then the horses are removed again, and they begin the fight. When there are only a few minutes left before killing Tecún, Tecún changes his mask, replacing it with one that makes it appear that Tecún is in agony, with a lot of blood on the face. More than anything else he is disfigured, a signal that he is going to die.

Tecún dying, Don Pedro takes away Tecún's lance and enters marching with two lances in front of his Spaniards. He makes three turns in this *sitio* and then arrives to occupy the place of the Indians.

Then Tecún is placed in a mortuary box. All the Indians are shouting and crying. Tecún is placed on the shoulders of the caciques. Huitzitzil takes the crown and carries it dancing, but it is a sad dance, the witch shouting, crying, and cursing the Spaniards.

Tecún now dead is in the presence of the great King Quiché. The witch speaks, saying that the great King Tecún has died, but this witch maltreats the Spaniards. Then Tzunún speaks with the King Quiché. The witch breaks his incensory, saying that all the *costumbres* that he has done to the gods were for naught. King Quiché, in a sad voice, acts as if he were crying. Then come the two daughters, singing very sadly and crying over the body of Tecún. The body of Tecún is removed from the presence of the King Quiché, and it is taken to its bier in the church. At the moment when the body of Tecún is taken by the caciques, the large church bells knell very sadly. At the moment when they deposit the body of Tecún in the coffin, they also throw flowers of *ruda* [a green plant that makes a yellow flower], tobacco leaves, and a lot of *aguardiente* to ward off evil spirits.

Then the drum and *chirimía* play very calmly with a sad sound. King Quiché dances very slowly, showing his pain and his sadness. His daughters sing to console him. Then King Quiché speaks with his two sons, ordering a commission to Don Pedro de Alvarado to tell him that their father, the king, accepts the baptism that the Spaniards come offering in the name of God and that now he doesn't want more fighting because his advanced age won't allow it.

Then the Spaniards enter dancing to the place where they meet the great King Quiché, the princes out in front as guides to show them the road. When the Spaniards arrive, they converse with King Quiché. Don Pedro has all the Indians kneel in columns and baptizes them saying, "I baptize you in the name of the Father, of the Son, and of the Holy Spirit, amen."

When the baptism is finished, King Quiché and Pedro de Alvarado enter dancing. All the dancers make two mixed lines, first an Indian, then a Spaniard, then an Indian, and so on.

After making lines, Spaniards and Indians take each others' hands like brothers and arrive together to finish in front where the musicians are, saying, "Here ends all this that we have prepared to celebrate the day of patron saint San Juan Bautista. Until another year, if God gives us life." And they say good-bye, embracing.[26]

—Ignacio Bizarro Ujpán

The Three Hombres Who Went to Look for *Pacayas*

This tale goes like this. Earlier, but much earlier, when there were more forests, before many trees had been cleared to plant crops and use for firewood, they say it was very dangerous because of the mountain lions and jaguars [*tigres*], which went into the towns to take out people. They entered the *potreros* [wide open spaces between the houses where children play and where the people keep chickens and large animals] to get the calves and sheep and eat them. The people were very much afraid to go out walking alone.

One time three hombres left to look for *pacayas* [palm fruit] in the mountains. But they didn't have shotguns in those days, just slings of *pita* [twine from agave] and flint knives. Thus, they went to the mountains, but *pacayas* were scarce. Two of them went together, and one went alone to see if he could get more.

The one who went alone saw a path that looked as if it had been used by humans. For the moment he forgot about the *pacayas* and continued on and on until the trail ended where there were many rocks. The hombre climbed up on the rocks and cast his vision and saw a cave with many jaguars, but they went back into the cave. Just one big jaguar remained above a big rock. But at the side of the jaguar was a lot of flesh of calves, sheep, and people. Also, there were many skulls that the same jaguar had eaten. This frightened the man very much, and he stopped in his tracks, unable to climb back down the rock where he had ascended. Finally, he regained his composure and descended down the same path and went looking for his two companions.

Later he found them and cried in front of them, and when he stopped crying, he told them what he had seen in the cave. The story says that the two companions wanted to see if it was true what the other one had said, and they told him to show them the place of the jaguars. "Yes," said the other, and the three of them left.

When they arrived, however, in this place of the jaguar, the jaguar had already changed his position. That is to say, now he was watching when the three hombres entered. When the jaguar saw the three men, he began to move his tail, lick his chops, and grind his teeth. Two of the hombres began to tremble with fear when they saw the jaguar and the skulls. But the other mustered strength and stayed with his sling and knife in hand. When the jaguar jumped over them, the two scared ones fell to the ground while the more valiant one backed up, looking the jaguar in the eye. He grabbed a rock, put it in his sling, twirled it many times in the air, threw the stone, and hit the jaguar right in the eye. The rock jammed in his eye, and the jaguar fell to the ground, rolling over among the stones. He wanted to run away but now he couldn't because he had a rock stuck in his eye. At this moment the hombre ran with his knife in hand and killed the jaguar. The two who were trembling little by little regained their composure when they saw that the jaguar now was dead.

Then the men climbed over the rocks and entered the cave to see if there were more jaguars, but there were only bones and more bones, and many skulls and clothing of men and women. Then, among the three of them, they decided to carry the jaguar to present it to the king.

They carried the jaguar on their backs through the mountain to the town where they found the king. When they arrived in the presence of the king, they said, "O King, here we bring this jaguar who has done much damage in the pueblo, eating a lot of the members of our relatives."

"How good!" said the king, and he became very content. He asked which of the three had killed this damned animal because this jaguar had eaten a daughter of the king. Previously, the king had ordered all the people of the town to go kill the jaguars, but the people had a lot of fear, and no one was able to do it. More for that reason, the king became happy when he saw this animal dead. He sent to call all the people of the pueblo and the other pueblos. He ordered a procession to the place where they had killed the jaguar.

When the people left walking in a procession, they carried the man who had killed the jaguar and the king went on foot because he felt inferior to that man. When they arrived at the place of the jaguars, the king recognized the clothing and the skeleton of his daughter, and they also carried it to bury it in the cemetery of the town.

When they returned, the king asked the people what prize that man deserved, and they all said, "He should be a son-in-law of the king because there is no one like him in the whole town."

"Very well," said the king. "It's certain that there is no man like you in this town. Now you are going to remain in my palace and soon you will marry my other daughter and be my son-in-law. But first you have to tell your parents, and you have to take them a gift."

The story says that the king filled six sacks with gold and sent his servants to put it over the backs of the mules. The king said, "Take this gift and return soon to live with my daughter because it is certain that you have saved many people from the mouth of the jaguar."

"Very well, Lord King," said the hombre. He took the road for his town with the three mules out in front and left his two companions behind the *rancho*. He traveled all day, but since it was distant, he wasn't able to arrive on the same day. Night came, and he had to sleep on the road. But on this night his two companions were planning evil against their companion, the real owner of the money, while he was sleeping. The two stole the three mules with the six sacks of money, and they left by another road. When they reached a town, they bought a *sitio* [homesite] and a house.

When the muchacho woke up, neither the mules nor the money were there. He ran away thinking of the mules and the money he had lost, and he left behind his travel bag. When he arrived in his town to ask his father if he had received the three mules with money, he told him no.

Then this man went to present himself before the king, and he said, "O Lord King, now I have come to live in your house. I'm going to be your son-in-law as you have spoken in front of all the people earlier."

"Very well," said the king. "You are going to stay with me as a son-in-law, but first what about my three mules and the six sacks of money that you took to your parents? And what did they say? Are they in agreement with my daughter?"

The hombre said, "Lord King, I'm the person who has killed the jaguar."

The king said, "I agree, but first I want my three mules and the sacks."

But the man didn't answer anymore.

The story says that the king became very angry with this man and sent him to jail because he thought he was another man because if he had been his son-in-law, without doubt he would have had the three mules and the sacks. The poor hombre landed in jail without a definite length of stay. There was no sentence for him. He just was put in jail.

The other two, his companions, were very clever. One said to the other, "You can stay here with the house and the money. I'm going in search of my *suerte* [fortune]."

"Very well," said the other, and he stayed with the *sitio*, the house, and the money.

The other one took the three mules and the empty sacks and went in the direction of the house of the king, and told the king, "I have come to remain with you as your son-in-law, and I will work as you want me to. I'm a very strong man because I have even killed a jaguar, and if there are more I will keep killing them."

"Very well," said the king. "Give me my three mules and six sacks."

"Here I have, Lord King, your mules and sacks."

"Fine," said the king. "You are the person who killed that dangerous jaguar in the cave."

"Yes, Lord King, remember when the whole town carried me in a procession."

"Certainly," said the king. "But there is one who is imprisoned who also says that he killed the jaguar. However, he didn't give me the three mules or the sacks."

"I don't know, Lord King. I only know that I'm the person who killed the jaguar."

The story says that the king sent to bring the other who

was imprisoned to find which of the two was the real person. The king, seated in his palace, said, "Which of you two killed the jaguar?"

"I, Señor King," said the thief, "to me you gave the gift of the six sacks of money."

"Lord, Lord King, I killed the jaguar, and you gave the six sacks of money to me, but what happened was that while I was sleeping, they robbed me."

"Well, I want to know which of you two killed the jaguar. Which one of you has the sling?"

"Here it is, Lord King," said the one who was in jail.

Then the king gave the sling to the one who had given him the mules and said, "Put a stone in the sling and hit the one in the eye who came to me first to say that he killed a jaguar." That is to say, the one who had been in jail.

"Fine, Lord King." And he put the stone in the sling and whirled it many times in the air. He threw it, but he didn't hit him in the eye.

The king then said to the other, "Come. Take the sling, put a stone in it, and hit a stone in the eye of your companion to prove you are the one who killed the jaguar."

"Fine," said he. He grabbed the sling and put a stone in it, whirled it many times in the air, and hit him right smack in the eye, proving that he was the real person and the other was a liar.

This story's meaning is to always tell the truth and that there is no reason to lie or steal because the lie will end in death and the truth will always come out.

—Lorenzo Pérez Hernández,[27]
Recorded by Ignacio Bizarro Ujpán

The Woman Who Loved Many Hombres and Died from Drinking a Lot of Water and a Piece of Sausage that She Had Eaten

They say that in a pueblo there had been a woman who loved many men. Not one husband was able to live with her because she had many other men clandestinely, or better said, she had many lovers. It was for this reason that her husbands did not want to put up with her.

The story goes that a strong man said, "I'm going to make this woman my wife. The rest of the men are afraid of me." Then he joined this woman. Thus it was that the man began to travel to the coast to sell fruit, but he did not realize that his woman had another mate. Each time that the husband went to the coast, the other hombre remained sleeping with the woman, but the real husband believed that his woman was honorable.

Then the story goes that the traveling fruit salesman and his wife had a son. When they baptized him, they looked for a *compadre* [co-parent, godfather to the son] as was the custom.

After they baptized the son, the husband of the woman continued as before, selling fruit on the *fincas* [farms] on the coast. And thus they were.

One day the husband talked to his *compadre* who asked, "How are you, *compadre*? How are your trips to the coast going? I'm seeing that you have a good business because you are hardly at home."

The *compadre* who was the fruit salesman answered, "*Compadre*, I'm not making much money, and it is far away. But what can I do? This is my life. At times I stay three to five days, suffering a lot."

"*Compadre*, I want to tell you something, but how I hope you won't get mad at me. It's a pity that each time you leave for the coast there is an hombre who remains sleeping with my *comadre*. I was much affected by these things, but there is nothing we could do to protest, and without doubt if we protested the *comadre* would get mad at us forever. Well, *compadre*, I tell you these things but with much care."

The story says that the *compadre* replied, "Don't tell me, *compadre*, I think that my woman has had a change of character. Well, earlier I knew that she liked men. But when we married, she swore to me that she would never do these things again. *Compadre*, many thanks for the news."

The *compadre* said, "If you want to confirm these things, you can carry your cargo someday and leave it in charge of someone in the village and then return at night. You will find the man sleeping with the *comadre*. But, *compadre*, take much care that he doesn't kill you because they say he's very dangerous."

"No, *compadre*, don't worry about me. I'm not a fool. First I have to think about what I'm going to do," he said.

Then the story goes that one day he told the woman, "I'm going to the coast to sell. Now we don't have any money to spend. I need to spend five days on the coast in order to return with some money."

"Very well," said the woman, who prepared food very happily.

The man left, carrying his cargo. But when he arrived in the village, he left his cargo in charge of someone, and he returned to the town during the day, but he was hiding in the mountains so that no one would see him.

When night fell, he got very close to his town. Seeing that the people of town were now sleeping, he got closer to where his house was, where he hid to see if what his *compadre* had told him was true. At ten at night when his neighbors were sleeping, the other hombre went straight for the house and entered. He slept with the woman. The real husband, however, felt a lot of pain in his heart, but he didn't pluck up the courage to enter the house. He just thought about killing the two with a knife he had in his hand, while he watched from behind the house. At times he had the courage, but at other times he lost his nerve. But the dogs were barking a lot, without doubt they were watching the husband who was waiting behind the house. The story says that the man and woman inside were talking, having sex.

Later the man said to the woman, "I'm going outside to pee."

The woman said, "No, don't go outside. I hear many dogs barking. Something bad can happen to you."

"Yes," said the man, and he lay back down.

But the need to urinate was urging him to go outside. Again he said to the woman, "I have to leave to pee."

Then the woman said, "Don't leave. There could be a *characotel* outside because the dogs are barking a lot. But you can urinate from here outside." Then she removed a cane from the frame of the rustic house and told the man, "You can do it from here to outside."

"Very well," he said, and he pulled out his penis, urinating from inside the house with the urine falling outside.

When the husband realized that the man was urinating,

he cut off his penis with the knife and took off running. The man fell down inside the house screaming. Then the woman got up to see what had happened to the man, but when she saw that the man now had no penis, she then began to cry and didn't know what to do because it was nighttime.

The story says that during this same night the man died in the *rancho*. The woman was frightened, but as it was in her house, she had to confront the situation. When she saw that the man was already dead, she began to dig a hole under her bed. She worked hard during the rest of the night. When the hole was ready, she buried the man under her bed.

Two days later, however, a foul odor began to come from the dead person because he was only buried under the bed, and the dogs sensed that inside the *rancho* there was some food for them. They began to dig behind the house. Also, the neighbors began to smell the repugnant odors of the dead person. Also, the buzzards began to land on the roof of the *rancho*.

Then the neighbors went to inform the mayor so that he would go to see what was happening. A commission went to see what the woman had inside. When they saw that there was a grave under the bed, they began to excavate and found the dead person. When they examined the body, he didn't have a penis. Then they asked her what she had done with his penis and why she had cut it off, but the woman didn't answer because it was not she who had cut off the penis of the man. But the mayor and the kin of the hombre continued asking her what had happened because she had buried the dead person under her bed. Finally she said, "The man came to sleep with me when my husband went to the coast. When my husband was away selling, this man came in the night and we slept together. When he needed to urinate, I told him not to go outside. Then he stuck his penis out and was urinating, but who knows who cut off his penis."

They heard only this, and they took the woman to jail. And they took the deceased to bury him in the cemetery.

But the story says that the husband, after cutting off the penis of the man, threw salt and lemon on it and put it out to dry in the sun like a sausage. He really went to sell for five days, and when he returned, he acted as if nothing had happened. He went directly for his house.

Then his neighbors told him, "Now, do you know what happened to your woman? She is in jail because she has buried a dead person under her bed."

The man, however, acted as if he didn't understand what they were telling him. He opened his *rancho,* but he could smell the foul odor. Then the man heated his tortillas and didn't give any importance to his woman's being in jail.

No one wanted to give the woman in jail her food because the people were afraid of her. Then the mayor ordered the husband to give the woman her food.

"Very well, Señor Mayor." Then he went to his rancho to warm up the tortillas, but then he remembered that he had a piece of penis. He roasted it and put it in *chirmol* [a sauce, eaten with or without meat]. Then he carried the food to his woman. When the husband arrived, the woman began to cry. Then the husband asked what had happened and why she had been put in jail. But the woman was not able to say what had happened. It could only be seen that there was a lump in her throat.

The husband told her, "Don't worry, because during the months and the years that you are going to be imprisoned I'm going to give you your food. And I'm going to take care of our son. Do you want to eat?"

"Yes," said the woman.

Then he gave her tortillas and her *chirmol,* and she began to eat without realizing that in the *chirmol* there was a piece of penis, and it was the same penis of the man that she had buried under her bed. The woman asked where he had bought the sausage, and the man told her, "I brought it from the coast."

"Very tasty," said the woman. And she ate very happily.

Then the man went to his rancho. He hardly felt sad for his woman who was imprisoned in jail. An hour after the woman had finished eating she felt very thirsty and asked for water from the *alguaciles* [attendants]. They gave her a lot of water, but it didn't quench her thirst. She begged and begged for more water until she died of thirst in the jail.

They say that this happened because she had eaten the penis of a man which had been treated with salt. Then the people said that it is bad to eat the flesh of people because the person who eats it will die of thirst. But the meaning of this story is also that women should not look for two or three men. They are able to live with just one husband, because if the woman looks for more men, she will die from her own hypocrisy.

—Bonifacio Ujpán Soto,[28]
Recorded by Ignacio Bizarro Ujpán

The Woman *Characotel*

My children, in this world there are many people with power. Each person, when he or she is born, has his own ability, or *suerte* [luck]. There are good *suertes* [fortunes] and bad *suertes*, like the *suerte* of the *characoteles*. There are always men and women *characoteles*. But this depends on the mothers.

When a woman is pregnant, she must take great care to sweep the house so that evil can't enter into it, pray to God that He help her in her hour of labor, kneel in front of the image [not important which, a saint], and not fail to have a cross near the bed so that the devil will not touch the body of the woman when the hour arrives to give birth to her child.[29] The pregnant woman should not speak bad words to prevent the devil from incarnating the body of the baby so it won't grow up to do bad things like becoming a *characotel*.

Thus, my aunt told us, "Take care so that when you are big you will not go around saying bad words and not get involved in bad things so that God will bless you and you will not give birth to children who are *brujos* or *characoteles* [both use evil power]." She said that the *characoteles* do the work of the devil. They carry spirits of the sick people to the cemetery and persecute sick persons in their houses in order to carry their spirits to the Dueño of Death, and they meet every twenty days to inform the *dueño* how many people in town are sick and when they are going to die.

Thus, she us told the following story.

Earlier in San José there lived a woman *characotel*. She wasn't the strongest, but she was fastidious. The story goes that this woman joined a man, but the man didn't know that she was a *characotel*. They had only been married a little while when she became constantly sick because she couldn't carry enough spirits to the Dueño of Death, and as punishment she didn't get her food, the bones of the dead. The husband gave her food and her medicine, but the woman didn't want to eat or heal herself because she knew that it wasn't a natural kind of illness. The man wanted the two of them to eat together, but the woman didn't want to eat with her husband. The man became sad and only thought about his woman every day, and he too didn't feel hungry because of his sadness.

Then a neighbor said, "Muchacho, what is happening to you? You are sad all the time. I never see you happy. Could it be that you are only fighting with your woman?"

"We aren't fighting," the husband answered. "It's true that I am sad, but it's because my woman doesn't want to eat with me. Each time I call her to come eat together, she moves away from me. She says that she's sick, and that's the way it is every day."

"You are an idiot," the neighbor responded. "Don't you realize that your woman is a *characotel*. Each Wednesday and Friday, she goes to the cemetery to eat the bones of the dead while you stay in bed. That's the reason she doesn't want to eat with you. If you like, I'll give you some advice."

"Very well, I will be grateful to you," said the husband.

"When night falls this Wednesday, be in bed with your woman, but don't go to sleep. Act as if you are fast asleep, and you will find out that your woman will grab the arm of the grinding stone and place it in bed with you, grab your nose to make sure you are sleeping, take off her *corte* [skirt], step over you in bed four times, and then cover you completely with her *corte*. Then she will go to the cemetery naked, and when she comes back she will do the same *secretos*. But be careful when she does these things. Don't move at all. When she goes to the cemetery, follow her steps, but stay far behind her so that she won't realize you are doing it."

The husband very gratefully said, "Many thanks. I'm going to see if what you have told me is true."

Then on Wednesday, the hombre wanted to see if it were true what the other one had said. When night fell, the two of them went to bed. The husband acted as if he were sleeping. When the hour arrived for the woman to leave for the cemetery, she first grabbed the nose of her husband to make sure he was asleep. The man breathed noisily, as if he were fast asleep. The woman got up, took off her *corte*, stepped naked over her husband four times, went to get the arm of the grinding stone, put it in the place where she was sleeping, and placed the *corte* over her husband. Naked, with just her *huipil* [blouse] on, she left for the cemetery.

When she arrived at the cemetery, the Dueño of Death came out and gave the woman her food. But the food was the bones of the dead. While she was eating them, the Dueño of Death asked her when she was going to bring him the spirit of some sick person because, "I too need my food."

"I don't know when," the woman replied. "It's true that there are sick persons, but the truth is that I don't know when they are going to die."

"Try to bring some spirits soon or else I won't give you your food. And you will die."

When the woman left for the cemetery, the husband followed her, but he stayed in the gate of the cemetery where he heard clearly what his wife was saying to the Dueño of Death. But as he heard these things, he felt a great cold in his entire body. He felt as if his head were heavy and his feet were heavy and swollen, and he couldn't move. He was frightened and didn't know what to do. Then he made the sign of the cross [touching his forehead and his heart in the center of his body and then back across to each shoulder]. Not until then was he able to move. He ran to get in bed again so that his woman wouldn't realize that he had seen and heard her in the cemetery.

When the woman came home, he made out as if he were fast asleep. Happily, the woman grabbed the nose of her husband to make sure he was asleep, stepped over him four times on the bed, removed the grinding arm, put her *corte* back on, and went back to bed, as before, and went to sleep. The man, however, didn't sleep at all from the time he returned from the cemetery.

The next morning, the woman got up, made a fire, prepared coffee, heated the tortillas, and told her husband to have breakfast. The man got up, washed his face, and sat next to the fire together with his woman so that they could eat breakfast together. Then he said, "We're going to eat our breakfast together."

But the woman told him, "I don't want to eat. I'm not hungry. My stomach is upset. You can eat by yourself."

When the woman spoke these words, the husband became very angry and told her what he had seen in the night. He declared, "You don't want to eat with me because you are a woman *characotel.* I remind you that last night you got up, grabbed my nose, took off your skirt, stepped over me four times, and in your place left the arm of the grinding stone. Naked, you opened the gate to the cemetery and went in. When you arrived, the Dueño of Death asked you when you were going to bring him the spirit of some dead person because he said that he needed his food too. Tell me it isn't true."

Upon hearing this, the woman didn't say another word. She took off her *corte* and threw it in the face of her husband. The man didn't say another word either. Then the woman grabbed her *corte* again, and, at this moment, the man was turned into a dog. The dog-man left the house and remained only in the patio, where he was kept by the woman.

One morning the mother of the man arrived to visit. The

dog-man began to wag his tail and said these words, "I'm your son. But now I'm a dog. Be careful with this woman. She's a *characotel.*" This is all he told her.

When a dog told her these things, the mother became very frightened. She ran inside the house and asked the woman what had happened.

Then the woman declared, "Take much care that you don't tell the people because, if you tell them, I'm going to turn you into a dog, too, for the rest of your life."

This scared the mother of the man, but the woman told her, "For your son, this is just a punishment. Friday, I'm going to cure him and turn him back into a man."

The mother of the man left very afraid, and she didn't tell anyone these things.

Friday arrived. At midnight the woman told the dog-man, "If you want to be cured, follow me to the cemetery."

When the two of them arrived, the woman talked again to the Dueño of Death. She told the *dueño* that she had punished her husband because she didn't want him to tell the people that she was a *characotel.*

"Fine," said the Dueño of Death. "We're going to cure him."

The woman stepped over the dog-man four times in the center of the cemetery. At the same time, he turned back into a man as before.

The Dueño of Death told him, "Don't tell anyone what has happened to you because, if you do, you're going to die."

"Very well," said the man. Together with his wife he went to his house, but the man was not the same as before. He had turned into a deranged idiot. He didn't work anymore. He just sat in the streets like a little boy. He didn't want to change his clothes or take a bath. But the man had good luck. The woman died. The Dueño of Death took her life because she wasn't a good worker for him. Not until then did the man tell the people what had happened to him with his wife, who was a *characotel.* And only then was he able to recuperate as he was before.

—María Ujpán Ramos,[30]
Recorded by Ignacio Bizarro Ujpán

The *Characoteles* Who Meet Every Twenty Days in the House of the True *Jefe*

The story says that the *characoteles* have a *jefe* [chief], one who has to have command over them and that the *characoteles* go to the house of their *jefe* for each of them to give information as to how many sick persons there are in each town where the *characoteles* reside and how many are ready to die. At the same time they celebrate a fiesta, eating in this house.

The story says that much earlier in past times, there had been an hombre who always went to other towns to sell *injertos* [soft, brilliant green fruit], avocados, and garlic. But he didn't know if his woman was a *characotel.* The man had been with the woman many years, but they didn't have a single child.

One time the man told the woman, "I'm going to the coast to sell avocados, *injertos,* and garlic."

"Very well," said the woman.

Then the hombre took to the road and said good-bye to

his woman, saying, "I'll return within a few days when I'm finished with my selling."

But the story says that the man carried a lot of cargo, and on the road he got very tired and couldn't bear to go on to where he had planned to go. In a pueblo, where he was when night was falling, he planned to ask for lodging. He asked a señora, "Please let me to spend the night in your house. I was planning to go farther, but I feel tired and can't stand to go farther. I need lodging."

Then the woman answered, "I'm very sorry, but I can't. It's that tonight I have to receive some persons invited to the house. For that reason, there's no place for you to sleep."

The man replied, "Señora, please, it's that now night is coming and the truth is that I can't endure this cargo anymore. It's that I have come a long way."

"I'm sorry about what's happening to you; there's only a place in the loft of the house. You can sleep there but on the condition that you have to remain very quiet. It's that I have a meeting and a fiesta for this night, and when you are sleeping in the loft, don't move much. My invited guests are very irritable. I don't want you to come down. They will hit you. Well, I'm going to do you a favor."

"Señora, thanks. I'm tired. I will remain asleep. And I don't want to bother or interrupt your fiesta. What I want to do is to take care of my body," said the hombre. Then he climbed up to the loft to sleep. But the house was very rustic, just of round sticks, so the man could see well what was going on below, that is to say, within the house.

The story says that the husband of the wife and the children went to sleep in the other house. The woman made a fire and put over it a clay bowl, but a big one. Before midnight, about eleven o'clock, women from other towns began to arrive. They spoke the same language and each one brought a chicken to eat.

When the man saw that the women had arrived, he didn't

sleep anymore. He felt a great fright. The woman of the man who was sleeping in the loft also arrived. She brought a chicken and gave it to the owner. Each one of the women did the same thing. Then they began to cook the meat. Each one also carried her little tamale. The man was very surprised at what he was seeing from the loft and that his woman was also one of those in this meeting.

When the meat was cooked, the owner of the house sat down in the middle of the women on the floor and said, "Now we're going to do our work. Remember that it has been twenty days since we met. Now each one go to the houses to see where there are sick persons and when they are going to die. This serves to inform the Dueño of Death when we go to the cemetery. You know what is our *suerte* [fate], and you have to comply."

Each one left, including the owner of the house. But before they left the door, the owner told them, "Make sure you return because we have to eat."

"Very well," said all the others.

The story says that the man just stayed in the loft, thinking about where and to what houses they had gone. But what was strangest for this man was that his woman was one of the women in this house, but her town was far away. The man felt bothered and wasn't able to sleep. He planned, however, to annoy them to see if it was certain that they would sense the smell or taste of his urine. Then he urinated from the loft, and his urine fell inside the bowl of stew, and then he lay down again face down to better see what the women would do when they returned.

First the owner of the house arrived. And that was the way it was with each. One by one they arrived. When they all were there, they all sat down on the floor. The owner of the house asked each one of the *characoteles* how things were going and how many sick persons were ready to die, saying, "Remember that some of you have not brought a spirit to the cemetery in these past twenty days."

Then the *characoteles* began to inform her. Some said, "We already brought spirits to the cemetery, and for sure they are going to die."

Others said, "We are struggling each night. Within a few days we are going to bring spirits to the cemetery."

Others said, "We have brought more spirits than the rest of you, and we need to rest a little."

Finally, they talked to the woman of the man, "What is happening with you? All the companions have fulfilled what they should do, but you have not been able to do so. Within these next twenty days, if you are not going to bring a spirit, you're going to die."

Then the woman answered, "It's true that I haven't been able. It's that I have dealt with very strong families. Each time that I get near the houses of the sick persons, they come out running with sticks to kill me, and I have to hide so they won't kill me. This has happened with many families."

"But you have to fight hard during these next twenty days. You have to bring at least a spirit because the Dueño of Death is very angry with you and for sure you're going to die."

Then the woman said, "For me it's very difficult, but such is my luck. I have to bring the spirit of my husband. I can't wait any longer."

The owner of the house asked her, "How can you bring the spirit of your husband? He's not sick!"

Then the woman said, "There I will need your help. This coming Friday, more or less about midnight, you are going to be stationed in the door of my house to wait. Then I inside am going to cry a lot and shout a lot and act as if I have a big stomachache. My husband will leave with me, but I'm going to tell him to leave first, to open the door. Then I'm going to push him to you, and you grab him and hit him. Only in this manner will his spirit be gained. With the blows they give him, he will fall ill and die."

"It's very well," said the *characoteles*. "We are going to help our companion."

"Very well," said the *jefe*. "I'm going to accompany you, and if you don't, well, you are going to be responsible."

"Don't worry. We're going to do it."

Then they began to eat, each woman eating a chicken. When they were eating, one of them sensed that the food had the odor of urine and said, "Something bad I sense in the food, some urine inside the bowl." But the others didn't find it to be the case, and they continued eating. But the other was insistent and said again, "Someone is in the loft, and it was he who urinated in the food."

"No," said the *dueña*, "there isn't anyone there."

The man felt very much afraid because of all that he had been seeing and more for what his woman had said—that she was going to deliver his spirit.

After the *characoteles* ate, they cleaned the bowl and other dishes and put them away, and then they said good-bye, each one. They said, "Until twenty days," and they left very content. And the *dueña* left for the other house where her family was sleeping.

The man, however, didn't sleep at all because he was just thinking about what he had heard—that he was going to die! When day broke, the man came down out of the loft. The owner of the house asked him, "Did you sleep well?"

"I slept well all night. I didn't feel a thing. It's that I was very tired."

But the owner of the house didn't know that this man was the husband of the woman *characotel*. The man very sadly carried his cargo and continued on his way.

When he returned to his house, he told his wife, "All went well and I made some money." Then the woman was very happy. She received her husband as if nothing had happened. They ate together.

The man, however, was afraid to sleep with his woman, but he plucked up the courage. Then Friday arrived, and he knew what was going to happen on the night. He continuously thought about what he was going to do to defend himself from the woman.

Then night fell, and together they were sleeping. It was the night of a Friday, as the *characoteles* had arranged. Then about midnight the woman of the man began to shout and cry. "A lot," she told her husband, "but a lot of pain I have in my stomach!" But it was a lie because this same night she had to deliver her husband into the hands of the rest of the *characoteles* as had been arranged at the last meeting. But the husband knew what was going to happen in this night. He acted as if he were fast asleep and didn't pay attention to his woman who was shouting a lot.

Then the woman woke up her husband saying, "Hombre, don't you realize that I'm dying of a great pain in my stomach? Please get up and go with me to look for leaves of nettles [some use this as a cure for aches but it hurts when they rub it on their bodies] to rub on my stomach."

But the hombre knew that in the door were *characoteles*, and he told his woman, "Better in the morning when the sun comes up. It's still very dark."

But the woman began to cry and shout as if it were the truth. She returned to say, "Get up. Come with me to look for leaves of *chichicastes* [nettles] for my stomach."

The man almost trembling with fear said, "But we can't see the leaves because it's night and we don't have a *candil* [a light, or oil or kerosene lamp]."

"Don't worry, get up! I'm going to light the *ocote* [pine with a lot of resin] to illuminate our way. It's that I'm dying of pain," said the woman.

"Very well," said the man, and he put on his clothing. "I'm going with you to look for the leaves of *chichicastes*, but don't light the *ocote*."

"Very well," answered the woman. Then the woman said, "Please go in front of me because I'm a woman. I'm in much pain. I ask you to go ahead of me. Please open the door."

The man said, "Let's go, don't worry."

When the man opened the door, it was he who pushed the woman and kicked her in the butt. She fell outside right where the *characoteles* were waiting. They thought it was the man, and then they fell right on her and gave her many blows, thinking that they were hitting the husband of the woman, as it was dark. They only realized it when the woman shouted, "No more blows, you are going to kill me. It is I, your companion. Please, no more blows!" But the other *characoteles* felt offended because the woman didn't fulfill what she had promised, and they hit her with more fury and more blows. And at this same moment they caught the spirit of the woman and went to leave it at the cemetery.

After the blows the woman entered the house, telling her husband, "Why didn't you help me? Some *characoteles* nearly killed me. Now I'm injured. Perhaps I'm going to die."

Only then did the hombre tell her, "That's what you wanted for me because earlier you had arranged with your *characotel* companions that it would be I who would be beaten in the dark. I know that you don't have a stomachache. Remember when they were eating chicken in the house of the woman, I was sleeping in the loft of the house. Remember when she asked each one how many sick persons they had and how many were going to die and each one gave her answer to the owner of the house. She also asked you whether within twenty days you would have a spirit and told you if you didn't bring a spirit to the cemetery within that time, you were going to die. You told her that you were dealing with strong families that chase you away with sticks. Finally, you said that this

Friday that you would deliver the spirit of your husband, but it wasn't possible."

When day was breaking, the woman now didn't get up. Once and for all she fell sick and in twenty days died of the blows that her *characotel* companions had given her. When the woman died, the husband criticized his woman to the other people saying that she was a *characotel*.

—Ignacio Bizarro Ujpán

The Two Real Children of God: There Were Only Two, the Grandfather and Grandmother

This is how a very old story goes. It says that God created the land, the trees, and the mountains. But first there was nothing more than mountains. On the land there was a great cold.

Then God sent to earth a man and woman in the form of persons without clothes. There had not been sin in the world at that time. God said to these two, "You are the ones in charge of finishing and creating what is not already done on earth. Just speak and it will all be done."

Then the man and woman just sat down under the trees like two children, each day more sad because in heaven there was a better life. They were very cold because on earth there was just wind and frigidness. But since they had been sent by God, they needed something to warm themselves, and they said in the night, "In the morning when it dawns there should be fire." Then they went to sleep.

When it dawned the following day, they got up and near them was a ball of fire. They went near it and felt its warmth. They threw more sticks on it, and that was when fire appeared. This is the same fire that is now found in the volcanoes. And with the fire they were able to be content, because it had been confirmed what had been said, "Just speak and it shall be done." The fire that they made remained for all time.

The first smoke that came out of the fire was converted into clouds. Then it rained. They were the first showers that fell in the world.

The man and woman, however, saw that there was only fire and rain. They became sad because all they could do was to warm themselves with the fire.

Later these two persons felt hungry and wanted to eat, but in the world there was nothing, but when they were sent to earth they were told to just speak and it will be done. Thus, when night fell, they said, "Tomorrow we want there to be species of all kinds of plants to eat." And they slept.

It dawned the following day, and when they got up they saw that all around them everything was covered with milpa, pumpkins, *chilacayote, güisquiles,* and greens of all kinds. That's the way it was when corn appeared, but the story says that it was in the mountains. Then these two persons were eating maize, and only maize, and finally they got tired of it.

One night before going to sleep they said, "God sent us to the world with the power to create and command what is needed. Now we have fire, clouds, rain, corn, and greens. But we need something good to eat. Tomorrow when it dawns, before we get up, we want there to be created other plant species to eat." And they slept.

The next day, when they got up, they saw a *frijolar* [field of beans] to harvest: black beans, white beans, and red beans. Then they became happy and said, "Our power has worked. Now we have beans to eat."

It was thus when the bean appeared. Then the man and woman ate just maize and beans for a long time. But as they were great and powerful, one night they said, "We are tired of eating just corn and beans. We need to eat something good." Before going to sleep, they said these words, "We want, when it dawns, with our sacred power, that birds of many species and animals of four legs appear." And they slept, always under the trees.

The following day when it dawned, they got up and went to where they kept the fire, where they now saw that there were many animals created—chickens, turkeys, hogs, sheep, and cattle. The two became happy and said, "We are the only ones who have the power to put the earth in order."

Thus it was when these animals appeared. That was also when the first two persons ate meat. And they say that for that reason we eat meat. Then they said, "Now we have everything to eat. Now we need two companions to help us eat and work."

As usual they had ordered in the night what they wanted done the following day. Night fell, and they said, "We are just two. We need companions. We want that our power be greater each day. When it dawns we want other beings like us." And they slept.

When they got up in the morning the next day, where they kept the fire, it was certain that what they had asked for had been done in the previous night. They saw their companions. But the story goes that their companions weren't able to speak or walk upright, just on all fours, on their hands. When the old man and old woman [ancestors] saw them, they became very frightened because their companions began to run many laps around them, making faces that they wanted to speak and walk, but they were unable. Then the story says that the two grabbed a stick and chased them to the mountains. That was when the monkey appeared.

Then the man and woman discussed why their power was failing and said, "The companions that appeared are not useful. They don't walk or speak, and their faces are very ugly." Again they said, "Now, our luck and our ability is failing."

When night came, they declared, "When day breaks, when it dawns, we want, with our power, to create and have appear companions, beings like us, men and women." Then they slept.

The following day they got up very early to see if their power and their wisdom worked during the night. When they arrived where the fire was, it's certain that some very big animals appeared with big teeth and with long whiskers. But they weren't humans. When the man and woman approached the animals, the animals began to grind their teeth, to lick their whiskers, and wanted to eat their creators. Then the man and woman remembered the fire and grabbed a half-burned stick to defend themselves, chasing the animals to the mountains. That was when the jaguars, lions, bears, and wolves appeared. But they say that at this same time, the whiskers of the jaguar and wolf had been burned in the fire, and for that reason these two animals don't grow whiskers.

Then the old man and old woman became sad because they felt they were failing in their works. They talked to God in heaven from whence they had come, and told Him, "You gave us the power to make and command the things. We made fire, clouds, rain, corn, beans, chickens, turkeys, swine, and cattle, but when we wanted companions like us to appear the next day, only ugly animals that can't walk or speak were created. We did it a second time so that human beings like us would appear, but what happened was that big animals were created and appeared that almost ate us."

Then God answered them, "You have the power, keep working until you make your companions." When they heard these things, they became sadder.

When night fell, the two said, "The time has come for us to use our heads and wisdom and our power to the fullest extent to do something better so that we will be able to create companions like us. While we are thinking, we shouldn't hear anything to distract us because tonight we need to and want to create creatures like ourselves. When it dawns, before the first rays of sun, our companions will appear." And they slept.

They say the next day they got up very early while it was still a little dark. Then they went to where they had the fire to see if during the night other people had appeared. But when they only saw big and small animals of different kinds, the old man and old woman became frightened. The animals, however, were very content, acting as if they wanted to talk, circling the two persons many times. But the two were mad and didn't want to be bothered by them. They grabbed sticks and chased them into the mountains. That was when the deer, wild boar, raccoons, paca, coati, mountain lions, and other animals appeared. And at the same time they were given their names.

But the story says that the animals went away very sad. They wanted to return, every little while looking back, but the man and woman chased them until they disappeared in the mountain. It was then that the animals were much afraid. And for that reason, now the animals run and hide when they see man because from the beginning they were scared.

Then the story says that the old man and old woman became more, but really more, sad and said, "Our power doesn't serve us, nor does our head. Each time we want to have companions like us, only animals appear."

Night came, and they said, "Darkness has come, and the

sun has already gone down. Now it is more serene. Our power and our wisdom begin to work. Before the sun comes out, before it dawns, we want human being companions to appear so that they will help us." And they slept during the night.

The following day they got up very early, before the first rays of light. They approached where the fire was and only saw ugly animals. They got very mad because they wanted to see human beings like themselves, but it was not so. The old man and old lady grabbed sticks on fire and chased them to the mountains. That was when opossums, foxes, rodents, and the dogs appeared. The rest of the animals went into the mountain, but the story says that the dogs were more clever. They only went in a circle and hid where the chickens and turkeys were. For that reason, the dogs leave to go to the mountains and return to the houses and watch the chickens and turkeys because the story says that they were their first friends. It says that the opossum and the fox previously were affected by the fire and for that reason now these animals have hair that smells like something burned and their meat has a foul odor.

Then the man and woman felt offended and told God in heaven, "You are mad at us and are punishing us. You told us that we are the ones who have the power to make everything. But now when we want to form companions like ourselves, we cannot. We are just able to make animals."

And again they talked to God in heaven, saying, "Here you have us on earth, and our hair is white with age. Before you told us that we have the power, but when we want to make and create companions, we only have created animals and more animals."

God said, "Continue working and commanding on earth until you are able to form and make your companions with your own power."

Night came. Before sleeping, they said, "The time has come when we can do a good work. Tomorrow before the light of day, before it dawns, we ask and want formed and to appear companions, human beings like ourselves." And the two slept.

They got up very early to see if their companions were formed and appeared, and they went to where they had the fire. But when they saw that near the fire were many snakes, toads, scorpions, rats, and buzzards, the old folks were very angry and chased them to the mountains. Only the buzzard was able to fly, and the others went into the holes of the earth, but very near.

The old man and old woman very angrily said, "Why stay here any longer? It's better to move." And they went walking and carrying the ball of fire, and behind them went the chickens, turkeys, pigs, sheep, and the dogs. But also, the story says that the rats followed them too. And for that reason, the rat lives inside the house. The snake and the toad remained sleeping in the holes. Also, for that reason, the chicken, turkey, pig, and sheep are domestic animals.

Then the two *viejitos* [old folks] were under a small tree, making their fire, and then said, "We are going to have a change. Now our power is great."

Night entered, and before sleeping they spoke, "In the hour of dawn, before the sun comes up, we need that human beings like us be formed and appear." And they slept.

They got up very early and went to where they had the fire to see if their companions had appeared. Instead what they saw ahead was that a great lake had appeared, where all the animals came to drink water. The two old folks saw inside the lake animals that were moving. And that's when the fish appeared.

Then they said, "Worse is our luck. What are we going to do? In place of companions, a great lake appears before us. We left the animals in the mountain, and now they have followed us."

Then God talked to them. "Cheer up! All is well. You have worked well during the nights. Continue working at night to form and make your companions the way you want them."

"Very well," they said. "Now is when our power and our wisdom is going to work well. Tomorrow we need and want to form and appear companions, human beings like ourselves." And they slept.

The next day they got up and went to where they always had the fire. But in place of companions, great hills and rocks appeared that now are the highlands because the story says that earlier it was just level land.

"Now we are tired," said the two. "We are going to do it for the last time, the last night. Let's hope that our thoughts, our power, and our wisdom function better. And now night enters. We want and ask that before daybreak, before the first rays of sunlight, before daylight, to form and appear companions."

The story says, however, that the man and the woman didn't sense, didn't realize, that they were having sex, and in the morning a son was born, whom they wanted as a companion. That is where they began to understand that they had the power to form and make their companions. They discovered that through sex they could make their own companions.

They say that our first two ancestors suffered a lot for us. Each day they had a child to form the world. For this reason, the old folks hair turned white because they had worked a lot, forming the rest of the world and the animals and people in it. And now in the night men sleep with the women. They say that for that reason in the nights, there is more use of sex between man and woman, and they say that for that reason the women get pregnant in the nights because in the beginning our first ancestors, a man and a woman, worked during the nights.

End.

—Bonifacio Ujpán Soto,
    Recorded by Ignacio Bizarro Ujpán

The Story of
Mariano the Buzzard

This story my grandma told me along with other grandchildren when we were little. It is one of the funny stories that grandfathers and grandmothers tell the children.

Little children, there is a man who is called Mariano—Mariano is a lazy person. They say that when Mariano was a child, his parents sent him to cut firewood. Instead of looking for firewood, however, he looked for shade and went to sleep. When he arrived home that night, they did not give him food.

As Mariano grew up, so did his laziness. When he became a man, he thought about looking for a woman. After all his travels, he was able to find a woman by the name of Pascuala.

Then Mariano and Pascuala joined [married] and intended to make a home. But the two were the same—neither wanted to work. Mariano would leave early in the morning to bring firewood, but he would not get back until late in the afternoon. He lost his jobs with the people. He delayed ten to fifteen days for each *cuerda* [.178 acre] of work. He suffered much poverty and sickness. Also, his woman went to houses to ask for work as a weaver, and when they gave her weavings to do, poor Pascuala took fifteen to twenty days for each piece. Thus it was. The unfortunate couple were two lazy persons.

For poor Mariano, dreaming was his major occupation. Then a day came when they gave him work by the day. As poor Mariano did not want to work, he lifted his face upward looking at the birds. Finally, he lay down over a large stone, gazing at some buzzards flying around. The buzzards thought that some dead person was lying on the stone, and they began to fly near him. Suddenly Mariano said happily, "The birds just pass their lives flying, and I work every day and do not earn a living. I would like to be happy like these buzzards who do not have to worry about building a house or planting or working; they pass their lives resting."

Mariano said these things without realizing that a buzzard was listening. Suddenly the buzzard lit above the stone where he found Mariano and greeted him.

The buzzard said to this man, "*Compadre* [Friend], what is it that you are thinking and saying? I was just listening to you from above."

Mariano answered, "I am very sad. Every day I have to work, and, if there is no work, there is no food."

"*Compadre,*" said the buzzard, "we also are suffering a lot. We eat when someone like a chicken dies, and when we do not find dead animals, from much hunger we eat dung. Your life is very nice because you work and you are able to eat a lot of good things. We buzzards like to work, but God was harsh on us, only giving us wings to fly."

"Friend," said Mariano, "eating dead animals or eating dung when necessary is not a problem but happiness because you do not work, but my life is a disgrace."

The buzzard saw that Mariano was worse than a dead person, and to give him the solution [to his troubles], the buzzard told him, "If you want to be happy, I will lend you my jacket so that you will be able to fly free in the air and see all that you wish, but you also have to give me your clothing to cover my body, and then I will have to work."

The story says that Mariano thought he was in heaven

when the buzzard told him these things. Then he took off his clothing and gave it to the buzzard. The buzzard did the same thing, taking off his jacket and giving it to the man. Then they said good-bye. Mariano went flying, and the buzzard began to work.

When the afternoon passed, the buzzard carried a backload of firewood, but he did not know which house to take it to. Luckily, Mariano passed by flying, and the buzzard said, *"Compadre,* I have problems; I am not familiar with your house."

"Friend," said Mariano, "I am going to guide you. Enter the house where I light. My woman is called Pascuala."

The buzzard-man carried the firewood on the road, and Mariano flew nearby. When the buzzard-man was about to arrive, Mariano lit on the house. The buzzard untied the wood and went inside the house.

Mariano had hardly gathered firewood, but the buzzard, who had converted into a person, had done a little.

"What a miracle you have brought firewood," said Pascuala. "You have hardly ever brought it."

"Ah, yes, I have brought firewood because now I am changing a lot," he said.

"But why have you come with you face black and very dirty and stinking?" Pascuala asked Mariano, although it was not Mariano.

Then he answered, "Yes, it is because the sun burned me a lot, and I worked hard today."

"My poor husband," said Pascuala, "if you would like, we can prepare the *temascal* [sweat house] so that we can bathe tonight."

"Very well, if you want to do it," the man said.

Then Pascuala heated the *temascal* to take off the dirt. When it was ready, the buzzard-man and Pascuala entered the *temascal.* But when he felt the intense heat, he shouted, "I am not Mariano! I am a buzzard! Your husband lent me his clothing, and I lent him my jacket. Thanks, but I have another jacket." He put on his new wings and flew away.

Poor Pascuala was left surprised inside the *temascal*. When she left she made the townsfolk realize that Mariano turned into a buzzard because of laziness.

Days later, poor Mariano, who was converted into a buzzard, wanted to talk to his woman, but he was not able to speak. All he was able to do was to say, "Utz, utz, utz," in the yard of the house. Pascuala became very angry and grabbed a piece of firewood and killed Mariano, the buzzard.

My grandma told me this story, which is very old. It served as an example for us to do work when our parents gave it to us without laziness. If they ordered us to work, we should work and not go to sleep. In our life it is difficult to earn a living. If a person works well, he is able to eat. The buzzard, who eats only dead animals and waste, is the laziest of all the animals.

My grandmother told us, "Children, this will serve you when you are adults, to be lazy is undesirable—it is better to die than to be lazy. So that you will not turn into buzzards, work and obey your parents."[31]

—Ignacio Bizarro Ujpán

Dance of the Mexicans

The Dance of the Mexicans is the
story of a farmer who has a woman,
servants, livestock breeding area, and a lot
of property. In the early morning, when they
begin to dance, the patron and the Maruca [a
comical name for his spouse, María, because it is
the name for someone who cannot be trusted] dance
three turns with each dancer until they finish with all twenty-
two, including the two bulls. The patron is at the head of one
line followed by a *mayordomo* [administrator], a dancer dressed
as a black, and the rest of the dancers with a bull at the end. In
the other line the Maruca is at the head, followed by a *caporal*
[leader], another dancer dressed as a black, and the rest as
cowboys with another bull at the end. Twelve are in each line.

The two elderly persons—the patron, who is really old,
and Maruca, who really is a young woman but who dances in
the order of an older spouse and is thus called old—begin to
dance with each person in each file until they complete both
lines. This takes about two hours. When they are finished
dancing with each dancer, two cowboys ask the patron to lend
them the two bravest bulls to celebrate the fiesta. The patron
responds, "With much pleasure," and he lends his large livestock. But beforehand the two cowboys have to erect a good
restaurant and throw a good banquet so that the patron's wife
can enjoy the fiesta.

Later, they have a bullfight. Then the first cowboy, who is
called Penacho and who owns the cantina named La Cantina

Resbalón [Slipup] de México, looks for the cowboys, who have gathered in his cantina to act as waiters.

When everything is prepared, the patron and the Maruca dance a lot on the corners of the square until they reach the cantina. When they arrive, they greet Don Penacho politely.

Then the patron asks, "What kinds of drinks are there in the cantina?"

Penacho responds, "Many different kinds of drinks."

Then Penacho gives two glasses to the patron and Maruca. As they drink their drinks, Don Penacho leaves the cantina to guard them, making sure they do not fall down in the street because the tequila is very strong. When the patron asks how much they owe for the drinks, Don Penacho answers that they do not owe anything because they own everything.

Then the patron and Maruca have to dance with each of the cowboys again until they arrive at their posts at the head of the file, which takes some time. When they finish, Don Penacho goes to the two waiters and leaves, dancing with a bottle, because his business was bad with the Mexicans, who acted like thieves and who left him with just a bottle. Don Penacho had been serving the Mexicans drinks, but they had not paid him sufficiently because they were dancers who just left and returned to the marimba. He says that he had to taste what the owners had been drinking, and he leaves with his own bottle. [But the truth is that not everyone drank liquor. Mostly they had sodas in their bottles. There was actually a mock-up of a small cantina with a sign, La Cantina Resbalón de México, with drinks of either liquor or soda pop, whichever a dancer wanted in reality, but the meaning of the dance was that they were all drinking beer or liquor and not paying for it because they were dancers.]

In this dance there are two persons with the masks of bulls. The cowboys set up a bullfight. They ask the patron to take out a tame bull. Then the *mayordomo, caporal,* the black,

and the rest of the cowboys bullfight. The last is the old patron.

The cowboys say that the patron's woman is very young
and that they want the patron to die. For that reason, they
take out a very mean bull so that they can have the woman
and all that she would inherit from the patron. The patron
dies, but before expiring, he calls together all the cowboys and
tells them that all his belongings are to go to them and to just
take care of his wife. Then he dies. They put the mask of death
[a mask with the face of a dead man] on him, and they put him
in a casket and take him for the burial.[32]

—Ignacio Bizarro Ujpán

Dance of the Flying Monkey

The peoples of these towns believe
in the *Baile del Mico Volador* [Dance of
the Flying Monkey]. It is a dance that is
very sacred because it deals with great animals
of the forest such as the jaguar, the puma, and
the monkey. It is a very old dance that in these
times the men are not lively enough to perform; the
dancers must fly from a long pole that measures forty meters
high by means of great lassos more than fifty meters long.

The dancers have to fly by means of a lasso until they
reach the ground. Before beginning the dance, they have to
make great sacrifices to look for a tree in the forest. When they

look for a tree, a shaman goes also and carries candles, myrrh, incense, and a lot of sugarcane liquor. Also, they take a lot of meat that they eat below the tree when they make the sacrifice. This serves to protect the tree from breaking when they cut it. Before felling the tree, they have to make three kinds of ceremonies, and the fourth time is when they are ready to cut. On the last night of the ritual all the dancers have to offer presents under the tree to ask for pardon of the god of the forest [for cutting down the tree]. At dawn they begin to chop down the tree.

After the tree is felled, they begin to strip off the bark or shell, and on the same day they carry it out. Not just the dancers, but the entire town helps because the pole is green and heavy.

In the morning the people have to walk three to five days to arrive at the point where they are going to perform this dance. When they reach the place, they allow the pole some time to dry. While it is drying, they guard it day and night against witches or other shamans. When it is time to plant the pole, they have to make other rituals to avoid danger to the fliers. The first dancer [monkey] is the main shaman of the group and in charge of laying the foundation where they plant the pole. When he is finished laying the foundation, they begin to burn candles, myrrh, incense, and offer a lot of rum. But before planting the pole, they first have to throw four living roosters inside the hole. The pole kills them when it falls inside the hole. Along with the four roosters they bury a liter of cane liquor. This serves as a sacrifice for the deity of the pole so that on the main day of the fiesta there will be no danger for the dancers.

When the pole is planted, they have to do four more rituals, and the pole has to be guarded by the authorities of the town, who are collaborating with the dancers. Furthermore, they believe that it is dangerous for women to cross over the pole before it is planted because the shaman says that if a woman passes over the pole, it is possible that on the main day of the fiesta it will break. Also, when the pole is planted, they do not permit a woman to pass under it. This is the reason they guard it until the end of the fiesta.

This Dance of the Flying Monkey they did in my town, but earlier, according to my grandma, who has lived in this world for 101 years![33] She said they did the Dance of the Monkey for the last time about 60 years ago when a son of hers, called Humberto Bizarro Temó, was a dancer. Also, she said that the first shaman of the dancers was called José Bizarro. Since Don José Bizarro died, no one has wanted to be in charge of the Dance of the Flying Monkey.

Well, what I know is that in the year 1952, when I was twelve years old, they did the Dance of the Flying Monkey in Santa Ana la Laguna. It was very beautiful, but at times one was afraid to look at the dancers. I went to watch the titular fiesta of this town, and what made me happy was the Dance of the Flying Monkey. I noticed that when the dancers erected the large pole, they gave it much respect. Before climbing they had to face and kiss the pole. Also, they had to pour good rum at the base of it, and each had to kneel at the foot of it. Around them were big candles that burned twenty-four hours.

During this time, the *jefe* of the monkeys was Señor Humberto Canajay, the main shaman, who guarded the surroundings of the pole and the dances. The first shaman placed himself on the reel. He was in charge of untying and uncoiling the big lassos from which the monkeys flew to the earth. In this dance there were jaguars, pumas, monkeys, and also dancers with the names of angels, who were dressed very differently from that of the monkeys.

When I asked why, in a dance of animals, some persons were dancing in the form of angels, the response was that the angels come from heaven and fly with their wings and protect the dancers from falling from the pole. I noticed that the angels flew toward earth, and when they reached halfway down the pole they began to sing a very beautiful song. However, it was difficult to comprehend what they said because they were about twenty-five meters above the ground when they sang. When they reached the ground, they finished the song. Then they went to kneel down at the foot of the large pole and began to sing in the year 1952.

Not until this year of 1979 did they perform again the Dance of the Flying Monkey. Twenty-seven years have passed since they have done this dance because no one wanted to be the first monkey. I do not know why it is that Don Humberto Canajay wanted to do it again, because he is very advanced in age, about eighty-five years old. Still, he is an elder who is very strong with the muscles of a younger man. It is true that I did not go to see the fiesta of Santa Ana, but I am acquainted with Señor Humberto Canajay because he has worked in my crew on the coast.

I am certain that in the history of these towns it was in the year of 1979 that they said good-bye to the Dance of the Flying Monkey, because in this fiesta of Santa Ana they performed the dance with fatal consequences. It happened on 11 August, the day before the fiesta. No one knows what happened to Don Humberto, the first shaman; that is, perhaps the first monkey failed with the rituals and was not able to control the reel that was on the point of the pole. They say that Don Humberto did not know why on this day a dancer released the lasso when he was still twenty-five meters from the ground and fell to his death. However, on this day, the eleventh, it was not as bad as what happened on the main day of the fiesta.

My close kin and my son José told me what they saw at about 1 P.M. on 12 August. They say that from the point of the pole, or from the reel, about forty meters high, the dancer Pablo Sicay fell. When the dancer fell to the earth, he was totally disfigured and unrecognizable because the bones of his face were all broken. Also, when Don Humberto realized that one of his companions had fallen, he also allowed himself to plunge toward the ground with the lasso, but when he reached midpoint, about seventeen meters from the ground, the lasso jammed and the reel of the wheel would not turn. Humberto lost control when the reel stuck, and he let go of the lasso and fell to the earth. However, this man with much luck did not die, but he broke his spinal column. The same car that carried the deceased also carried Don Humberto, who was in critical condition, to the hospital in Sololá.

Señor Don José García informed me that Don Humberto Canajay spent weeks in the hospital of Sololá. But he still lives. However, he lost all his strength, and he walks with a cane because he suffers with his vertebral column. Don José García was chatting with Don Humberto Canajay about the dance and what he had suffered in the past year and why two of his friends of the dance had died. The answer that Don Humberto gave was that they were bewitched by some men of Santo Tomás Chichicastenango, who do the Dance of the Flying Monkey but not as well as the Santanecos. The *brujos* of Chichicastenango are still young and able to make witchcraft to prevent him and his fellow Santanecos from performing a better dance. Don Humberto said that he had lost two of his companions of the dance but that now he is making rituals to bewitch these men of Chichicastenango. He knows very well that his companions suffered the mishap because of these *brujos*.

This information of Don Humberto was taken at the end of August of this year [1979]. Don José García arrived in Santa Ana soon after the fiesta to buy old things. When it was opportune, I recommended that he get the information from Don Humberto. When Don José got these facts, he told them to me. It is certain that it will be difficult for them to perform this kind of dance in the highlands again because it will be hard to find men strong enough.

—Ignacio Bizarro Ujpán

The Four Indians of Samayac

The story says that around here in our region, the Indians are always telling stories. And it says that there is a story that is called "The Four Indians of Samayac." It says that in this town, well, there are many people who can't speak *Castilla* [Castilian Spanish].[34] They can't speak or understand.

There were four men who couldn't speak *Castilla* and couldn't understand. They were illiterate; never had they been in school. Then, tired of life, the four of them said, "What will become of us if we are very poor? We don't have money; we can't speak or understand *Castilla*."

Then one of them said, "Look, why don't we go to the coast to work? They say that on the coast much money is earned. Around Mazatenango and Retalhuleu is where one can work well."

But then the three said, "But why do we go to the coast if we don't know how to speak *Castilla,* or understand? And there on the coast there are only Ladinos. They don't understand our language. If we go to the coast, it seems that we are going to suffer," said the three to the other comrade.

"No, *muchá,*[35] don't be so foolish. Let's be a little smart. *Castilla* can be learned. We can learn it as we walk, because also all things can be learned." Like that the four spoke among themselves.

They were convinced that they had to go out to the coast the next day. Like that, they left at three in the morning, leaving Samayac and passing by all the coast.

The story goes that every little while they would say along the way, "We will learn *Castilla*. To learn Spanish is easy. When we return, we will be able to speak well like the Ladinos," they would say. Like that, they would talk among themselves.

When they were approaching Mazatenango, the smartest told the other three, "*Muchá*, now we are arriving in Mazatenango. Now each one of us has to learn a word, and, little by little, we will be learning more, and, like that, it won't be hard for us among the Ladinos. So they will give us work."

"Very well," said the other three. "That's good."

The story says that they passed very close by a group of muchachos speaking Spanish, saying, "We four."

Then the smartest of them said that he heard the same words, "We four." Then he told his comrades, "Look, *muchá*, I can already speak the *Castilla*," he said. "I can already say, 'We four,' " he said.

"Ah, how good," said the three. "Then like that we will also do."

They continued walking and walking, and they passed by another group of señores who were talking about money, who were saying, "For the money."

And another one of Samayac managed to hear, "For the money."

"Well," he said, "I also learned how to speak *Castilla*," he told his comrades. "I now can say, 'For the money.' Now it's two of us who know *Castilla*," he said.

"Good, *muchá*, act smart, because we must learn *Castilla*," they said to the other two.

"Very good," said the two, "right."

They continued walking and walking around Mazatenango.

The story says that there a man was bothering a woman, but the angry woman told the abusive man, "Don't be bothering me because I'll send you to the can [jail]."

Then one of the Indians of Samayac managed to hear, "To the can."

"Look, *muchá*," said he to his comrades, "I also can speak the *Castilla*. I can now say, 'To the can.'"

"Ah, how good! Then that's three of us already. Now only one is lacking."

Well, they continued like that, repeating the same words. "We four," would say one. "For the money," the other would say. "To the can," said the other. "But our other comrade has to learn how to talk," they said.

Well, the story says that they were walking around Mazatenango when there a señorita and a muchacho passed. Then the muchacho told the señorita, "I am accompanying you, my love."

"With much pleasure," said the señorita.

Then the last one of the four Indians of Samayac retained the words, "With much pleasure."

"Well, *muchá*," he said, "I also now know *Castilla*. I can now say, 'With much pleasure.' That's what I learned."

"Ah, it's good," they said.

The story goes that they were very happy, saying among themselves, "Now we can speak *Castilla*."

"So that we won't forget what we have learned," said the smartest, "we have to speak according to the order we learned the words. The one who learned first has to speak first; the one who learned second has to speak second; the one who learned third has to speak third; the one who learned fourth has to speak last."

"Very well," they said, and they went on. "Now we will see if we can speak," they said.

"When the Ladinos speak to us, I will say, 'We four,'" said the first Indian of Samayac.

"Very good."

"Then I will speak," said the second. I will say, 'For the money.'"

"Ah, very good, we can speak," said another.

And the third one said, "I will say, 'To the can.' "

The fourth one said, "I also have to say, 'With much pleasure.' "

"Ah, well, then we now know how to speak," they said, "now there is no worry. With that we can work well and earn money to take to our town in Samayac." Like that they talked contentedly.

These were the words that each of them learned. The story says that every little while they repeated them so that they would not forget them:

The first: "I'm going to say, 'We four.' "

The second: "I'm going to say, 'For the money.' "

The third: "I'm going to say, 'To the can.' "

The fourth: "I'm going to say, 'With much pleasure.' "

The story says that upon entering the city center of Mazatenango, the four Indians of Samayac passed near a cadaver, a dead person. They, more than anything else, right, didn't know that being near a dead person might make them look suspicious, and they stopped to see. They laughed and laughed, watching the dead person. The policemen, however, were making an investigation as to who assassinated the man, but the Indians of Samayac didn't realize that the police were looking for the assassins. They were there just watching the dead person, laughing and laughing.

Then the police suspected the four Indians of Samayac. "Why are these men laughing?" they said. "Could it be they are the ones who killed the person?"

A policeman went to them and said, "Well, *muchá*, what are you laughing at?"

They didn't speak.

"Which of you killed this man?" is what he said.

The first, the most clever Indian of Samayac spoke, "We four," he said.

"Ah, well," said the policeman, "good, and why did you kill him?"

"For the money," the other Indian of Samayac said.

"Ah, now it's two," he said.

"Now, what will we do with these men?" said one policeman to the other.

The other Indian of Samayac spoke. "To the can," is what he said.

"Ah, my God, then truly you killed the man. Well, accompany me," said the policeman.

"With much pleasure," said the fourth one.

Then that's the way it was with these hombres. They were taken to jail for saying the words they learned in Spanish, and for speaking the *Castilla* that they learned on the road: we four, for the money, to the can, and with much pleasure, these poor Indians of Samayac, they took to the can. Since they couldn't speak, they said the same things to the judge. Because of that, they spent the next twenty years in the prison instead of earning money to take to their family.

This is the story of "The Four Indians of Samayac."

—Ignacio Bizarro Ujpán

The Two Lazy Men

The story says that in a town there were two disobedient and lazy brothers who didn't want to work. They only spent their days sleeping.

One day their father, tired of giving them food, got very mad at them and said, "You have to get out of my house because you don't want to work. In reality you are my sons, but I can no longer bear to support you because you are lazy." And he threw them out of his house.

"That's okay," they said.

They went walking and walking and walking through many pueblos, but no one would give them work, because when the people would ask them what they could do, they would say only that they wanted to work, but not what work they could do. They went to many towns, but when the people saw their dirty clothes, they would not give them work, because more than anything else, they feared them.

The story says that they arrived at a house of a señora, and they told her, "Señora, please, be kind to us. Give us free shelter! It's that we come from afar."

And the señora told them, "Ah, I can't."

And they said again, "Please, give us shelter."

"Well, and do you bring suitcases, then, because I don't want to give shelter to people who are just vagabonds. It's that my husband is very cross," the señora said.

"Look, señora," they said, "it's that some damned thieves

stole our suitcases, but here we have two sacks to put on the floor and we can sleep, if you wish, on the corridor of the house, but please give us shelter."

"Ah, well," she said, "it's okay; you can stay. But how many nights of shelter do you want?"

"One week, señora, because we have to work in this pueblo. Here we have to earn some money. Look, it's that we have no clothes, because our clothing was stolen by the thieves," they said.

"Ah, well, very good," she said, "you can stay there inside in this corner, but with the condition that tomorrow you have to sweep the house and *sitio* for me, so that my husband doesn't get angry with me. It's that I don't have time to do the cleaning because every day I go out to sell rice."

"Señora, tell us what to do, and we will do everything that we can."

"Well, okay," said the señora.

Then the following day the lazy men got up very early. They swept the floor and the *sitio* well. The señora became very happy with them. She went to sell the rice in milk, and they went to sleep under the trees.

That's what they would do. At night they would come in because the señora would come back very late. When night was falling, she came home, and at that time they would arrive also. They had greater expectations with the señora. They didn't like the husband because the woman had more confidence in them.

Then each time that they would arrive, they would ask her, "Look, señora, by chance, did you have any leftover rice in milk? Give us a little bit. It's that we are hungry."

"Very good," is what she would say. She had leftover rice, and always she would give it to the two lazy men.

Like that it was for one day, two days, three days. But the señora also got angry because they only wanted the rice in milk given to them.

Then one day they asked her, "Look, señora, by chance did you have any leftover rice? Give it to us, it's that we are hungry."

"Look, I can't give you anything now. If you want, sleep here and, if not, well, I don't have rice," is what she said.

But they saw that the señora had rice leftover from the market. One night the two lazy men took notice where the señora had put away the leftover rice. Then they planned what to do. "Look, you," said one to the other comrade, "we will wait until the old man and old woman go to sleep, and then we will fill ourselves with rice."

"Now with the oil lamp, let's see well where the rice is kept so that in the darkness we can go get it," said the other.

"Very well."

And that's the way it was.

First, the *viejito* [little old man], the husband, went to sleep, and afterward the señora. They calmly turned off the oil lamp, but the lazy men lay waiting. One of them fell asleep, and the other was awake because hunger was bothering him. Then the one who wasn't asleep said to the other, "Pst, you, get up. Let's go get rice. Already the *vieja* [old woman] is asleep."

But the story goes that the other, who was sound asleep, didn't hear anything. Instead he was snoring.

"You, indeed, are fucked up. But I'm hungry; I, indeed, will eat my rice," said the other. He got up, crawling, crawling, looking for the direction where the rice was, because, since it was dark, he couldn't control his footsteps well.

At last he arrived where the pot of rice was. He grabbed a glass and he began to drink rice with milk until he was full. Then, he said, "Ah, I already got full, but my comrade, without doubt, is hungry." In the darkness he brought a glass of rice in milk, looking, looking, for the comrade, but since it was dark, he lost his direction to where his comrade was.

"Where is my comrade?" he said. But when the man lost his way, he went to where the señora was sleeping.

Luck would have it that the señora was sleeping sideways. Who knows how the *corte* unfolded, but the señora was sleeping nude. So the woman was like that lying on her side. *Púchica* [Goodness]! The man was taking a glass of rice.

"Look," he told him, "you, get up," and, no, it wasn't his comrade, rather, it was the señora. But everything was silent; she didn't answer. And he touched her, "Pst, you, what happened to you?" he told him. "*Púchica,* why do you have such fat cheeks; you are getting too fat." That's what he said. "Not only are you hungry, you are getting fatter." But it wasn't the face of the comrade, instead, it was the butt of the señora that he was touching with his hands.

"Get up! *Púchica,* is that, you? It seems that you are sick, why are you already so fat? You weren't like that when we went to sleep." But he wasn't touching the face of his companion. He was touching her ass.

But the story says that the señora didn't feel anything because she was fast asleep. Suddenly, he got tired. "You, open your mouth," he told him, touching the bottom of the señora. "Open your mouth, hombre. Here is your rice," he would tell him. "*Púchica,* you caused your mouth to have a different shape? It is in a vertical form. Mine isn't like that, like yours. What happened to you?"

The señora didn't feel a thing.

"You, I opened your mouth. Little by little I'm going to pour the rice in milk into it." And he poured the rice in milk, but not into his mouth but into the behind of the señora. "Surely, things are screwed up with you. Take your rice!"

At last he realized that the rice was spread out. "Ihh," he said, and he got frightened. Little by little, however, the story says that he went to sleep where he was.

After a while, when the woman woke up, she began to cry in the darkness. She was crying, crying, and crying.

Later, her husband got up and asked her, "What happened to you?"

"Look, *m'hijo* [my dear]," she told him, "now I'm going to die."

"Why?"

"My love, I'm going to die. This may be the last night of my life with you. You are going to be alone in this house. Without doubt this is a bad sign!"

"What? What happened to you?"

"It's that who knows how it was? Imagine that when I was sleeping, I didn't sense when I was having a bowel movement in my *corte*. I didn't even have any pain or anything in my stomach. Nor did I eat much. I don't know why I defecated inside my *corte*, which I've never done in my life," she said.

"You don't say," he said.

But the señora distressfully kept on crying, crying. She thought that she was the one who crapped in her *corte*, but, no, instead it was rice that the lazy man had poured on her posterior.

Then, also, the husband got scared and started to cry. The two were crying because, without doubt, they thought it was a bad sign, a temptation of the devil, what happened there with them, because now there was something inside the *corte* of the señora. But it was only the rice in milk that the lazy man had poured on her derriere.

When it dawned, the two lazy men asked her, "Señora, what happened last night, because you were crying?"

Then the woman answered, saying, "I had a bad sign. I didn't sense when I did my necessity in my *corte*. Now there is no one who will wash my *corte*. I'm sad. It seems that I'm going to die, because never before has something like this happened to me."

But the story says that the two lazy men knew that it was not excrement that the señora had in her *corte*, and they said, "If you like we will go to the lake to wash your *corte.*"

"Very well," said the señora, and she gave her *corte* to the two lazy men. They went to wash it, and, for that favor, they gave them another week of lodging.

This is the story of the two lazy men.

—Ignacio Bizarro Ujpán

The Padre Pícaro

The story says that in a town there was a sly priest from Spain who liked the indigenous women. Each Sunday he would stand at the door of the church to wait for the prettiest indigenous women. He would embrace them and seat them on the first benches of the church. But he wouldn't do this with all the women, rather, only with the young, pretty ones. Now, the *viejitas*, he didn't even want to see. The father only wanted young women and was annoyed with the men.

Then, that's how it was for some time. Each time that he would arrive, always he would have the pretty muchachas on the first benches of the church. The story says that in this town lived a very attractive woman who seemed like a virgin and who also went to masses. But when the father became aware of this woman, he asked her, "What's your name?"

"I'm called Vicenta."

"Look, Vicenta, I tell you that each Sunday you have to confess your sins in front of me."

"Very well, Father," she told him. "I will do what's possible. Sometimes I have much work, but I will do what's possible. Now that you are the priest who advises me well, I will do the confession."

But when Vicenta would arrive to confess herself, the father didn't want to receive the confession; he would only tell her, "After mass, daughter, we will go to the convent. I have a gift for you."

Out of respect to the priest, the woman would say, "Very well."

Then, at the end of each mass he would tell her, "Let's slip over to the convent."

"Very well, Father."

"Oh, very good, let's go," he would say.

Then he would give her bread and chocolate. "Oh, you seem like a virgin," he would say to the woman.

Then, one morning, while they ate bread and drank chocolate, he said, "Look, Vicenta, how delightful it would be to spend the night with you! You are the most beautiful woman in this pueblo."

"Father, don't talk like that. Don't be *pícaro* [naughty]," she told him.

"Oh, I'm not *pícaro*," he told her, "I'm the priest. What I'm telling you isn't *pícaro*. Every man in the whole world needs a woman."

"No, I have a husband; I'm married by the church, and, in addition, on Sundays I'm receiving communion with you," she said. "If this is the way you are going to talk to me, I won't come again to mass."

"Nothing is happening. There's been no sin," said the priest.

"No, Father. I won't come here again to you," she told him.

"No, no, no, no, don't worry. You can come to mass. Every Sunday you need to confess your sins to me," he told her, because, without doubt, the father thought that the woman was going to criticize him for what he had said to her.

And the woman went to her house. But the story says that the woman was disgusted with the words the priest had said to her.

The next Sunday came, and Vicenta went to the church to confess, but the father didn't want to hear her confession. In the confessional he told her, "How delightful a night with you would be."

"Don't be *pícaro*. Instead of listening to my confession, you tell me other things."

"No, daughter, don't worry. I'm the father. I can forgive your sins, but what I want you to do is sleep with me."

Then the woman got scared when the padre told her directly that he wanted to sleep with her. "Father, are you a *pícaro* [rogue]?"

"No," said the padre. "What I'm telling you is a good thing, because I will give you money with which to buy your *corte*, to buy your blouse, to buy your shawl. Also, I will give you money so that you can live more tranquilly with your husband."

Another Sunday, the same thing happened. Another Sunday, the same thing happened. The priest was obstinate.

Then the story says that Vicenta cried and told her husband what the priest had said to her.

"Look, *m'hijo*," she told him, "imagine what is happening. The priest is *pícaro*."

"Why?"

"Because each time that the mass ends, he takes me to the convent and tells me that he wants to sleep with me, that it would be delightful to spend a night with me. But how is it that I can do these things if I know that I am married by the church and you are my husband? I can't do things that are not proper."

"Ah, well," he said. "Next Sunday you have to go," he told her.

"I don't want to go anymore," said the woman.

"You have to go."

Sunday arrived. "Are you going to mass?" he told his wife.

"It's that the priest bothers me much; he's *pícaro*."

"Don't be foolish," he told her, "ask him for *pisto* [money]. Ask him for 50 or 100 quetzales of money and bring it here. We need money," the husband said.

"It's okay?" she said. "You aren't going to get angry with me."

"No, because nothing will happen. You will only take the money. We will see what to do here. Next Sunday you are going to tell the father to give you money and that he can come to sleep with you, but tell him to come at ten or eleven o'clock at night."

"Ay, no, because you will beat me!"

"No," said the hombre, "I'm not going to hit you. What I want is that the padre give us money because we are very poor, and he has a lot of money," said her husband.

"Well, then, if you are not going to strike me, I'm going to ask for money from the *pícaro* padre," she said.

Then Sunday arrived, and Vicenta went to mass. The story says that the father was waiting in front of the church. "Now you have come, Vicenta. I've been waiting for you to begin the mass." Then he embraced her and took her to the first bench of the church and said, "After mass I have a gift for you."

"Very well, Padre," she said.

Then after mass, Vicenta went to the convent to talk to the father.

"Now you have come, Vicenta."

"Yes, Father," she said. And they drank chocolate.

"Oh, you seem like a virgin. How delightful it would be to spend a night of my dreams with you. Have you thought anything about what I have told you?"

"Padre, you are a *pícaro!* Well, now you have convinced me. Now what is it that you want with me?"

"What I want is to sleep a night with you."

"Well, then give me money!"

"Very well, how much do you need?"

"Fifty quetzales," said the woman.

"Good," said the priest, and he gave her fifty quetzales.

Then the woman said, "Father, you can come sleep with me. My husband is not there now, but you must come about ten or eleven at night when the people are sleeping, because if they see you, tomorrow morning they will criticize you."

"Oh, don't worry. I can come at ten o'clock, because I have my horse," said the priest.

"Very well, Father. Then I will wait for you, but don't you trick me," said the woman.

"No, no, no, no, I can't trick anyone."

"Okay."

Then the woman left for her house and took the fifty quetzales she had received to give to her husband. "Look, here is the money that the reverend gave me," she told him.

"How much?"

"Fifty quetzales," she said.

"Fifty quetzales is very little," said the husband, "you should have asked for a hundred. He's a priest who makes money by only sitting down, not like us, who labor under the sun. At mass he is paid well. You should have asked 100 quetzales, but since you only asked for fifty, well, that's all right," said her mate. "It will serve for our living expenses. When will he come?"

"At ten at night," she said.

"Good," he said.

Then, night fell. The story says that the man told his woman, "You need to make chocolate and buy bread," he said. "We are going to eat afterward, later, around eleven at night when the father leaves," said the husband.

"Very well," said the woman, and she went to buy chocolate and bread. Then the two of them communicated. "At the hour when the priest comes, I'm going to be outside. Wait inside for the reverend. When he arrives, tell him to take off his clothes before going to bed and that you will take off your clothes. Then tell him to take off his underwear and that you will take off your underwear. I will be outside listening, and I will know when to come in. I know what I will do," said the husband.

"But you aren't going to hit me," the woman said.

"No, no, no, with you there is nothing because I know that the father is *pícaro,* and he will answer to me."

"Very well," said the woman.

The story says that at nine-thirty the husband went outside. And then at ten the priest came mounted on his horse. Slowly, he entered the *sitio.* He left his horse tied to a tree, went to the door of the house, and went inside.

"Oh, Daughter Vicenta, there you are. This night will be delightful," said the padre when he went in.

"Come on in, Father, come on in."

"No one else is here?" he asked.

"No one. I can't trick you. You are a priest," said the woman.

"Oh, how good! How good!"

Then the story says that they sat down.

"Oh, how I want to go to bed now," said the reverend.

"One moment, Father," said the woman. "We still need much to talk," she said.

"Okay, I need my delightful nights, my pleasure," is what he said.

"Wait a moment," said the woman. She was controlling

the padre so that her husband outside could do another job. While the priest was sitting inside, the husband went to bring a bull, and he took the saddle off the horse and put it on the bull. The husband untied the horse, and it ran to the pasture. Instead of the horse, it was the bull that was there with a saddle on it. The woman was calculating the time when the husband would be finished.

"Now, Father, let's go to bed," she said.

"Oh, sure," said the priest, "let's go to bed."

"Only on my condition; see if you accept," is what the woman said.

"And what is it?" said the priest.

"I want you to take off your cassock," she told him, "because my husband and I have the habit of sleeping naked."

"Very well," said the priest, and he took off his cassock.

"To bed then," said the father.

"Take off your shirt," she told him, "and I will take off my blouse."

"Oh no," he said.

"If you don't take off the shirt, I won't sleep with you," she said.

"Ah, and why?" he said.

"My husband and I are accustomed to sleeping like that, without clothing."

"Ah, how good," said the priest, he took off the shirt.

And the woman took off her blouse.

"Take off your pants," she told him.

"Ah, it's a little bit risky to take my pants off."

"No, it's that we are accustomed to it. We sleep nude. If you don't take your pants off, you aren't going to sleep with me," said the woman. "Take off your pants, and I'll take off my skirt."

"Very well," said the priest, and he took off his pants.

And the woman took off her skirt.

"Now take off the T-shirt," she said, "and I'll take off my brassiere."

"Very well." He took off the T-shirt.

And the woman took off her brassiere.

"Now the shorts are lacking," she said. "Take off your shorts and I'll take off my panties."

"Oh, my shorts, no; it can't be," he said.

"No, you have to take off your underwear. If you don't take off the underwear, you can't sleep with me."

"Very good," he said. He was taking off his shorts . . .

"Pum, pum, pum!" went a pound on the door.

"Father, there comes my husband," said the woman, acting as if she was scared, but it was a lie. "Father, now we're going to die! Here comes my husband!"

"Uhhh," said the priest, but now he didn't have on any clothes. Frightened, he said, "My God, I'm going to die; my God, I'm going to die!"

"Well, Father *pícaro*, what are you doing here?" the husband told him. "Get out. What the fuck! Right now I'm going to kill you," is what the man said.

"No, I'm sorry, my God. I'm sorry, my God. I'm leaving; I'm leaving," he said.

The husband landed two kicks on the father's ass, and the priest left running. He grabbed and grabbed at the reins and mounted the bull, but he thought he had climbed on a horse. Instead of a horse, it was a bull! And the bull was very *bravo* [mean]. The padre said, "My God, my God, on this devil I've mounted. My God, my God, on this devil I got on." And he couldn't dismount because the bull was too *bravo*. Thus he spent the rest of the night in the pasture without any clothes.

After the reverend had gone, the couple, the story says, ate the bread and chocolate that the woman had bought earlier.

Very early in the morning the sacristans went to look for

the priest. They found the padre nude, on top of a bull. The cowboys had to go grab the bull to get him off.

Mounted nude on a bull all night was the delight of the *pícaro* priest.

And this is the story of padre *pícaro*.

—Ignacio Bizarro Ujpán

The Padre Who Wants the Wealth

 This is how the story goes. A Spanish priest was coming to celebrate mass in these pueblos. But he looked upon the hombres with despising; that is, he was very *bravo* to the men. But one time he fell in love with a pretty Indian woman named María. She, however, was married. Each time that the father arrived in the pueblo, he remained for three days, and each time he arrived he always bothered the woman before and after mass. He told her, *"Hijita* [Dear Daughter], I love you and appreciate you. I will be the *dueño* [owner] of your wealth."

But the woman only listened and didn't want to answer because she respected her marriage.

Then the priest told her, "María, your wealth is mine. You will give me what I ask."

"But look, Father, I don't have any wealth," the woman answered, "I'm poor. My husband has no riches."

"Ah, no, it's that you don't understand," he said. "I want your fortune."

"*Púchica,* and what wealth could it be that the father is talking about?" the woman would ask the other women.

Since they didn't know how to speak Spanish, they would say, "We don't know what the padre is telling you. 'Wealth,' he says, but who knows what wealth it is."

And afterward it is said that María went to mass. "*Hijita* María," he told her, "could you go with me to the convent? I have a present for you."

"Very well, Father," said María, but it was out of respect, right. The people were expected to respect their priest. The woman, however, didn't know the intentions of the reverend.

It is said that after mass, María went to the convent.

"Oh, let's go have breakfast," is what the priest said to her.

"Thank you, Father," she said, "and why only me?"

"Ah, it's only you because it's only your wealth that I want," he said.

"Father, and why do you tell me wealth if I don't have any riches and my husband is poor?"

"Oh, you don't understand. I want your fortune," he said.

"Oh," said María.

Then it is said that the woman ate but not with pleasure. It bothered her, that thing about wealth. She ate but anxiously. Afterward, she went to her house.

Another Sunday, it is said that the priest arrived again in the town, and also María went to mass. "Ah, now we will see the mass," he said.

"That's good," said María.

"Today I will stay sleeping here," he said, "in the convent. I will not go out to another town, rather, I will be here," said the padre.

"That's good, Father," said María. And the reverend seated María on the front bench where the preachers sit.

"Ay, my daughter," he said, *"malaya* [*malhaya*, damn it] your wealth," said the father.

"But, Father, don't talk to me about wealth because right now the mass will begin," said the woman.

"Ah, I don't think about mass," he said. "I think only about your wealth," said the priest.

Well, like that it was. Finishing the mass, the padre said, *"Hijita* María, I need for you to come with me to the convent. I have something prepared for you," he said.

"Good, Father," she said. The woman went with him again.

"Now give me your wealth. I will make you happy. I will buy you your *corte;* I will buy you your blouse; I will buy you your shawl. I will give you money so that you will be happy with your husband," said the priest.

"Uy, Father, how is it that I give you my wealth if I am poor?" said the woman.

"No, woman. It's not wealth of this world, rather, it's wealth that God has given to you. That's the wealth I want," he said.

"No, Father," she told him, "I don't understand what you are telling me. I had better leave," said the woman; she went out.

And she went to tell the husband. "Look," she said, "the priest is very abusive."

"Why?"

"He says that he wants my wealth, but I don't know what my wealth is, since we are poor," said the woman to her husband.

"Ah, I know what your wealth is," said the husband. He thought, "That priest is quite without shame. He wants the fortune between her legs."

"Go! Go another Sunday," he said, "and see if he tells you that again. If so, you tell me."

"Very well," said the woman, and she went to mass.

And the priest was waiting in front of the church. "Oh, *Hijita* María, you have come now," he said.

"Well, yes, Father," she said.

"Ay, *malaya*, your wealth," he said.

"And, Father, why do you speak to me of wealth, if I am poor?"

"No, you are poor of this world, but the wealth that God has given you is great," is what the priest said.

But the woman didn't understand that, and they went to place her inside. After the mass ended, the priest told her, "*Hijita* María, to the convent please. Let's have a refreshment."

"Very well, Father."

They went to the convent and had cake and soda. "Well, *Hijita* María," he said, "I will make you happy. Give me your wealth."

"But, Father, I don't have any wealth. I'm poor."

"I want to be the *dueño* of the wealth that you have in the middle of your legs. For this wealth I will give you whatever you ask for. I'll give you money with which to buy a *corte*. I will buy you a blouse, a shawl. I will give you money for your husband."

"Father, it's sinful, what you are telling me! I am a married lady, and each time you come to celebrate mass, I always confide in you."

"*Hijita*, there's sin all over the whole world, and God will forgive us. What I want you to do is come sleep with me to enjoy your riches. I don't want your wealth all the time, rather once in a while. You can ask me for money. I love you very much. Because of you I haven't been able to sleep. I am suffering for you. *Hijita*, I have a lot of money. I will give to you and your husband whatever you wish, so that you won't suffer poverty anymore."

"Father," she said, "out of respect I came inside this convent. From now on, I will not come back here. I'm going to tell my husband all of these things."

"Oh, you have to come to mass. It's your obligation to come to mass."

"Yes, but with these words, now I feel sad," said the woman, and she started to cry.

"Don't cry," he said, "don't cry. There's been no sin."

And the woman left for her house. She told her husband, "Look, m'hijo," she said, "the priest is abusive. He keeps bothering me, telling me he wants my fortune."

But it is said that the husband was clever and told his woman that early in the morning she should go to mass so that the padre would offer her money. The woman, however, was scared and said, "No, because you will have a falling out with me and beat me."

"No, we can use the money that this damned priest is offering you. Tomorrow when you arrive for mass if the priest offers you money, tell him that you are going to spend a night with him but to give you 100 quetzales. But you have to tell him that you are going to arrive at ten at night when the people are asleep so that no one will realize it. Tell him, 'I will fix bread and meat for my husband so that he will be happy when I come to see you.'

"Tell the priest to give you money, and we will see what we will do."

"But you will hit me," said the woman.

"No, you will not sleep with the priest there. I know what I will do," said the husband.

"Very well," said the woman.

The following day the woman went again to mass, and the father was waiting in front of the church. "Hijita, you are so beautiful, I want to savor the riches that you bring. I didn't sleep all night, and for that reason, I have been waiting for you."

And it is said that the reverend hugged her and took her to the first bench of the church. Before finishing mass, the father told her, "After mass you can have breakfast."

After mass the woman headed for the convent, as it had been arranged with her husband. It is said that the padre and the lady had breakfast together, and in the middle of it, he offered her money, saying, "Now that you are with me, you can ask me for all the money that you need. The truth is that I want to taste your wealth before leaving this pueblo. You can come sleep with me a night."

"Very well, now you have convinced me," said the woman, "but right now you have to give me money."

"With much pleasure," he said, "100, 200 quetzales; how much do you want?" He got out his money.

"For the moment give me 100 quetzales to buy food and drinks for my husband. Afterward you can give me more. When my husband is good and drunk, I'll come to sleep with you. I will be able to come, but not until 10 P.M. when it is quiet so that the people won't be aware of us. I don't have a watch but I will calculate the time."

"Very well, *Hijita*. That's very well. One hundred quetzales is nothing. You can take 200 quetzales so that you can buy enough *aguardiente* [firewater] for your mate."

"Very well," said the woman, and she took the 200 quetzales to her man. The story says that he was very happy because he was able to buy clothing and food, and they had a good lunch.

And the story says that in the afternoon, the man looked for a big, stiff whip, made from the penis of a bull. The couple ate peacefully, because they didn't have children. They had been married only four months.

When night fell the woman said, "My heart aches because the priest is waiting for me, but I won't arrive."

"Well, it's nine-thirty. Give me a *corte*," said the man.

"Very well," said the woman, and she gave him a *corte*.

"Now give me a blouse," he said.

"Fine," said the woman, and she gave him a blouse. The man was not hairy. He tied his head with a scarf so that he would look like a woman. He put on the *corte*, the blouse, and the shawl. But inside the *corte*, he put the whip. Then he left at about eleven at night.

The priest had been waiting since ten o'clock. He knew very well the hour when the woman was to arrive. So he said to the sacristan, since there are two who sleep in the convent, "Look, do me a favor. Stay outside because I have to receive a woman. I have a special guest for this evening. When the woman leaves, you can come in to sleep."

"Very well," said the sacristan. He went outside, and he was in the garden. He saw when the woman was coming. "Ay, the priest sure is going to score tonight," said the sacristan, holding back his own desires.

Then the priest said to himself, "Ah, my wealth is coming. My fortune is coming; how fortunate am I! Today I will partake of life. I've been punished because I don't have a woman, but today is the day of my reward."

Then the door went pum, pum, pum!

"Oh, *Hijita* María, now you have arrived," said the padre, and he opened the door of the convent.

The man was dressed like his wife, and he answered in her voice.

"Good evening, Father. I've come to stay and sleep with you."

"Very well, *Hijita*, come in," and he embraced her.

"Don't kiss me because there is no need to kiss," said the disguised man.

"That's fine. Now you have come."

"Yes."

"Ah good. Now, your riches are mine. *Hijita*, God will forgive us. I can't hold back my desires; let's go to bed."

"Yes, indeed. It's yours," said the man. "The wealth is yours," but he meant the whip that he was carrying.

"Take off your cassock," he said.

"Very well," said the father.

"Take off your shirt and trousers; get naked," said the man disguised as a woman.

"Very well," said the priest, and he took off his shirt and pants.

"I only will take off my blouse, not my *corte*," said the man, because he had something hidden there.

"No," said the padre. "Look, I took off my clothes, and you don't want to take off yours."

"No, it's my custom. You are the one who has to get naked," said the man in disguise. "Take off your T-shirt and shorts."

"Very well," said the reverend, "now we are going to bed." And he took them off.

"Yes, now we are going to bed," said the husband, or that is, the man dressed like a woman.

"Yes," said the padre, "now, for my wealth."

"Indeed," said the husband, "now for your wealth," and he took out the big whip, which was a bull's penis, from under his *corte*.

"Slash!" but he gave it to him hard.

And it is said that the sacristan was holding back his desires outside.

And the priest, the story goes, said, "Uy, my God, ay, no more! Ay, no more! My God, no more! My God, no more!" But the husband gave him who knows how many whiplashes.

"That's what you are getting," he said. "This is your wealth," said the husband of the woman. "You get yours to-day. This is your fortune."

It was a big torment for the priest, being whipped with the penis of the bull. He could no longer get up from the many blows, saying, "My God, my God, it's really big; I ache. No more penis!"

The story goes that the sacristan was listening outside to the voice that said, "It is really big; it hurts a lot." And the sacristan said, "The father is sticking the woman very hard. Poor woman, she's crying. Without doubt the father has a big penis." But it wasn't the woman; it was the father crying from lashes. The sacristan could not hold back his desires, thinking that the padre was enjoying the woman. But the reverend was speaking in a low voice because of the blows.

Then the husband dressed like his woman took a candle that was lit on a table and let drops of wax fall on the butt of the priest. In great pain, the father said, "By an Indian woman I'm given a penis and my ass is burned with wax."

"Don't bother my woman again," the husband told him. "I am not the wife, I am the husband. She gave me the 200 quetzales. You were asking for the wealth of my woman. This is your fortune. Now you are shamefully naked. And if you continue bothering my wife, I will give it to you again, and more. It will be worse. This will be only the beginning of your fortune. You have already felt this wealth."

But the priest now could not talk; he just cried a lot from the blows.

The man, then, put back on the blouse, placed the whip inside the *corte*, and went outside.

The sacristan, waiting outside and seeing the woman leaving, called to her, "Sht, sht, sht," he said, "sht, a little for me, a little for me. I want a little."

The husband heard him.

"Sht, a little for me; I want a little," the sacristan was saying.

"Very well," said the man disguised as a woman. He also gave the bull's penis to the sacristan. He hit him hard, and when the sacristan fell to the ground, the husband ran to the convent to bring the candle, and he let hot wax drop on the butt of the sacristan.

This is what happened to the padre and the sacristan for the love of an Indian woman. They were beaten with a bull's penis and had their bottoms burned with hot wax.

This story ends.

—Ignacio Bizarro Ujpán

The Woman and the Guardian

It is said that in two neighboring towns, there was one couple—a man and woman. The man got a job as a guardian. He had to go out of his house at six in the afternoon because he worked at night. Then he would leave his woman in the house. But he didn't know if the woman had another man. He always thought there was no problem, that his woman was honest, and he told her, "Look, *m'hija* [my dear], stay with the baby. I'll go work."

"That's okay," she would say.

And each time that he would go to work at night, it is said that a man would pass by. He would see the man pass, but they wouldn't talk to each other since he was the guardian.

Then one night he told him, "You, each time I see you pass by here. Where are you going?"

"Look, I have a woman there in the other town. And her husband is a guardian who works at night. Thus we have the agreement that when the husband goes out to work, I go to stay with her to sleep."

"Really, you? Where does she live?"

"She lives there, in the town," said the other man.

"Ah, good," he said.

It was like that for a while, the story goes. The muchacho would leave his own house at six in the afternoon to go to the house he was guarding, and the other man would come almost every night, sometimes every three nights, to sleep with the guardian's woman.

Finally, the guardian asked him, "You, where are you going, really?"

"Well, I already told you that I'm going to sleep with a woman whose husband is a guardian."

"Ah, yes," he said. Then the man thought to himself, "Couldn't it be my woman, because he says that it's a woman of a guardian, and I am a guardian? Who else could it be in the town? Could there be another guardian in the town, or only I?" the man would say. This he would say to himself, thinking.

Well, another night passed. "You, where are you going?" he asked him.

"Ha, right now I am going to sleep with the woman, owing to the husband working at night. I'm going to sleep there."

"That's good," said the guardian to himself, "but I will follow him. Maybe he's going to sleep with my woman."

And it's said that he followed him. When he arrived at his house, he knocked on the door.

"Ih, my husband is coming," the woman told the man who was sleeping with her. "There comes my husband; what will we do?" she said.

The man was scared because the house only had one door. He couldn't escape.

"Look," she told him, "get in there. There, there are many leaves of dry milpa for the *chivos* [young goats]. Get in there," the woman told him.

"Very well," said the man; he got in.

Then the woman opened the door. "What do you want?" she asked her husband.

"Ah, no, I've only come to see," he told her, "if only you are inside. It's that I have a doubt."

"And what is your doubt?" she asked him.

"It's that a señor tells me, when he passes there, by me, that he comes to sleep with a woman, and he tells me that he comes to sleep with a woman of a guardian, and since I am guardian, couldn't it be that he comes to sleep with you, this hombre?" said the husband.

"No, look, there is nothing. Check in the bed; there is nothing. I am only sleeping with the baby," she said.

"Ah, very well," he said. "Well, continue sleeping, then. Take care of the baby. I will go. Be careful!" he said.

"Very well," said the woman. She closed the door, and the man came out from where he was hiding. He continued sleeping with the woman, the story says.

At four in the morning, he passed there, where the guardian was, and the guardian asked him, "You, how did it go?"

"Ha, look, you, it seems that the husband of the woman already knows because today in the night he arrived to knock on the door. But, damn, that woman was smart. She hid me under some dry leaves that she had inside the house. She says that those leaves are used for the young goats, and there I was hiding, because if he finds me in the bed, maybe he will kill me, because he carries a machete," is what the man said.

"Ah, good," he said.

"Good-bye," he said.

"Good-bye, then." Then the man kept thinking, *"Púchica,*

this *pícaro* [rogue], in my house! He's going to my house, because in my house there are these dry leaves," said the husband, the guardian. "Well, now yes," he said, "I will take good care of them."

"When is it that you are going to come back?" is what he asked him.

"The day after tomorrow," the man told him, now far away.

It is said that day the guardian sharpened his machete.

Then by night the man passed. "Where are you going?" he asked him.

"There, the same place where I had told you before, to sleep with the woman, the woman of the guardian," he told him.

"Ah, yes," he told him. "And her husband doesn't come home?"

"Well, I hope that he doesn't arrive tonight. The last time he did arrive, but he didn't find me," said the man.

"Well," he said. The man went, and the husband, the guardian followed, followed. About an hour later, the husband arrived, says the story.

"You, the door! Open the door!" he told his wife.

"My husband is coming," the wife told her lover.

"Now, yes, now yes, he will kill us because he has a machete. Now what will I do?" said the man. "I can't escape from here because the house has only one door, what can I do?"

"Get in, get in this *petate* [weaving] of *tule*." There was a big *petate* there. "Get in there!" she told him.

"That's good," said the man. He got inside the *petate* of *tule*; there he stayed, without moving for anything.

And when the husband came in, the story goes that there directly where the dry leaves were, he parted them with the machete. He thought that the man was underneath it, but, no, because the woman was very smart, she hid him in another place.

"What happened to you? Are you crazy?" his woman asked him.

"No, I know someone is here," he said.

"No, here there is no one," she said. "What's happening to you? Nobody is here."

"Ah good, then. It's that there is a man there that tells me that he comes to sleep with the woman of a guardian. Because of that, I think it's to you he's coming. And he told me when he went by that the woman had hid him under some dry leaves, and I know that there are some dry leaves inside the house. That's why I hit the machete there," he said.

"No," she said, "there's nothing."

"Well," he said. The man returned to his work.

And at four in the morning, the story says, when the man passed there, the guardian said, "You, how did it go?"

"Shut up, you," he told him, "he almost got to kill me. But, damn, that the woman was smart! She hid me inside a *petate* of *tule*. If she had hidden me where I was the day before yesterday, under the dry leaves, right now I would be dead," said the man.

"Really, you?"

"Yes."

"Damned," said the guardian to himself, "the *petate* of *tule* is inside my house, and I parted the leaves with my machete."

"Imagine, he arrived," the man who was telling the guardian said, "and parted the leaves with a machete. What if I had been there? Surely the husband would have killed me."

"Well," the guardian said to the man, "when are you coming again?"

"The day after tomorrow," he said.

"Very well," he said.

The day after tomorrow arrived, the story goes, and the

guardian was at work as usual. The man came again, and the guardian asked him, "You, was it the same there?" he said.

"Ah, there, it was the same with the woman of the guardian," he said.

"Ah, good, have a good day," he said.

"Thank you," he told him, and the man arrived at the guardian's house.

The guardian followed him, followed him, followed him, and an hour later, he knocked on the door. "I am your husband," he said.

"Ih, my God, my husband is coming," said the woman to the man.

"Now what are we going to do?" he said.

"Get underneath the bed," she said.

"Very well," said the man. He got down and stretched under the bed.

"Well, hurry up, open the door!" the guardian demanded.

"Right now, only I'm nursing the baby," she said, and she opened the door.

"Well, what's with you?" he asked her.

"Nothing."

And the husband goes directly to where the *petate* of *tule* was.

"Swish," he gave it with the machete, and there was nothing there.

"And what happened to you?"

"I knew that there was someone in the *petate* of *tule*," he told her.

"There's no one," said the woman.

"Well, if there's no one, I will go work some more. Continue sleeping," said the husband.

"It's okay," she said, and the man came out from under the bed and continued sleeping with the woman.

At four in the morning, he passed where the guardian was. "You, how did it go?" he asked him.

"Ha, shut up, you. It's good that the woman of the guardian is smart," he told him. "She told me to hide under the bed. Had I hidden in the *petate* of *tule* where I was the day before yesterday, the husband would have killed me, because the husband arrived very *bravo* and hit the *petate* of *tule* with the cutting edge of his machete and shredded it into pieces," he said.

"Damned," he said to himself, "that was me. Then it's my woman." He said to the man, "Well, when will you return again?"

"Always every three days," he said, "since the woman is almost my woman."

And it is said that the guardian felt bothered when he spoke to him like that, his wife was almost his woman.

Well, the story says that one day the woman went to wash the clothes of her mother, and she put them near the bed. And that night, the man arrived. And there were the clothes of her mother.

"Look," the man said, "where will you hide me now, if your husband comes."

"Ah, don't be a fool," she told him. "A man has to be smarter than a woman."

"Yes, but you have your ideas of where I should hide," said the man.

"Now, I won't hide you in any place because we no longer can. The house is very small and the man already knows the hiding places. Better, what you will do now, when he knocks on the door, if he comes, is to put on the *corte* and the blouse of my mother, tie your head with a handkerchief, and you will sleep with me on the bed. I will tell him that it's my mother who is sleeping with me."

"Very well," said the man. "Doing it like that is good."

And surely, the story says, the husband arrived.

"Open the door!" he said. "Open the door!"

The woman was listening, but didn't want to open the

door because she was giving time to the man inside to put on the *corte,* her mother's clothing.

"Open the door!" he demanded.

"What?" said the woman. She saw that the man already had the clothes on. He lay down on the bed and covered himself with the blanket.

"Well, you, are you going to open the door?"

"Yes, right now." She opened the door. "Come in."

"Who is with you?" he told her.

"There is no one. Only my mother is sleeping with me."

"How can that be, if last night your mother wasn't with you."

"Later, she came, around ten at night. She says she came to see the baby, and since it was already night, she was afraid to leave because she didn't have a light. That's why she stayed sleeping with me," she said. "Take off the blanket!"

The man took off the blanket and saw that it was his mother-in-law. But it wasn't his mother-in-law, instead it was the other man. "Well, it's okay. Tomorrow, early, get up and give coffee to your mother. Thank her for coming to sleep with you."

"Yes, she's my mother," said the woman.

"Good, go back to sleep. I will go work some more," the man said.

Then the story says that at four in the morning the man again passed by where the guardian was taking care of the house. "You, how did it go?" he said.

"Indeed, I now will not return, because he will surely kill me."

"Why?"

"Because today the husband arrived again. Damn that woman was smart! Yesterday, she went to wash the clothes of her mother and that's what I put on. I lay on the bed. I was sleeping, when the husband arrived, but he didn't recognize that it was me. He thought that it was his mother-in-law. Because of that I no longer will go back."

"Hum, damn my wife," said the man. The same night, it is said, he went to her. Her mother's clothes were there, but not her mother. He told her, "You have no shame. Go to hell,"[36] and he chased her out with kicks.

And that is the story of this woman of the guardian.

—Ignacio Bizarro Ujpán

Story of Don Chebo

Don Chebo is the surname, but the story says that he was named Don Eusebio Ibarra. This story is old. The people would tell it often, but now it's told very little, maybe because there are new stories.

Don Chebo, the story goes, was from Quezaltenango and was very rich. He had a hacienda and a lot of money; but he also was the most foolish.

When the first automobile arrived around Quezaltenango, Don Chebo adored it and asked the owner how much it had cost him.

The owner answered, "One thousand five hundred quetzales, and the motor has twenty horsepower." Then, it is said, Don Chebo did many rounds around the car to see where the horses were.

At last he was convinced, and he went to his house. And

he told his woman, "Now we are in good times; now there is the automobile. Well, we will build a car so as not to have to go buy [one] in Guatemala."

The story goes that Don Chebo bought boards and he looked for a carpenter to construct the car. When the carpenter finished, Don Chebo sold twenty mules and bought twenty horses, which he put inside the wooden car, and he started to whip the horses. He thought that the car would start to roll. But it wasn't like that. The horses got very *bravo* because they would run in the same place. Don Chebo got angry when he saw that the car would not move. It is said that the people got to laughing for all that Don Chebo did.

Don Chebo was a wealthy man, and he sent his son to study at the University of San Carlos of Guatemala. But it is said that the son spent all the money; his shoes were now torn, and he no longer had decent clothes.

Then the story says that the son sent a telegram saying, "Father, urgent! Send me money. Shoes torn. I have much need."

The story says that Don Chebo received the telegram, exclaiming, "My God, my son's without money, without shoes and clothes!" But the story goes that in these times there hardly were cars. Then Don Chebo thought, "If I wait for a car, who knows how long it will take. And if I go on foot, worse, I will need more time." Then he knew that the telegrams were faster and said, "I am not an idiot, better I will send the things by telegram."

The story says that he went to the store, bought a pair of boots, good clothes, and put money in an envelope. Later, he got on a post where the telegraph line goes by. There he left the shoes, the clothes, and the money hanging.

Don Chebo, very content, arrived in his house and he told his woman, "I already sent the things to our son, and I sent them by telegram so that they will arrive soon."

"How good!" said the wife.

But the story says that at noon, a very poor but clever *muchachito* [little boy] passed by. He saw that on the wire there were tied new shoes and clothes. Soon the muchacho got the things down, put on the clothes and shoes, and made himself owner of the money, but since he was very smart, he once again went up the post to leave his old clothes and the torn shoes hanging on the wire. And, very content, he left for his house, thinking that for him it was a blessing.

By the afternoon, Don Chebo went to see the things that he had left hanging, to see if the telegram took it. When Don Chebo saw on the wire old shoes and dirty, torn clothes, he ran to take them down, and said, "Thanks to God I sent them by telegram, and he sent me by telegram the shoes and clothes that no longer serve." He ran to his house, and he told his woman, "Look, the shoes and the clothes that our son had on at the university."

The story says that the two were very trusting because the things for the son went by telegram. But two days later, Don Chebo received another telegram, saying, "Father, be conscientious. I find myself with torn shoes; I need clothes and money."

Then Don Chebo realized that the things can't be sent by telegram.

Another time, Don Chebo was found on the second floor of the house when he received a telegram from one of his sons, telling him, "Papá, I wait for you. Come here."

Don Chebo thought that they were telling him to come down, and he threw himself from the second floor to the ground where he broke his neck.

Then the family told him, "How many times are you not going to do things right?" But he always was a fool.

One time Don Chebo received an invitation to attend a wedding of a *compadre*. Then Don Chebo told his woman so that she would prepare his suit. The day of the wedding arrived. Don Chebo put on a pair of new boots and his *tacuche* [elegant suit].

But before going out, his daughter told him, "Papá, please take care to do the things right. When you arrive at the invitational, be careful not to put your foot in so that the people will not laugh at you."

"Very good, daughter, I will take much care not to put my feet in," said Don Chebo.

For more clarity, the daughter told him not to do inappropriate things. But he thought that the feet were his own feet.

Soon he went to the invitational, but the story says that when he was arriving, he got on his knees and like that he went to the place where the people were. But the people got frightened; they thought that Don Chebo was a loco because he went in on his knees.

Then the owners of the house told Don Chebo, "Why do you do this thing? You come in on your knees, scaring the people."

And Don Chebo answered, "It's that my daughter told me to take more care not put my feet in, and because of that, I came in on my knees."

All the guests started to laugh. There Don Chebo received another ridicule.

In Quezaltenango, the story goes, an order of the government arrived. All the owners of big properties were now obligated to register the *escrituras* [title deeds] in the property registry to comply with the taxes.

It is said that Don Chebo was a landowner. Then he took all the *escrituras* in a portfolio to register them in the capital of Guatemala. From Quezaltenango he went on mule to Mazatenango. There he stayed sleeping in a boardinghouse to get on a train the following day.

Don Chebo got up the next day. Later, he went to the restaurant to have breakfast, but the story goes that the breakfast was very delicious and because of that, Don Chebo left his portfolio forgotten. Very content, he boarded the train in the station. On the train he met some amigos, and he got to talking. The train was passing by the Pantaleón when he realized that he had left all the *escrituras* in the restaurant. He became worse than a loco, turning around in the train, but the train continued advancing. Don Chebo, seeing the trees that were being left behind, thought that the trees were returning to Mazatenango; and he said, "If I go on foot, when will I arrive at Mazatenango? Better I will go on a tree because I am seeing that the trees run the same as the train," he said. He opened a window, and he jumped out to grab the tree. The train left. "I also am already far," he said. It was a matter of his hugging the tree for two hours before some women passed by underneath, and he asked them, "How much further to arrive at Mazatenango?"

The women started to laugh and told him, "Señor, you are loco. Here we are in Pantaleón. You need three days on foot to arrive at Mazatenango. Get off the tree; that tree is in the same place."

Then Don Chebo understood that the trees remain in the same place when the train passes nearby.

One time Don Chebo went with the *mozos* [helpers] to Palogordo to bring sugar. They took twenty-five mules. Don Chebo was mounted on one mule, and ahead went the other twenty-four. Later, he started to count the mules, but he would only count twenty-four, and he told the *mozos*, "Careless hombres, you didn't realize, on the road one mule was lost." The story says that Don Chebo returned to look for it, but the mule that he was looking for was the one that he had mounted, but he had not realized it. Again, he went to the *mozos* to scold them so that they would look for the lost mule.

Then the *mozos* told him, "Patron, what is this, being such a mule you can't count. Ahead go twenty-four, and there are twenty-five, including the one you have mounted."

Don Chebo started to count again and the same thing he got—twenty-four mules. Then he said, "It's better to go on foot so that the mules can be counted exactly." When he went on foot, again he counted the mules and then, yes, he did get twenty-five.

One day, the story says, some diviners arrived near Quezaltenango to resolve the people's problems. Many people went to the diviners to consult about their personal problems.

Don Chebo decided to ask the diviners when he was going to die, because earlier he had had a bad dream. Then the diviners predicted the death to Don Chebo, telling him like this, "Don Chebo, take much care. Your death will be on the road. You have many enemies that have bewitched you. That is why you on the road will die within a few days."

Don Chebo asked again what kind of death it would be—gunfire, machete, or over a cliff. The diviners answered, "Don Chebo, you will die when you are traveling mounted on a mule. When that animal throws twelve farts, your death will be certain."

When Don Chebo arrived at his house, he told his family what he had been told. The story says that the family got sad. Don Chebo went to buy his coffin where they were going to put his body when on the road he died.

Three days later Don Chebo left mounted on a mule for a town where he had to go up a hill. When the hill started, the mule gave the first fart.

Then soon Don Chebo remembered his death and said, "Now is the day that I have to die. Now there are only missing eleven farts." When the mule threw the second fart, "Now only ten are lacking," said Don Chebo.

It was like that all the way, Don Chebo getting closer to death according to the animal's throwing the farts. When the mule threw the eleventh fart, Don Chebo thought that he was in agony, and he said, "My God, now I am going to die. Now only one fart is left. My body will stay on the road."

The story says that when the mule completed the twelve farts, Don Chebo said, "Here is my death. Eusebio Ibarra already died," and he got off the mule, lay down in the shade, and covered his face with the sombrero at the edge of the road.

Near him passed some campesinos who said, "This poor man is drunk."

And he answered, "I am dead, fools."

The story says that some persons arrived to give notice to the family. The family got alarmed, looked for *mozos*, and they took the casket to bring the cadaver. It's true that when they arrived, Don Chebo was extended as if dead. The family prayed for the recommendation of his soul. Later, they put him in the box as a dead person.

Then the people would offer themselves to carry him on their shoulders. The carriers said, "Should we take the dead person on the main road or should we take him through the shortcut to arrive sooner," they said.

It is said that Don Chebo spoke, saying from within the box, "Better if you take me through the shortcut so that you can arrive sooner."

The carriers got frightened and threw the box down. Don Chebo received a great bump. Only then did the people realize that Don Chebo was a fool or a loco.

Apologizing to the people, Don Chebo said, "It's that some diviners had told me that when the mule throws twelve farts it would be the hour of my death. But I'm thankful it wasn't like that."

—Ignacio Bizarro Ujpán

The Story of
the Lazy Man Who Got
to Be King of a Town

Earlier, there was a man by the name of Tomás, but mostly they called him Lazy Man, because this man didn't want to work; more than anything else, he would pass the time underneath the trees, sleeping.

His father told him, "Tomás, go to work. We need corn and other things for the maintenance of the house."

Tomás answered his father, "I don't want to work. Each time that I work, my stomach hurts. For me it's better to rest all the time; I like to be lazy."

His father replied, "Tomás, what is this, you don't want to work? We men have the obligation to work, and through work we eat."

The son answered his father, "Papá, I don't have desire, nor do I want to work. I prefer to be the best lazy man of the town." And he told him, "Papá, I am lazy, but I know that the lazy men also find their food, and like that, I will do it."

Then the father told him, "Tomás, I have loved you more than your brothers, but from now on, you can go to hell, because you are my dishonor. Don't you see that in the town they have much respect for me? I even receive reverence."

Tomás told his father, "My good father, from now on you

won't have to look at me anymore. I have to leave the house. I already said that I will be the best lazy man."

He grabbed his bundle and went out of the house. Then his father told him, "My son, how dare you abandon the house, but if you think like that, you must leave. There's no other recourse. What I can give you is only a little bit of money to buy your food. When you finish this money, you will remember me, but it is no longer possible to have you in my house."

Tomás took to the road, but with the money that his father gave him, he bought four *veladoras* [short, thick candles]. Upon arriving at the foot of the hill where one could see his town, he said, "I light the first *veladora* to ask for forgiveness for not respecting my father." After than, he stated, "I light the second *veladora* so that my mother will forgive me. To her I owe my life." And last, he said, "I light the third *veladora* in the name of my town because there I was born, there I grew up, and I don't know if I will see it again."

Tomás, with much laziness climbed up the slope until he arrived at the summit of the hill. There the night fell upon him and he slept under some trees. At midnight, Tomás got up and lit the last *veladora* for the *dueño* of this hill, saying, "This *veladora* is to ask the *dueño* of this hill for the blessing of my protection. The truth is that in life I don't want to work. Better, in life I want to be Lazy Tomás. I hope that the *dueño* of the hill talks to me in my sleep." He lit the *veladora* and continued sleeping.

And, suddenly, a very tall man with white hair came to him and told him, "Tomás, I am the *dueño* of this hill; to me you offer this *veladora*. Well, what do you want me to do for you?"

Tomás, very frightened, answered, "Señor, if you are the *dueño* of this hill, for you is this *veladora* as a present. I want a blessing for my protection in my life. The truth is, I don't want to work, only to be a lazy man."

The *dueño* of the hill told him, "Tomás, you are lazy. Well,

I will help you in your life but with the condition that you not forget me. Always light my *veladora* when you find money."

Tomás told him, "Señor of white hairs, tell me, how can I obtain money without work?"

Then the *dueño* of the hill answered him, "When you arrive in the very next town, remain seated close to the *lavadero* [public wash place] in the center of the town. Then the daughter of the king will arrive to wash clothes. You will see well which side she goes to place herself when she washes the clothes. The daughter of the king is tall, slender, and well dressed. She won't realize when she loses the ring of gold that she is wearing. I will numb her senses. When she finds out about the ring, then she will start to look but won't find it. Then her father, the king, will send to call all the magicians of the town to prophesy where the ring is found. But for the hell of it, they will not tell the truth. I will nullify the science of the magicians. Then the king will release a public announcement throughout all the town, 'The one who hands over the gold ring will receive a grand prize, half the goods of the kingdom.' But no one will hand it over. Find a long cane and sit in the streets, always like a lazy man. In the dream I will tell you what you will do."

"Thank you, señor. I will do all that you tell me," replied Tomás.

When it dawned, Tomás continued on his way until arriving at the town. There he sat close to the *lavadero* of the town, but on that day, not one woman came to wash. Tomás was all day and all night, sleeping there. He thought, "Maybe the woman will arrive at night to wash," but no.

It dawned. Tomás sat again to watch. As the sun came out, the daughter of the king arrived to wash clothes. Tomás took good notice where the woman was washing.

The following day, there was a great commotion in the house of the king because his daughter had lost the gold ring. The daughter of the king offered a lot of money to the person who could find the ring, but it was not possible to find it. Then the king sent to call all the magicians of the town to divine where the ring was to be found, but the magicians could not foresee. Then the king sent a public announcement to all the town to find out who picked up the ring. "The one who returns it will have a reward that is half of the kingdom," but no one could hand over the gold ring.

By the night of that day, Tomás remained sleeping in the hallway of a house, when in his sleep, the señor of white hairs, *dueño* of the hill, spoke to him, telling him, "I am the *dueño* of the hill where you lit a *veladora* as a present. Also, I talked to you on the hill, and I told you that in the dream I will tell you what you will do. Well now, when it dawns, you will be seated at the entrance of the palace of the king, always with the cane in your hand. I will make sure that she talks to you. When she asks you who you are, you will tell her that you are 'Tomás, the wisest.' She will ask you whether with science you can predict the finding of the gold ring that she had lost. You tell her with much assurance that within two days you will tell her where the ring is. She will tell her father. Then when the king receives you in his palace and asks you, 'Who are you?' you will tell him that you are 'Tomás, the wisest.' He will tell you about the ring, and you will tell him with much assurance that within the two days you will tell him where the lost object can be found. When the day arrives, tell the king to gather all the people so that you will do these things in their presence. You go ahead with the cane in your hand, and when you reach the *lavadero*, stick the cane inside the pool. Act as if the cane were advising you of something—shake your head. When you arrive in the place where the daughter of the king was washing, there will be the ring, but always have the cane in the water. Stand on that place and tell the king to order a soldier to get into the pool to take out the gold ring. Then hand it over to the woman. In this matter, you will beat all the best magicians of the town, and when they give you your prize, don't forget my *veladora*, always there on the hill where you slept beneath the trees when I talked to you."

Tomás sat down at the entrance of the palace. When the daughter of the king came out, she asked him, "Hombre, why are you seated here? Who are you?"

And Tomás answered her, "I am Tomás, the wisest of all."

Then the daughter of the king told him, "If you are wise, I want you to tell me the truth. Who has my gold ring that I lost a few days ago?"

Tomás answered her, "Well, I can tell you where the ring is found, but I need two days to not fail."

Then the daughter of the king ran to tell her father that at the entrance of the palace there was a wise man. Then, moved, the king sent a soldier to call Tomás.

In the palace, the king asked him, "Who are you? From where did you come?"

And he answered, "I come from a town. I am the wisest of all."

Then the king told him, "My daughter lost her gold ring. We have looked through all the town, and I sent to call all the magicians of the town, but no one could tell the truth where it was. Now if you are wise, I want you to tell me where the lost ring is, and I will give you a prize, half of my goods."

Tomás told him, "Señor, if you are the king of this town, with much pleasure, within two days I will tell you with assurance where the ring is found, so get my prize ready."

When the day arrived, Tomás told the king to gather the people of the town so that they see how a wise man acts. The king did all that Tomás told him. When the town was already gathered, Tomás told them, "Let's go," and he went ahead with the cane in his hand up to where the *lavadero* of the town was located.

The people gathered around and he started to stick the cane inside the *lavadero*, acting as if he were receiving notices from the cane. Tomás, shaking his head, made turns around the *lavadero*. At last, he arrived in the place where the daughter of the king had been washing. There he remained standing with the cane inside the pool, and he told the king, "The ring is here inside the *lavadero*. Your daughter lost the ring when she was washing clothes." Tomás found the ring directly and handed it to the daughter of the king. There then was the fame of Tomás, the wise.

The king told him, "Tomás, you are the wisest one; there is no other wise man like you. Now I give you half of my land, half my young bulls, plus half the money that I have in the treasury. And if I had two women, I would give you one, but I only have one. But, when I die, you stay in my place."

When all that the *dueño* of the hill had told him had been fulfilled, Tomás took more *veladoras*. He went to the hill at midnight, lit the *veladoras*, and soon, the *dueño* of the hill came out and told him, "Thank you for the *veladoras*. I provided all that I promised you. Now you are the best lazy man in the town. The king will die within twenty days, and then you will be king. Then what you want will be fulfilled: only seated you will be like a lazy man because kings don't work, only seated they spend their lives in their palaces."

The king died at the end of twenty days. Then Lazy Tomás remained in place of the king. That is how Lazy Tomás got to be king.

—Ignacio Bizarro Ujpán[37]

Story of Chema Tamales

 The story goes like this. In a town there lived a man who called himself Chema Tamales. He would pass the time only betting; more than anything else, that was his job, and he would always end up winning because he had much luck. He would win a lot of money, land, horses, and even women, only by gambling with those who had aspirations in this business. Always he would come out winning.

The story says that the losers got together and went to accuse Chema Tamales before the king, to see if they could succeed in recouping the goods that they had lost. They told him, "O Great King, greatest in all this town, we have come here to your palace to denounce Chema Tamales. He is a bad man and astute at gambling. We wanted to beat him, but lost everything—our money, land, horses, and even our women. Now we have nothing."

The king, very *bravo*, answered them, "Who obligated you to bet with that man? Now that you've lost your goods and your women, you come here to my palace. But if you had beaten this man, whom you say is called Chema Tamales, you would never come, not even to greet me."

The accusers spoke again. "King, we have come, and we ask for justice so that this man will return our goods and our women. On the contrary, all the people will continue losing because this man will continue to bet with the people with his cleverness."

"I understand," said the king, "what is happening in the

town is something serious," and he sent to call Chema Tama-les.

Chema presented himself in the palace very humbly while the king went up in his throne to dictate a sentence. Later he asked Chema, "Is it true of what they are accusing you of, having much money, land, horses, and even women that you have gained through bets?"

The story says that Chema responded, "O King, you deserve reverences," and Chema kneeled and kissed the feet of the king, saying, "These men accuse me of winning money, land, and even women, but they are the ones who asked me to bet. Luck helps me a lot, and I come out winning."

The king, the story goes, acted with great interest. He required Chema Tamales to hand over all the goods that he had won from those men. The accusers got very happy when the king obliged Chema. They thought that the king was going to hand over their goods and their women that they had lost. But it wasn't like that.

Instead, the king put in the treasury of the town all that was recovered. Then the accusers remained with sad faces. And the king told them, "Damned accusers, you never beat this man. Now you will spend two years in jail for losing your wives in betting and one year in jail for losing your goods." And he told Chema Tamales, "Damned man, you want to be rich and powerful with the goods of others. Now you will stay in the jail until you die."

Then it was that they ended up in jail. But the story says that Chema was content to be in jail, always making bets with the other prisoners and always coming out winning.

But the story goes that the king had a problem with his woman. The king wanted to have a son, but each time his woman only would bear daughters. The king was desperate and sad because all the other kings always had sons. Mainly because of that, the king only fought with his woman. He was angry and wanted his wife to give him a son by force.

Then the king sent to call the diviners, wise men, *zajorines* [seers] and *brujos* to find out the future of the king and his wife, to see if it were possible to have a son. The diviners, magicians, *zajorines*, and *brujos* brought only more discomfort because they predicted that the woman and the king would never have a son and they would have to resign themselves to having only daughters.

Like that it was. The woman of the king was pregnant again, and he now knew that a daughter would be born.

Then the story goes that one day the king wanted to kill Chema, who was in jail, and he sent a soldier to get him. Then Chema Tamales arrived at the palace very frightened, thinking that they were going to kill him.

The king told him, "Chema, now you are in my palace; we will make a bet. The bet that I will make with you will be for your liberty. If you lose, however, you will die burned."

"Let's make the bet," replied Chema.

Then the king sent to call his wife. Soon the wife arrived, and the king told Chema, "This is my woman. See how she is."

Chema answered, "Your woman is pregnant."

The king told him, "Yes, my woman is pregnant, very good, but I want you to bet on what my woman will have, a son or daughter, and when it will be born."

The story goes that Chema Tamales very calmly gave the response. He said, just like that, "Your woman is pregnant. She will be relieved with no problem. Tomorrow at sunrise your woman will give birth to a gorgeous boy, and I beg you to give him your name."

When the king heard what Chema told him, he was surprised because he had already received the response from the diviners, wise men, *zajorines*, and *brujos* that his woman would have a daughter. Then the king told him, "Chema, I bet that my woman won't give birth until five more days and that she will give birth to a girl. Let's see which of us two will win. If tomorrow a son is not born at sunrise, I will win. Then that same hour I will send soldiers to execute you by burning you in a blazing oven."

"Very well," said Chema, "if tomorrow a son is born at sunrise, then I will win; then you will sign for my liberty."

Like that remained the bet. They took Chema Tamales again to the jail, but the story says that he got very scared and regretful for all that he had said.

Exactly at sunrise the following day a gorgeous baby was born. The king and his woman got very content when they saw a son, and soon they remembered the bet. Then the story says the king sent to get Chema out of jail, ordering his liberty and calling him to his palace as a free man, not a prisoner. And he told him, "You have won the bet, a son was born at sunrise. Now I lost my intentions of killing you by fire. It's that some lying wise men, *zajorines*, and *brujos* divined that to my wife would be born a daughter. Because of them, I lost this bet."

The story says that Chema was very content because he had won his liberty. The king sent to call some musicians and had good young bulls killed for a fiesta for all the town, but he also sent to call the wise men, diviners, *zajorines*, and *brujos*, who each took 100 whiplashes for lying to the king.

After the fiesta, Chema Tamales remained a great amigo of the king, and the king told him that he had the right to go out with him when he went to visit other towns. Then one day the king received an invitation from a town and accepted. He sent to call Chema and he told him, "Tomorrow very early you will go with me. We are going to an invitational. Prepare your horse because we are going on horseback."

"Very well," said Chema Tamales, accepting the invitation.

The following day Chema very early got ready his white horse. He put on a new saddle and adorned his horse a lot, because he was doing nothing less than going out with a king. Also he put on a pair of new boots, shirt, and pants. The king also sent a servant to prepare his horse. But when the two got on their horses, Chema went out more elegant than the king. The story says that the people of the town belittled the king and applauded Chema.

The two went on the road talking, but Chema was very astute and he told the king when they were about to arrive at the town to which they were going, "Amigo, King, I need to investigate how the people of this town are. It could be that there are enemies who are planning an attempt against your life. They could kill you. Better I go to see how the entrance of this town is. I will return, and together we will enter."

"Very well," said the king, "that's what I want to do—go with a smart man like you. Go to see, and I will wait for you here."

Then the story says that Chema Tamales went alone, entering the town. There the people were waiting with a *chirimía* and marimba. When they saw Chema arriving mounted on his horse, they thought that he was the king. The people started to ignite *bombas*, and the musicians played. Also the people rang the bells, went to get Chema down from his horse, and carried him in their arms up to the place of the invitational. Chema, however, told them that he wasn't the king, only a *compadre*, and that he had come to see if there were enemies in the town.

Then the inhabitants of the town got scared, and they all had sad faces. They thought that they had welcomed the real king. It was all a mockery for them.

Chema, after the great welcome that the people had given him, returned up to the place where he had left the king and he told him, "Amigo, King, in the town there are no enemies; moreover, there is a big fiesta with a lot of *bombas*, a marimba, and a *chirimía*. Very happily they are awaiting for you."

"Very well," said the king.

The king went in front and Chema in back, but the story says that when they entered in the town, everything was silent. There was no more igniting *bombas*, nor marimba, nor *chirimía*. They had finished all of it when Chema had arrived earlier.

They did not give any importance to the welcoming of the king.

Then when they returned on the road, the king told Chema, "You are a clever person, you humiliated me. When you entered in the town, it was my welcome, and when I arrived, they welcomed me as a simple campesino. Now that we have arrived, I'm putting you in jail."

Chema told him, "Amigo, King, I didn't do it with intention. I beg your pardon for this fault."

"There is no pardon," said the king. When they arrived in the town, they put Chema in the jail, and the king sent soldiers to torture him as a punishment for having mocked a king.

Then the story says that one day in the morning the king went to mass. When he returned, he passed by a *sitio* and suddenly he saw a hen standing with only one leg and the other she had drawn in within her feathers. The king was astonished, thinking that the hen had only one leg. When he arrived in his palace, he was continually preoccupied with the hen, because never in his life had he seen anything like it.

Then he wanted to harm Chema, to kill him; he sent to get him out of jail, and he told him, "Amigo, Chema, now I have decided to sentence you to death inside an oven."

Chema told him, "That's all right, if your conscience allows you to burn a friend. The order of a king will be carried out without recourse."

"Very well, Chema, I will not kill you; you are a great amigo, but only if within fifteen days you bring to my palace a hen with only one leg from birth. And if fifteen days pass and you haven't brought the hen, you will die cremated in a blazing oven."

Then Chema answered, "Very well, amigo, King; if luck helps me, I will find the hen, and if not, then my life is already lost."

Then the story says that Chema very happily left jail, arriving at his house. Soon he grabbed a hen and cut off a leg and put sap of aloe vera to make a scar. Then in ten days it was all scarred, and, well, it was believed that the hen had only one leg from birth. And the story says that the hen could stand with only one leg.

Then for Chema the designated day arrived. Very proudly, he presented himself at the palace of the king, taking the hen in his arms and handing it over to the king saying, "Amigo, King, it cost me much to find that hen. I had to go to the other side of the sea; with luck I found her."

The story says that the king, very convinced, received the hen and put it on his desk, and the hen stood on only one leg. "Very well," said the king, "you are a man of much luck. Now you can go to your house. You're free." At that moment the king signed for the liberty of Chema Tamales.

Since that time, they were again like new friends. Then one day before the first birthday of the son of the king, the king invited Chema, saying, "Tomorrow we will lunch together here in my palace, but beforehand, the two us will have go out to take a stroll in the town on horseback. Prepare your horse for tomorrow."

"Very well," said Chema, "we will go."

The king, however, planned to annoy Chema by ridiculing him. By night, the king sent his servant to cut off the ears of the horse of Chema Tamales. The servant did all that he was ordered to do.

Very early Chema went to fetch his horse, but now it had no ears. Since he only had that horse, he had to go like that, on his horse without ears. When Chema presented himself before the king, the king was dying of laughter saying, "Amigo, Chema, why did you eat the ears of your horse?"

Chema embarrassed, bowed, but he had the courage to go out to stroll with the king like that, on his horse with no ears. Throughout all the town, the people humiliated Chema and applauded the king. The king smiled when the people ridiculed Chema.

The story says that another day the king sent to invite Chema. Accordingly, he wanted to belittle him, and he told him, "Tomorrow will be the baptism of my son, before lunch, we will have to take a stroll through all the town on horseback. It's a special invitation."

"Very well, amigo, King," said Chema, and he went to his house, saying to himself, "The king wants to humiliate me again because he himself sent to have the ears cut off my horse. There's no recourse. I will have to go out like this, on my horse without ears."

But the story goes that by the night an evil idea was born to Chema to bother the king. He grabbed a knife and rope and went to the pasture. He tied up all the horses and mules of the king, and he cut the skin that covers the upper part of the teeth. All the horses and mules had their teeth peeled as if they were smiling with laughter.

When it dawned, the king sent a servant to bring a horse, because he had to go out to stroll through the town with Chema. But the servant got frightened when he saw the horses with the skin of the teeth peeled. He didn't return. At once he fled, thinking that they were going to kill him.

Then Chema, mounted on his horse without ears, arrived and said to the king, "Amigo, King, it's already the hour, let's go take a stroll." But the king was angry because the servant had not arrived with the horse. But Chema, knowing what had happened to the animals, to annoy the king said, "You're breaking your word. You told me that early in the morning would be the stroll around the town."

And the story says that Chema climbed up a tree that he had grasped to see the pasture, and he gave a great whistle. When the animals heard the whistle, they looked toward him. And he told the king, "Amigo, King, come up here with me! Come see your horses and mules! All are in a festive mood, very content, even laughing. You can see their teeth. When I gave the whistle, all of them looked at me."

Then the king yelled, "Never in my life I have seen horses and mules laugh!" Later he went up the tree and gave another whistle, and the horses and mules turned to look with teeth that made them appear as if they were laughing hard. And the king soon came down from the tree, ran to the pasture, but when he arrived, the horses and mules were not laughing. Instead their upper [top] lip had been cut. There was no other remedy for the king other than to mount a horse like that, with the teeth peeled.

Then it is said that the two went out to stroll through the town on horseback, Chema with his horse without ears and the king with the horse with the teeth peeled. The townspeople became very scared. All went into their houses; they thought that they were two locos.

The king felt much shame and he told Chema, "Today, yes, the people ridiculed me because they cut the lips of all my horses and mules, but I will find out who peeled the teeth of the animals and I will command that they burn him and his family. For this thing there is no forgiveness."

Then the story says that Chema got very much scared when he heard these things. He abandoned his woman and children and left his horse without ears. Chema Tamales passed through many towns always betting with the people, but at last, the story says, he lost his luck. No longer did he win at gambling. He lost all his money and remained a beggar.

One day very early, he went to another town, and from afar he saw coming a priest mounted on his horse. To Chema was born the bad thought of taking away the horse of the priest. He got to shitting in the middle of the road and soon he covered the excrement with his hat. He had it held with one hand while the priest was arriving.

Chema told him, "Good morning, Father."

The priest answered, "Good morning, *hijito* [dear son], what is that you have in the hat?"

Chema answered, "Father, underneath the hat I have a

dove of seven colors, very beautiful. It came flying, and I trapped it with the hat."

The priest told him, "Very well, this dove will be for me; in the convent I need to have a dove of seven colors," and the priest got off his horse very content.

Chema told him, "Father, with much pleasure the dove is yours, but lend me your horse only for a while to go bring a cage that I have in my house. It's that it's somewhat far, but on horseback, I travel fast."

"Very well," said the priest.

But the story says that the horse would not allow Chema to mount him because he knew his owner well. Then Chema told him, "Father, please lend me your cassock. It's that the horse doesn't know me and won't allow me to mount.

"Very well," said the priest. He took off the cassock, and he gave it to Chema. Chema put on the cassock and dressed like a priest. Later he climbed on the horse, and he told him, "Father, grasp the hat hard while I return with the cage."

Then the priest answered, "Run, my son, it's that in the town they are already waiting for me to celebrate mass." Like that it happened, the priest waiting for the cage, grasping the hat very hard.

Chema, very content, took the horse at once. When he arrived in the town, the people started to sound the bells, thinking that it was the real priest. It was a great welcome that they gave to Chema Tamales because he had on the dress of a priest. The people kissed his hand and greeted him with the good mornings. Chema told the people, "Now there will not be mass. All I need is all the money that you have. It's that in the hospital there are many sick people and they need medicine."

The people were moved. They gathered much money in the town plus the alms of the church, and they handed it over to Chema Tamales. Very pleased, he told them, "Sunday I will come to celebrate mass," and he withdrew. Farther away, he took off the cassock, and he left looking like a cowboy.

While the priest was waiting and waiting for the hour when Chema would arrive, his hand got tired. He wanted to pick up the hat, but he was afraid that the dove would escape. But it was not a dove, but shit that had been left underneath the hat. And the priest said to himself, "That damned guy now isn't returning. Better, I will grab the dove."

The story says that with one hand he lifted the hat and with the other grabbed the excrement that was in the hat instead of a dove. Only then did he realize that he had been tricked.

The story says that he smeared the feces on his fingers. He began crying for his horse and his cassock. Sitting on a rock, thinking, he put his hand on his jaw without realizing that on his hand he had shit.

A man approached him asked, "Señor, why do you put your hand on your jaw? Don't you see that on your hand you have a lot of crap?"

And he answered, "I am a priest, but a damned thief stole my horse and my cassock from me; he never came back."

Then, the story says, the priest started to shake his fingers when suddenly, he hit the fingers against the rock. Because of the pain, he didn't realize it when he stuck his fingers in his mouth with all the defecation on them.

And this story ends here.

—Ignacio Bizarro Ujpán

Tale of Two Compadres

There were a poor *compadre* [ritual
co-parent, male friend] and a rich *compadre*. The rich *compadre* had a lot of wealth.
There was more than enough money to waste.
But he was a stingy man, envious and angry. The
poor *compadre* came to ask the rich *compadre* for
work to support his family. The rich man said, "Fine,
amigo, I have a lot of work and you can have a job. I will pay
you twenty-five centavos daily. My godson also can work, and
I will pay him ten centavos daily."

The poor *compadre*, because he was very much in need,
had to accept and said, "Very well, *compadre*. We will work
even if it's just enough for a few pounds of corn."*

Well the poor *compadre* and his son began to work on the
lands of the rich *compadre*. Then when they finished the first
week, they received their pay. Father and son, it is said, only
spent on the house the twenty-five centavos that the father
earned, and the ten centavos that the son earned, they put
away in order to save. Little by little they were able to put
together the cost of a sheep, and they bought one. But when
the rich *compadre* found out, he became full of jealousy, seeing
the poor *compadre* could buy a sheep.

The rich *compadre* looked for a trick to annoy the poor
compadre so that he would lose his only sheep. Then one day
the rich *compadre* said to the poor friend, *"Compadre*, when is
the birthday of my godson?"

"In fifteen days," the poor amigo told him.

"Very well," said the rich *compadre*, "then for that day you are going to cut the throat of the sheep to make a party to celebrate the birthday of my godson. Then I am going to buy a lot of wine and drinks, and thus we are going to celebrate together."

The poor amigo told him, "*Compadre*, I don't have more than one sheep, besides we have bought it with the boy's money."

The rich *compadre* told him, "Now see, *compadre*, if it is from the boy, well then spend it for him."

The intention of the rich *compadre* was that the poor *compadre* lose his sheep. At the end of the talk, the poor *compadre* agreed to have a fiesta. When the day arrived, he slaughtered the sheep. He looked for many women to prepare the meal and make *tamalitos* [small tamales], and when everything was ready, he sent to call the rich *compadre*.

Well, the rich *compadre*, very happy with his wife, left for the house of the poor *compadre*. Later they sat at the table and were served lunch. The poor *compadre* said, "*Compadre*, we are eating lunch, but first I want us to drink the wine and the *tragos* [shots of liquor] so that both of us fulfill our promise."

The rich *compadre* answered, "*Compadre*, we are eating lunch now that you killed the sheep for this birthday of my godson, and I was supposed to bring the wine and the drinks, but it's a shame what happened. Last night thieves entered in my house, took my key, and took all the money and gold that I had. *Compadre*, it seems that I have become poorer than you because of this. Now I cannot buy the wine or the drinks that I had offered."

The poor *compadre* thought that it was true, what the friend was telling him, and said, "*Compadre*, do not worry. *Compadre*, now let's eat lunch." And they ate lunch. After lunch the rich *compadre* and his wife said good-bye to the poor *compadre*.

On the road the rich *compadre* said to his wife, "Now I

beat the *compadre*. He killed his only sheep, and we ate it to-gether, and we did not spend anything. This I did so that he would lose his only sheep, because if he did not, he would keep on buying more, and afterward he would not work for us, and suddenly he would be more wealthy than us."

Days later the poor *compadre* went another time to the rich *compadre* to ask him for work. The rich *compadre* replied, "With much pleasure there is work for you and my godson. Now you are going to earn well—one quetzal a day for you and fifty centavos for the boy," he said.

Thus were the poor *compadre* and his son. They began to work again. Later, upon finishing the week, the rich *compadre* paid them according to the amount on which they had agreed. After they received their pay, they said to each other, "Now that we have lost the sheep, we should be more smart. We're going to buy a bull so that it will be something to show for our work." And this they did.

But when the rich *compadre* realized this, he became full of envy. He was looking for another trick to molest the poor *compadre* so that he would lose his only bull. Then one day the rich *compadre* began to talk with the poor *compadre*, telling him his story about how the earlier people were and how things are now. The poor *compadre*, out of curiosity asked him the ques-tion, "*Compadre*, excuse me, what did you do to earn the wealth that you now have? I admire the fact that you have many things and I only have one bull. *Compadre*, give me just an idea how to gain something in life. I am tired of working day after day in the fields underneath the strong sun."

When the poor *compadre* was talking, the rich *compadre* looked for a new trick to annoy the poor *compadre* so that he would lose his bull. In good time he gave him a response and said, "*Compadre*, before I was poorer. All I had was a bull; it was that which I dispatched. We ate the meat, but the penis and the two testicles I carried to another country and sold them to the president of that nation. There it was where they gave me a lot, but a lot, of money, and with this money I bought that which I have. *Compadre*, if you want to have money and one day be rich like me, well then, you can kill the bull that you have and go to a foreign land to sell the penis and the two testicles to the president of the nation. If they ask you if you are poor, say yes; then they will give you a lot of money. And with this money you can buy what you want." But these things he told him so that the poor *compadre* would lose the only bull he had.

One day the poor *compadre* decided to butcher his bull. Giving meat to the people didn't even matter to him. The following day he left for a foreign land to sell the penis and the two testicles. He thought that it was real advice which the rich *compadre* had given him. This poor man left on foot and stayed sleeping in the towns where he entered at night. One night when he was sleeping in the corridor of a building, when he was very tired, he became careless and did not realize that some dogs ate the testicles and the penis of the bull. He was very calm when he woke up in the morning, but when he realized what had happened, he became like a crazy person. Now he couldn't do anything, and to top it all he had to return.

Much later on he found a policeman who was a little drunk and told him what had happened. The policeman had compassion for him, and they went to a bar to drink. But as the policeman already had been drinking, he later became drunk and stayed drunk. The warmth of the drinks gave the poor *compadre* the courage to remove the uniform of the policeman and put it on. Dressed like a policeman, he continued to walk home.

On the road, he approached two men who were bringing two mules packed with money, without knowing they were thieves. When they saw that a policeman was coming, they became very frightened. They thought that the policeman was coming to surprise and capture them because of the booty that they were bringing. They escaped, leaving the mules abandoned. The man was happy that he became the owner of the two mules packed with money. When he was about to arrive at his house, he removed the police uniform. He was simply the poor *compadre*. With the money that he gained, he could do many things, and it resulted that he was the richest in the town, much richer than the rich *compadre*.

The rich *compadre* was always expressing his envy, but now he could do nothing. Finally, one day he went to talk with the *compadre* who was once poor and said to him, "Compadre how was the business? Was the advice any good? I find it very odd that you have many things."

The *compadre* answered him, "Compadre, your advice served me well; the business went very well for the penis and the two testicles of the bull. They gave me two mules packed with money. It's a shame, *compadre*, that I only had one bull because if not, they could have given me more money. In the foreign land they asked me if I would return, but it seems that now I will not go because now I have a lot of money and I do not need to get more. *Compadre*, if you want, you can go now that you have many bulls, and you can earn more than they gave me."

"Thank you, *compadre*," said the rich *compadre*.

One day the rich *compadre* butchered three very fat bulls, giving all the meat to the people of the town. He thought that with six testicles and three penises he could earn more money than his *compadre*. The rich *compadre* left for a foreign land, taking many days to arrive. But when he was offering the penises and testicles, the people only looked, and they were scared, thinking he was loco. The things that he had brought now had a bad odor; no one wanted to talk to him. Later the people of the town went to complain to the police because of the stench that they smelled through the streets where that man passed. The police ran to capture him. When they interrogated him, he answered that the six testicles and the three penises were to sell to the president. When the police heard these things, they became full of ire and ordered the man flogged. Then they put him in a jail where he stayed until he died.

And this story is finished.

—Ignacio Bizarro Ujpán

Story of
the Enchanted Hill,
Tun Abaj

Tun Abaj, the story says, is an enchanted hill that is found between Totonicapán and Quezaltenango. The story goes like this.

There was a very poor man who with great difficulty could earn a living each day. One day he said to his wife that he was going to go to other places to look for work and *suerte* [luck]. This he did.

The story says that when he was passing by the hill, Tun Abaj, the poor man asked for help from the hill and that suddenly the *dueño* of the hill came out. It was a man with white hair and a white beard, and he spoke saying, "Man, where are you going, where do you come from, and what are you looking for?"

The poor man answered, "Señor with white hair and white beard, maybe you are the *dueño* of this hill, Tun Abaj. Well, I am a poor man in search of luck and work."

"Fine," said the *dueño* of the hill. "I will give you work. From now on you are not going to suffer much."

"Thank you, señor," said the poor man, and the two went walking until they were inside of the hill.

When they were inside, the *dueño* of the hill told him, "Tomorrow early, you are going to dispatch a very fat pig so that my woman and I can always eat meat of the pig daily."

"Very well, señor, I will do what you order," he said. The following day, very early, the *dueño* of the hill awoke, and he woke up the poor man.

They arrived at the pigsty where they found the fat sow and he said, "Here are the pigs. Each day you are going to kill a hog. I will pay you well and there will be a lot of money for your family."

"Very well," said the poor man.

He entered the pigsty in order to remove the fattest swine, but the story says that the pigs began to talk among themselves to say good-bye to the fattest pig, saying, "Go amigo, God protect you from pain. Today, they are going to slaughter you. Tomorrow and later, us also." The story says that they kissed the fattest pig.

Then the poor man removed from the corral the plumpest hog in order to butcher it, without realizing that the fat pig was really his friend. The story says that previously the poor man had a rich friend named Macario, who had died. The rich friend, when he was in this life had a lot of wealth and money to spare. But the money was of the enchanted hill that is called Tun Abaj, and when he died, his spirit changed into a pig and went to stay in the hill, Tun Abaj.

The poor man removed the pig from the pigsty, not imagining it was his friend. He tied up the legs of the boar and put them over the table in order to decapitate him, and suddenly the pig spoke, telling his friend, "Amigo, do not kill me, have compassion for me. I was your friend when I was alive. Remember me. My name is Macario. Remember when I was alive I gave you work and I paid you well. I was very rich. I had a lot of money and land. But now I am here in a tormenting punishment, suffering that does not end, each two or three days they kill us, and the *dueños* of the hill eat our meat. After they eat our meat, they return to throw our bones in the pigsty and reincarnate us again. This is the way we are all the time."

They say that the poor man began to cry for the life of his amigo. The friend told him, "Amigo, please, if the *dueño* offers you gold and silver, do not take it because then it is certain that you are going to be very rich, but then when you will die, you will come here with us, and the *dueño* of the hill will make use of your meat."

"Thank you, friend, for the advice," the poor man said then.

When the *dueño* of the hill came back again to get the meat, the story says that the two friends were talking. Later the *dueño* told the poor man, "Why haven't you done your work? You told me that you wanted work."

The man answered, "I am very afraid to behead the animal. It's not a real pig. It's my amigo, Macario. When he was alive, he was the godfather of my children."

"Now that you are here," said the *dueño* of the hill, "do you want gold or silver or a lot of money?"

The poor man said, "No, señor, I don't want anything. It's better for me to continue with my life of poverty. I don't want gold or silver. I would turn into a swine."

The *dueño* of the hill became mad and began to beat the poor man, and he threw him from the hill.

Then it was observed that when the rich persons who

take money from the enchanted hills die, their spirits stay in those hills in order to pay for all the fortune that they had in this life.

And this story ends.

—Ignacio Bizarro Ujpán

The Story of
the Hunter *Compadre*

In a town there was a famous hunter. He was rich with a lot of money and land. He was the only one in the town who sold meat of animals of every kind: venison, wild pig, *tepezucintle* [wild animal the size of a pup that looks like a wild dog], spotted cavy, paca, and other animals of the mountains. But it was strange that he did not use a shotgun or dogs to hunt the animals. His work was always to hunt animals in the mountain, but in order to hunt, he used certain *secretos* [sacred rites]. He killed the animals with one bite. With the passage of time, this man had a *compadre*. Later this *compadre* asked for work from the hunter *compadre*. Well, he gave him work. His work was to skin animals and sell them to the houses and to be a *mozo* [helper] in the campo.

The story says that the hunter *compadre* sold a lot of meat, but he never gave a little to his *compadre*. One day the poor *compadre* said to the rich one: "You eat and sell a lot of meat, but we don't eat anything. *Compadre,* show me how to hunt the animals in the mountain.

"*Compadre,* you can't learn it, it's very difficult."

"Whatever the cost, indeed I want to learn it."

Finally, one time when the hunter *compadre* returned from the mountain, he brought two dead deer. Curiosity overcame the other who said, "Hunter *compadre,* I want to go with you to the mountain in order to hunt animals, to see if luck helps me."

The hunter *compadre* answered him, "Very well, *compadre,* if you want, then tomorrow we will go. Prepare your rope and porter's leather strap to carry on our backs the animals we are able to get." The *compadre* was very happy, but the hunter *compadre* had doubts because he did not want his *secretos* to be discovered.

The following day, the two *compadres* left very early for the mountain. When they were close to the place, the hunter *compadre* said to the other, "Here in this place there are many deer, wild boars of the mountain, spotted cavy, and more. But we are going to do one thing. We are going one by one in order to see who has more luck. *Compadre,* I will stay here while you go to hunt the animal that you most like. When you find the animal, grab the ears and give it a bite, and with this it dies."

"Very, very well, *compadre,*" said the other and he went in the mountain. He walked and walked, but he couldn't see any deer.

What he did was to return to where he had left the hunter *compadre* and told him, "*Compadre,* I walked a lot in the mountain, but I did not even see a single animal. I had to return because it is now late."

"Very well, *compadre,* now, as far as I am concerned, you can stay here waiting." And the hunter *compadre* left for the mountain. In a while, he brought back on his shoulders a very large deer and told his *compadre,* "Here is the first deer, this is enough for you." Later he left again and without taking a long time, he arrived with another deer and told the *compadre*, "This deer is enough for me."

"Then we will go to our houses," they said, very content, each one carrying his deer.

In a few days, the *compadre* went to the house of the hunter *compadre* and told him, "Compadre, the meat of the deer is very tasty. When are we going another time?"

The hunter *compadre* answered him, "Compadre, then with much pleasure, day after tomorrow we will go but on the condition that each one of us has to hunt something."

The other said, "Compadre, I hope luck helps me. Well, we will go."

The day arrived, and they left for the mountain. When they arrived in the same place, the hunter *compadre* said to the other, "I will stay waiting while you go to the mountain to hunt the animal that you will find there."

"Very well," said the *compadre*, and he went to the mountain. He walked a lot, and from bad luck instead of finding a deer or a spotted cavy, he found a furious jaguar. Hopelessly, he returned scared to death and told his friend, "Compadre, I only have such bad luck. I encountered a damned jaguar that nearly killed me."

"Very well," said the hunter *compadre*, "now I will go. You stay and take care of things. But be careful not to follow me because it could be bad. I don't want you to die."

Then the hunter *compadre* went to the mountain. In half an hour, he returned with two wild pigs on his shoulder. Later he left another time, and without taking long he returned with two spotted cavy and said to the *compadre*, "This is how hunting is done. The next time you have to do the same thing." And he gave him the two spotted cavy and took for himself the two wild boars.

The story says that another time the *compadre* went to the house of the hunter *compadre* and said to him, "Compadre, many thanks for the two spotted cavy. We ate them and the meat was very tasty. When we will go again?"

The hunter *compadre* answered, *"Compadre,* now I do not feel like going with you, because luck does not help you. Well, I will give you the last opportunity. Tomorrow we will go."

The following day, the two left for the mountain. But the *compadre* of bad luck was very clever. He brought two bottles of liquor. When they arrived in the place, they felt like eating lunch. "Fine," said the clever *compadre,* and he took the first bottle and gave it to the hunter *compadre* who enjoyed it, dining and drinking.

It happened that the hunter *compadre* got drunk. The other was very smart. He only drank a little because the poor *compadre* wanted to discover the *secreto* of the rich *compadre.*

After the lunch, the hunter *compadre* said to his *compadre,* "Fine, for hunting there are certain *secretos,* but they are very risky. I can kill any animal with only one bite because it is my luck. Now I will go. You stay taking care of things, but be very careful that you do not follow me because if you do, suddenly something bad is going to happen."

"Very well, *compadre,"* said the other. Then the hunter *compadre* left to the mountain drunk. But the other, as he is very intelligent, followed him from a distance to watch and discover the *secreto* that he did to hunt animals. Then the hunter *compadre* entered the mountain without realizing that the other was following him. When he arrived underneath a tree, he rolled over four times on the ground, only thinking of animals, until he converted himself in the form of a big jaguar. He took off running, and, in a little while, returned with a deer. Then he rolled around on the ground and turned back into a man as before.

When he arrived, he told his *compadre,* "Here is the deer."

The other answered, *"Compadre,* now I discovered the *secreto* that you do. Before going into the mountain, you roll over on the ground and convert yourself into a jaguar and because of this, you do not find it hard to catch the animals."

"*Compadre*, very well you discovered me. It's true that I have certain *secretos*. In order to hunt deer, I have to turn myself into a jaguar. To hunt spotted cavy I have to turn myself into a coyote, and to hunt small animals like rabbits, raccoons, armadillos, and opossums, I only convert into a dog. *Compadre*, now that you saw me, then with much pleasure I taught you the *secreto*. Then let's go." Then the two left for the usual place.

When they arrived, the hunter *compadre* said to the other, "Now we are going to do the *secreto*. Both of us have to convert ourselves into jaguars since both of us are going to hunt deer. *Compadre*, be careful, however, when you convert yourself into a jaguar. When you find a deer, run after it, catch it, and bite it in the neck, but with caution. Do not drink the blood of the animal or eat the meat because if you do, you will see what will happen to you."

Thinking only of animals, the two rolled over on the ground four times and each turned into a jaguar. Then they each went running in his own direction to hunt deer. Well, the hunter *compadre* after a while returned bringing a big deer to the place where they did the *secreto*. Then he converted himself back into a man. There he was hoping that his *compadre* would return. But he did not return, and finally he went to look for him. When he found him, he was drinking the blood and devouring the deer, lacking only a little to having finished it.

The hunter *compadre* became frightened and asked his *compadre*, "What are you doing? I told you not to drink the blood of or eat the meat of the animals, and now you are doing it."

The jaguar was very *bravo* [brash] and continued eating until he was full. Then he made signals for the rich *compadre* to help him to turn back into a man again.

Then his hunter *compadre* said, "*Compadre,* I'm very sorry, but I'm unable to help you anymore because you didn't respect the *secreto* that I told you. Now your life is changed. You will go into the mountains and the *barrancas* and sleep among the rocks. Forget your wife and your children. If you are lucky, *compadre,* you will find a female jaguar for your wife." Then the hunter *compadre* said good-bye to his poor *compadre.*

The jaguarman remained crying in the mountains. He could talk no more.

The story says that thus the jaguar became an enemy of man. When a jaguar encounters a man, he smacks his snout and wants to eat him. It is a resentment of the jaguar. When he sees a man, he thinks he's the rich *compadre* and for that reason he wants to eat him because it was the rich *compadre's* fault that he lost his life and family and remained a jaguar forever.

This ends the story.[38]

—Ignacio Bizarro Ujpán,
Tzutuhil *Joseño*

The Good-natured Father
and His Little Horses
of Gold

A priest lived very happily in his
convent. This padre had a good heart
with all the people, the poor as well as the
wealthy. After celebrating mass, he went to the
market to buy tortillas and food to give to the
forsaken. But to do these things, the priest had to
walk a lot since the marketplace was far away.

Then one day a nun said, "*Padrecito* [Dear Father], it's a
shame that you walk a lot every day to buy food for the sake of
the helpless. I don't know whether you realize it, but in time
you will get sick. What you should do is buy a horse to help
you a little."

The father answered, "*Hijita* [Dear Daughter] in order
for me to buy a horse, I would need a lot of money, and I
wouldn't have any money left for the poor."

The sacristan told him the same thing. "It would be better
if you bought a horse to help you a little. I have noticed that
the padres of the other pueblos always go mounted on their
horses to the other towns to celebrate mass."

The nun and the sacristan convinced the father. Then he
left to look for a horse to buy. At last he arrived at the place
where the animals were sold. Very happily he bought a white
horse with a saddle for 200 quetzales, without realizing that in

those parts were three thieves, casing the people who bought things, and these thieves knew when the father bought his horse.

The priest very happily mounted his horse and steered him on his way for his return trip to his convent. The thieves followed pretty far behind. When they were far from the town, they set up a trick to rob the father of his horse. The most clever told his two companions, "Stay here and meet me later in the house. Give me some time."

"Yes," said the two.

The most clever thief ran to where the padre was resting and said, "Father, please, we are some forsaken persons. We want to eat something. We are very hungry. My two brothers aren't able to walk. They are at the bend of the road. We know that you always give food."

The padre answered, "Son, right now I am unable. I don't have money with which to buy you food because I had to buy myself a horse."

"Padre," said the thief, "please get down from your horse. At least give a blessing to my two brothers before they die in sin. Put your hand on them so that they can go to heaven when they present themselves in the other life."

"Where are your brothers?"

"They are at the bend in the road. Get off your horse. They need your blessing."

"Very well," answered the priest, and he dismounted. "Take care of my horse while I go to bless your brothers."

The reverend went to the bend in the road where the two were acting as if they were very sick. Then the father put his hand on them, and he returned to where he had left his horse. But when he returned, he discovered that they had stolen his horse. The priest shouted, "Satan, Satan, you have robbed my horse." Without any recourse the padre continued walking until reaching the convent.

Then the sacristan and the nun asked him, "Padre, what

happened? Why didn't you buy a horse. You promised, and now you haven't brought one."

The priest answered, "My children, it's that Satan is very clever. He robbed me of the horse on the road, and now all is lost. Now I am madder than the devil."

The people of the town realized what had happened to the father. In this pueblo there was a family that had a pair of white horses that were twins, the two looked very much alike. Then this family said, "They robbed the father of his horse, but we out of love and affection are going to give him two little horses."

The members of this family went to the convent to the father and said, "Padre, you lost your horse, but we are going to express our love and affection. Here take these two beautiful horses that are twins. When they are grown, you can ride them."

"Oh! *Hijitos,* [Dear Sons] thank you very much. May God bless you. The little horses are very pretty. I won't give up the hope that some day that I will ride a little horse."

Then he gave them to the sacristan to take them out to pasture. But because of the reverend's bad luck, the two little horses didn't get any bigger since they were twins. The father was desperate and cursed, because he didn't have the fortune to ride his little horses.

Finally, the father bought a harness for one of the little horses and took him to the market. When he arrived at the market, the priest bought vegetables and other things to eat. After buying them, he threw them on the horse. He was leaving the pueblo when he met the three thieves. The father was very clever, and he recognized them. He very happily slackened the reins of his horse.

Then the three thieves asked the father, "Padre, how much did your horse cost? It is very pretty, and it can carry vegetables and other things."

The priest, since he recognized that they were the thieves

that had stolen his first horse, got a shrewd idea to punish them, although it would require him to lose his little horse. He answered, "My little horse is of gold. Trained, he cost me 1,000 quetzales. I load the cargo on him here, and from here he will go to convent by himself where the nuns and sacristan will unload him. Later I will arrive at the *sitio* [homesite] of the convent. Here it goes," said the padre. *"Arre, arre,* [spurring on the horse] horse of gold. Carry the vegetables so that the sacristan and the nuns can unload your cargo. I will come later."

And the little horse of gold took off on the road without realizing what his owner was doing. But the reverend had confidence in the other little horse that he had left at the *sitio* of the convent.

The three thieves out of curiosity followed the priest, but he acted as if he had other commitments, allowing enough time to lose his little horse. Finally, the father returned to his convent, and the thieves said, "We are going to continue accompanying you to the convent to see if the little horse of gold arrived there with the vegetables."

"Very well, let's go," said the priest, and they continued to the convent. When they arrived, the nun and sacristan were taking the cargo off a little horse, but it was the other one, the twin. The thieves thought it was the same little horse that had brought the vegetables from the market. They were very curious and wished to buy it. Since they were thieves and they had swindled a lot of people, without doubt they had a lot of money.

They told the father, "Padre, your horse of gold is really intelligent and clever. Will you sell it to us? With much pleasure we will pay you now."

The father, smiling, told them, "My little horse is gold. He can travel by himself, and for that reason, he costs 1,000 quetzales. If you pay me this amount, with much pleasure."

The thieves really thought that this horse was very intelligent and among themselves decided that they would be able to sell it at a higher price. And they paid in cash the 1,000 quetzales and took the horse to their house. The padre was very content and treated the money as if it were a gift from heaven, because he had not bought the little horse.

Then one day the thieves thought about doing the same thing. They harnessed the little horse and took it to the market. Then they bought corn, beans, meat, and vegetables, and they put them on the back of the horse. Very arrogantly in front of the people they said, *"Arre, arre,* little horse of gold. Carry the cargo home, and we will come later."

The little horse carried the cargo without knowing where to go. Later the three thieves went home. They were content, thinking that the little horse had arrived with the cargo. When they arrived, they asked whether the little horse had come with the cargo. Those at home said no. That was when the three thieves lost all of their earnings.

There is a saying, "For each clever person, there is someone more clever."

—Ignacio Bizarro Ujpán[39]

Notes

1. Clyde M. Woods initiated the project at UCLA in 1969. I joined it a year later. Since my first field research, I have returned to the area ten times over the past twenty years. For an examination of our research results, see Sexton (1972, 1978, 1979a, 1979b), Woods (1975), Sexton and Woods (1977, 1982), and Sexton (1982, 1985, 1990, 1992).

2. Most of these tales Ignacio learned from interacting with friends and relatives, especially the *viejitos*, or old folks. Seven of the tales were taped by Ignacio from five other native Tzutuhiles living in his town of San José, as I have indicated after the text of each tale. For the sake of anonymity, the names of Ignacio, his collaborators, and his town are pseudonyms. All of the tales have titles that Bizarro and Sahon gave them, and most have never been published. Another version of Bizarro's tale, "Sebastiana," appears in Orellana's (1975) work from the Tzutuhil Maya of Santiago Atitlán as "The Dog Who Cooked a Little Boy." Ignacio's version of "Mariano the Buzzard" is a different version of Orellana's (1975) Tzutuhil fable titled, "The Man Who Turned into a Buzzard." In addition, Shaw (1971) has published an *Aguacatec* (Guatemalan) version of the buzzard man, and she states that there is a slightly different *Mixtec* (Mexican) version. Also, Goosen (1974) and Laughlin and Karasik (1988) have published Tzotzil (Mexican) versions of the buzzard man. Since informants in Honduras, El Salvador, and Costa Rica told me that they were familiar with this tale, it appears to be widely known throughout Middle Amer-

ica. Laughlin's book of tales from Zinacantán also includes a tale that he titled "A Bellyful," which is a different version of Bizarro's tale, "The Woman Who Loved Many Men and Died from Drinking a Piece of Sausage She Had Eaten." Finally, Bizarro's version of Don Chebo is a different version of Valdeavellano's (1984) "The Adventures of Don Chebo," from western Guatemala.

3. During two field trips in the summer of 1987 and a fall sabbatical of 1988 I collected twenty-one tales from Ignacio, which I translated in the field. I carried back to the United States five additional tales that I didn't have time to translate before I left. Soon after returning, Ignacio sent three more tales by mail, for which Mimi Hugh, a research assistant, who holds dual U.S. and Honduran citizenship, did a literal translation. After Mimi returned to Honduras, I received three more tales from Ignacio in the mail. Gwenn Gallenstein, also a research assistant, did a literal translation of these tales. Word for word, I checked the translations of Mimi and Gwenn, and then I edited all of the tales into a free translation in standard English.

My goal has been to make the folktales as readable as possible. Thus I have made the tenses of verbs in a paragraph consistent, have ensured that the subject and verb in a sentence agree in number, and have deleted some obvious repetitions that arise when the storyteller is repeating himself while thinking of what comes next in the story. However, I have included the repetition when the narrator repeated a statement for greater emphasis. Also, I have stayed as close as possible to the teller's own words and local expressions.

Folktales have been translated and edited into both verse (Tedlock 1983; Hymes 1977) and prose (Shaw 1971; Orellana 1977; Mattina 1985; Sexton 1985; Goosen 1974; Laughlin and Karasik 1988). While each style has its virtues, depending on the text in question, I have translated and edited the tales I collected from the Lake Atitlán region into a free translation of English prose rather than verse because, as Mattina (1987) points out, identifying a pattern of verse often seems arbitrary and because a free translation of English prose will make the tales more readable and thus reach a wider audience. Moreover, the primary value of these stories is in the cultural richness of their content and themes rather than an exact literal translation that would be useful mainly to Mayan scholars. Since the tales contain information about the natural habitat, geography, social conditions, history, political relations, and mythology, they should be of interest to biologists, botanists, geographers, sociologists, historians, political scientists, and folklorists as well as anthropologists in general and Mayanists in particular. They will also appeal to the general reader who is simply interested in learning about other cultures.

4. When I asked Ignacio about this dance, he explained that it was a typical dance he heard about from his grandmother, which isn't done anymore, and in which men, women, and children participate, and sing in verse about corn, the hills, lake, and towns of the lake.

5. Participation in civil and religious offices was mandatory in San José until the 1944 Revolution separated the functions of church and state. While participation in religious office is no longer mandatory, social pressure to participate is still strong among folk Catholics and Catholic Actionists. And while the top offices such as *alcalde*, syndic, and *regidor* are elected, young men may still be forced into service as *alguaciles* and as soldiers.

6. Here Ignacio refers to Tecún Umán as *rey*, or king, instead of a *príncipe*, or prince. Also in the text to the dance drama of the conquest, Tecún Umán is again referred to as a king along with King Quiché. It is uncertain whether current lore has

simply elevated Tecún Umán to the status of a king (see also Asociación Tikal 1981) or whether those retelling the story of the conquest are following earlier scholars such as Fuentes y Guzmán (in Carmack 1981:20), who said that at the time of conquest in 1524 Tecún was king. In my introduction to the current book, my identification of Tecún Umán as a warrior prince follows the more recent scholarship of Miles (1965:282), Gordillo Barrios (1982:110), and Carmack (1981:179–171). According to Carmack, Tecún Umán was the grandson of the Quiché *ajpop* (supreme ruler, or "king"). Tecún Umán held the next highest office, *nima rajpop achij* (great military captain), and was next in line to succeed his grandfather, the king.

7. Ignacio, like other Joseños, believes *characoteles* exist. He told me the following story:

This was something that happened some time back that I have not written in the two books [*Son of Tecún Umán* and *Campesino*]. For me it was very strange when I went to a cantina just to accompany Señor Martín, who reared me. It happened in 1958. He had owed twenty-five *quetzales* in a cantina. Because he made canoes, and I worked a period of time with him, we were able to sell a canoe. Then he told me, "Come with me, we are going to pay the debt." And I went with him. We left about eight o'clock at night. "It'll just take a little while," he told me. But when we arrived, he began to drink his *tragos* again.

Then I told him, "Let's go, let's go, I'm sleepy. It's late. Let's go." He still drank two more drinks. He wasn't good and drunk. He was just talking and drinking a little in the cantina. We left about 12:15 A.M. But when we left, we went near the municipal building, where we met a woman whose hair was partly on her back and partly in her face. We knew the woman, Señora Ana; we could see her well, because we carried a candle. There wasn't any electricity, but we carried a candle, and her body passed closed to us. We then ran to catch up with her, but we weren't able. What was very strange was that she was not running, just walking, and we ran, but we weren't able to catch up with her. Then, what was even stranger, when she got near the door, it opened for her by itself and shut by itself when she went inside. Don Martín wanted to grab her and inspect her, but when we knocked hard on the door, no one answered. We couldn't do anything.

Then he went to wake up Don Juan. "Don Juan, get up, I'm your friend here to give you a drink, I'm Martín. The family, however, was fast asleep. Then, Don Martín was very frightened because no one answered, and we had seen that the woman had entered there. Then with a pocketknife Martín cut two lassos that tied two backloads of firewood, thinking the noise would wake them up. But nothing happened. He said, "I'm going to pay for the lassos, and I'm going to tell Don Juan that his daughter is a *characotel*, because she has scared us this night." But afterward there was nothing, no news or complaint about cutting the lassos, nothing. It was as if nothing had happened. We realized that this woman is a *characotel*. She is still alive; most strangely, she only seems sick. *Characoteles* are weakened when they can't carry a spirit to the cemetery for the bones of the dead, which is their food. They say that when the *characoteles* are just sick, they don't have a lot of power to bewitch someone, and it is for that reason they remain sick. This seems true because this woman now is just ill, and we met her in the middle of the night. In 1958, not like now, a woman was not supposed to be out walking in the middle of the night. Strangest of all was that part of her hair was in her face and part on her back.

One thing more, I have seen other *characoteles*. I saw them in 1965 during a night when we were renting a house from Nicolás R., but this was after we had seen Señora Ana. This was when sleep had not come, and I went outside. I walked a little there, and I saw three women in the street at midnight. I saw them passing by my house headed toward the house of Juanito M. I continued to follow them, but I was hidden. One of them I recognized. The next day, the one that I recognized arrived with the mother of my wife. I said, "Señor Clara, good morning."

"*Buenos días.*"

"Why were you walking in the night?"

"No, Ignacio, it was not I," she told me, "some *characotel.*"

"I don't know if you are a *characotel,* but I saw you walking; I indeed saw you walking in the night."

"With whom?" she told me.

"With two other women. I didn't recognize the other two women, but indeed I recognized you," I told her.

"No, no, no, no, no, I wasn't to blame. It wasn't I. What I did was leave my clothing in the patio. It could have been another person who put on my clothing and left as a *characotel,* but it wasn't I." What was very strange to me was her telling me she left her clothing in the patio and that another *characotel* could have put on her clothing, and her saying "It was not I." Well, it is certain that there are persons who can change or leave as *characoteles.*

A characotel is different from a *brujo.* They both have *naguales,* they both can change into other forms, but a *characotel* acts more like a spy to go see what is happening in another family or something.

8. According to Ignacio, this story is more than a hundred years old. It was taped by Ignacio in Tzutuhil on Saturday, 11 July 1987. He translated it for me in Spanish on 13 July 1987.

9. According to Laughlin and Karasik (1988:17), Zinacantecos fear of blacks is reflected in their folktales. They pro-

fess that this in part derives from Spanish political rather than religious motives. The conquerors told horrendous stories about black cannibalism and supersexuality to prevent an alliance between fugitive slaves and the native Indian population. While this in part could also explain the role of the black man in the Tzutuhil tale, another explanation is that there aren't any blacks living in the Lake Atitlán area. Most of the blacks who reside in Guatemala are on the distant northern coast, and they are something of a mystery. In San Cristóbal, Chiapas, blacks historically were treated more as confidants than slaves. They were allowed to wear daggers and dress like Europeans. Also they might have been placed in the role of foreman and might have physically punished the master's Indian serfs (Laughlin and Karasik 1988:266). It is interesting to note that the Dance of the Mexicans, which is popular in the midwestern highlands of Guatemala, has two dancers who are blacks—a *mayordomo* (administrator) and a *caporal* (leader).

10. The word in Spanish is *abogado,* which could be translated as lawyer. However, Ignacio said the meaning here is defender.

11. This story was told to Ignacio Bizarro Ujpán by Miguel Gonzáles Mendoza. Ignacio gave me a written version in Spanish on 14 July 1987, which I translated in Panajachel.

12. This tale has a more familiar European ring than others in the collection. As Laughlin and Karasik (1988) point out, if a person were meticulous, European elements could be found in most of the tales of Zinacantán, Mexico. The same argument could be made for tales from the Tzutuhil town of San José and the Cakchiquel town of Panajachel. Magical adventures, animal tales, and kings and queens are found in Spanish folktales. However, the Tzotzils of Mexico and the Tzutuhiles and Cakchiqueles of Guatemala have had more than four centuries

to adapt such themes into their local versions. And the Tzu-tuhiles, Cakchiqueles, and more northerly Quichés were not unfamiliar with royalty at the time of the Spanish conquest of Guatemala in 1524. The importance of lords, kings, and animals in the precontact world of the Mayas is well documented in surviving native texts such as the *Popol Vuh* (Recinos, Goetz, and Morley 1950) and *The Annals of the Cakchiqueles* (Recinos and Goetz 1953).

13. When Ignacio began to write the next story, he introduced it by giving the place and date, San José la Laguna of Department of Sololá, 23 August 1987. He then wrote the following, "As a remembrance of this day we are going to write some *cuentos folklóricos* [folktales] of our Tzutuhil ancestors. These I'm going to tell both to entertain and educate our children to avoid laziness and other defects."

14. Ignacio added the following explanation for the meaning of this tale:

This tale is meant to be an example for the women not to be lazy or arrogant, because lazy and arrogant women are evil. And the *dueño* of evil in all parts and places can present himself and make the animals talk and be able to do what he did with the female dog, giving her feet, hands, and a mouth to speak and enabling it to cook a human being. To this day it is forbidden for women to talk to dogs and allow a little baby to be alone in the house when its mother leaves to go on errands and worse when she goes to wash.

This story is very old, and the women of fifty to sixty years of age tell it. Now the women of thirty to forty years hardly tell it because the idea of educating is different, not like earlier.

Señora Elena Cholotío Meza was sixty-three years of age when Ignacio recorded this tale from her on Saturday, 22 August 1987. I translated it into English on Sunday, 23 August 1987.

15. The entrance is a cave and inside is the store.

16. Ignacio added the following commentary about the Dance of the Deer:

This kind of dance is very entertaining because most of the people understand its meaning since it's in Tzutuhil. For this kind of dance, they say it is a very delicate situation before the rehearsals. The one who is going to turn out to be the old man has to make a real *costumbre* by a shaman in a most sacred place according to the old folks. Some Tzutuhiles believe there are many places to do *costumbres* in the hills. But for others, there are more special places for doing *costumbres* such as Pacristalín, Patzalú, Chui'aynom, and Chui'ajaú, Panatzam, Pachicoc, Chua Cruz, Tzan Juy. These places have special features like rocks or caves.

In 1950, when I was nine years old, I was a dancer in the Dance of the Deer. I was dancing as a little dog. We went to rent my dancing clothes at the *morería* [store where they make costumes for the dancers] of San Cristóbol, Totonicapán. We left San José on foot to San Cristóbol. I was very small; with great difficulty was I able to arrive in this place. I remember well that we left at three in the morning from San José, and we arrived in Totonicapán at five in the afternoon. There we slept. Not until the next morning did we arrive in San Cristóbal. The clothing we rented in the *morería* of Don Alejandro Tistoj. The cost of my clothing was Q1.50. Two days going and two days returning, in four days we returned to our town.

This deed is certain. The *tutor* of the dance, who rests in peace, was Don Nicolás; the old man was Andrés C., who also rests in peace. Catarina, the old woman, was Juan G., who didn't finish it. Thus the one who finished it was Don Diego C.; little dogs, Ignacio Bizarro Ujpán and Domingo M.;

pastor, or shepherd boys, Diego P., and in peace he rests, Domingo P.; the deer were, from one to four: in peace he rests, Don Antonio, Francisco, Luciano, and Pedro; tigers, in peace they rest, Clemente and Esteban; lions, Domingo C., and others; monkeys, Victoriano, and Andrés M. What I have forgotten is the names of the other lions and monkeys; I hardly remember because I was very young.

In this dance, the two shamans, Marcos and Domingo C., were doing *costumbres* four days before the fiesta. When they took us to the hill, Chua Cristalín, the shamans had all the little and big dancers kneel down in pairs.

The old man and the old woman together on their knees were presented to the *dueño* of the hill; they put the two shepherd boys together on their knees; and they put us two little dogs together on our knees. That's the way it was with everyone until finishing with the lions and the monkeys.

The *costumbre* began at three in the morning, and each dancer carried his clothing and placed it when his turn arrived to kneel. Also, those who played the tunes came with us. They were two men of San Martín la Laguna, who now rest in peace, Don Mariano with his cane flute and Don Juan C. who played the marimba of *tecomate*, executed by just one person.

The two old people had their tunes just for them and their two dogs. The shepherd boys had their very separate dances, and the dancers of the jaguars, lions, and monkeys were all very different.

After kneeling where we did the *costumbre*, each dancer had to dance in the same place, although it was short. When he finished dancing, he was given a *trago*. It was an obligation because they say it was a *secreto*. When everything was finished, we returned in file, a shaman in front and one in back. When we arrived in the place called Chi Cua, we put on the dance clothing and entered the town dancing, until we reached the church to make another *costumbre* in the presence of the patron saint, San Juan Bautista, because the dance is prepared to celebrate the titular fiesta, or the birth of the saint.

The shamans do the same things that they did in the hills. By pairs the dancers kneel down, presenting themselves and saying what position they have in the dance. In the church they don't dance, although indeed the *tragos* they have to drink. In the church they don't put on their dance masks, but in the hills they put them on.

When this *costumbre* is finished in the church, the dancers leave the church in two lines, dancing until they reach the house of the *tutor*, where they take off their costumes and masks. Then each dancer carries his costume to his house. This act ends more or less at nine in the morning. It takes about twelve hours to do the *costumbres*. Most of the day they drink as a way to rest. These things they do four days before the main day of the fiesta, that is to say, they do them on 21 June. On the eve of this day, the twenty-second, at night, the one who plays the marimba and the one who plays the flute, accompanied by some monkey dancers, begin. They go to the house of each dancer to play for dancing. Three times they play the same dance that corresponds to the dancer. When they have finished playing, they serve coffee or chocolate with plenty of bread. When they eat bread, the dancer is inspected with his dance clothing, but since it is night, he doesn't put on his mask.

Then they continue to the house of the dancer whose turn is next. They do this until day breaks. Lastly, they go to get the two *viejitos* [old folks] and go to the house of the *tutor* of the dance, where all of them put on their masks and then go to the *sitio* of the church to present the dance formally. But before the dancers leave the *sitio* of the *tutor*, they have to perform two rounds, forming a circle. In front of the musicians, the wife of the *tutor* (author) carries an incensory in her hand, with much respect, until reaching the front of the church. Then they perform two more rounds, always forming a circle as a signal of entry of the dancers. Then the musicians get in their positions. When the dancers begin to dance, the shamans go right next to the musicians to protect them from anything bad happening. For this dance that we presented, there is one person who knows the story. He is the one who teaches each dancer what he's going to do when they play the tunes to dance. The maestro of the Dance of the Deer is a very funny person, and the old man in the dance has to be even funnier than his teacher.

In 1950, the maestro of the Dance of the Deer was Don Félix, who rests in peace. But when the day arrived when the dancers formally presented the dance, the teacher didn't teach anymore, he only observed and during rest periods he pointed out the faults.

During the three days, twenty-second, twenty-third, and twenty-fourth, the dancers are obliged to dance in front of the church. After these three days, they are able to dance in private *sitios*. That is to say, one is able to invite the dancers to dance in one's homesite, with the conditions that this person has to be in charge of giving the drinks to the musicians and the dancers, more than two *quetzales* worth.

The last day of dancing in front of the church is 2 July, which is eight days after the fiesta has begun [24 June]. Everyone enters the church, kneels in front of the patron saint, and says good-bye, embracing in pairs, saying to God until another year, if God permits him. Many of them are crying, but this is already in the afternoon.

When this is finished, the wife of the *tutor* arrives, always with her incensory, positions herself in front of the musicians, and leads the dance to the house of the *tutor*. They say good-bye with big drunken parties.

I only observed as a child what the big folks were doing. This is all that I am writing about the story of the deer. The last Dance of the Deer was done more than twenty years ago. The *tutor* was Pablo. The person who was the old man of the dance was the same person, Andrés C., but he died fifteen years ago. This is a story that the Tzutuhiles of San Jorge and San Luis still conserve, but very little. Now in San José, who knows if it will be done again. Only in San Benito la Laguna are there two persons who play for the Dance of the Deer. The flute is still of cane, but the marimba now is not of *tecomate*. It's of wood. In all the towns around the lake, there are no more musicians, just in San Benito.

17. The *intendente* was the *jefe* of the municipality before there were *alcaldes*, or mayors.

18. According to Ignacio, in these times there was a lot of corn and no one wanted to eat black corn. They, however, do now.

19. La Malinche was the name of Cortés's mistress.

20. They do this *costumbre* in the same order, switching back and forth from Indian to conqueror.

21. The *tutor* is not the teacher, just the guardian or person in charge of the dance.

22. Out of respect of the shaman, he is not called "shaman" in the dance. Rather the shaman is addressed with these euphemistic titles.

23. A *cruzada* (cross) is just going diagonally once. Making an "X" is entering with one *cruzada* and leaving with another.

24. "Tun" added as a suffix to Quiché indicates respect similar to "Señor" before a name in Spanish.

25. Just as there is no fast agreement in the literature about the actual status of Tecún Umán at the time of conquest, there is some uncertainty as to how he actually died. Carmack (1973:303) points out that the *Título C'oyoi* says only that Tecún Umán was fatally pierced by Pedro de Alvarado. Sapia Martina (1964:40) and Stuart and Stuart (1977:131) suggest Tecún Umán was killed by Alvarado's steel sword. Gordillo Barrios (1982:109) and the text to Ignacio's account of the dance drama suggest that Tecún Umán and Alvarado fought with lances and that Tecún Umán was pierced with Alvarado's steel lance.

26. This dance closes eight days after the main day of the fiesta. The dancers, musicians, and *tutor* finish it, drinking *aguardiente*. It begins three days before the main day of the fiesta, but this varies somewhat.

27. Ignacio taped this tale and translated it into Spanish from Lorenzo Pérez Hernández, a native-born Indian of San José la Laguna who doesn't know how to read or write Spanish and who is sixty-two years of age. I did the translation into English also on 20 October 1988.

28. Bonifacio Ujpán Soto, eighty years of age, is a pure Tzutuhil Maya born in San José, first son of Ignacio's grandmother, Isabel Soto Tuc. The tale was translated by Ignacio into Spanish and by me into English on 21 October 1988.

29. The cross must be on a desk or table nearby, not on the wall over the bed, which has another significance of warding off the spirit of a relative who was *bravo* in life and who might like to come around to molest the surviving relatives.

30. María Ujpán Ramos was Ignacio's deceased aunt and foster mother who reared him. He said that María told the story

to him and his sister, Tonita, when they were young. They always liked to hear stories that the old folks told, and when they asked their aunt to tell them something, she told them this story. Ignacio retold the story to me in Spanish on 21 October 1988.

31. This folktale was originally published in *Campesino*. It was the first folktale that Ignacio told me. When he wrote this tale, he mentioned the tales of the coyote and rabbit, the woman so lazy that she made her dog help her but cooks her baby, and the story of the Hill of Chuitinamit. He said that these were all amusing tales and that we should write about them someday. All three of these tales appear in the present book.

32. This text was first published in *Campesino*. Ignacio explained how it felt when he was the patron who was killed by the bull and put in the casket:

It was very nice when they put me in a casket and carried me to the church. It was 24 June, and many people saw them put me into the coffin. A lot of people cried, but many people laughed. I was well aware when they put me down in the coffin, but they waited about a half hour before they took me out. In about twenty minutes I lost consciousness. [I do not know whether it was from weariness or sleepiness.] I did not feel a thing when they opened the box. When I came to, I was on a bench, and my wife was guarding me. They told me I was in a deep sleep: I did not feel a thing when they took me out. I woke up about an hour later, and my wife asked me if I wanted a beer or an eighth of a liter [of *aguardiente*]. Gradually, I realized that I was in the convent [a room of the church], and I asked my wife to give me the eighth, and about five minutes later I felt good again. I do not know if some spirit captured my soul because when they put me in the casket, they began to sound the death knell. It could have been this, or it could have been the eyes of the people. We believe in the captive eye and the captive word. Words and eyes have an ability or power of the blood.

The climax of the dance is when the patron dies, and there were many people outside of the church from all the different towns, including San Jorge and San Martín, who had come to watch the fiesta.

33. The text of the Dance of the Flying Monkeys was first published in *Campesino* in an episode of 1979. Ignacio's grandmother, Elena, died in 1984 at 104 years of age. An episode about her death and the ancient customs surrounding her burial appear in *Ignacio*.

34. This is a Guatemalan expression meaning "El Castellano," or Spanish. See Armas (1971).

35. *"Muchá"* is a short exclamatory synonym, or apocope for "Muchachos." See Rubio (1982) and Armas (1971).

36. The expression Ignacio used was, *"¡Andante a la chingada!"* According to Armas (1971:74), this expression alludes to a distant, undetermined place that could be Hell.

37. Ignacio introduced this story by saying it was his own arrangement.

38. Ignacio introduced this story by stating it was an old one. He said that thirty-five years ago Señor José Ixtamer Hernández, of Tzutuhil race, told it to him. Some parts he had already forgotten; it was difficult for him to remember all of it. In 1987 he was completing the story but he lost the notebook and speculated that one of his children liked reading the story, although it wasn't finished. One day he went to Señor José Ixtamer Hernández to get him to tell it to him again, but José

told him he had forgotten everything because he was already seventy years old. Ignacio returned a little sad because he had not recorded the story when it was first told to him.

39. Ignacio said that this tale is neither old nor copied from someone else but invented by him.

References Cited

Armas, Daniel. 1971. *Diccionario de la Expresión Popular Guatemalteco.* Tipografí a Nacional de Guatemala, Centroamérica.

Asociación Tikal. 1981. *El Baile de la Conquista.* Guatemala City: Piedra Santa.

Carmack, Robert M. 1973. *Quichean Civilization: The Ethnohistoric, Ethnographic, and Archaeological Sources.* Berkeley and Los Angeles: University of California Press.

———. 1981. *The Quiché Mayas of Utatlán: The Evolution of a Highland Guatemala Kingdom.* Norman: University of Oklahoma Press.

De Borhegyi, Stephan F. 1965. "Archaeological Synthesis of the Guatemalan Highlands." In *Handbook of Middle American Indians*, vol. 2. Robert Wauchope, gen. ed.; Gordon Willey, vol. ed. of *Archaeology of Southern Mesoamerica*, part 1. Austin: University of Texas Press.

Díaz, Bernal. 1972. "Appendix II." In *An Account of the Conquest of Guatemala.* Sedley J. Mackie, ed. Boston: Milford House.

Geografía Visualizada. n.d. Guatemala City: Piedra Santa.

Goosen, Gary H. 1974. *Chamulas in the World of the Sun: Time and Space in Maya Oral Tradition.* Cambridge: Harvard University Press.

Gordillo Barrios, Gerardo. 1982. *Guatemala: Historia Gráfica.* Guatemala City: Editorial Piedra Santa.

Hymes, Dell H. 1977. "Discovering Oral Performance and Measured Verse in American Indian Narrative." *New Literary History* 8:431–57.

256

Laughlin, Robert M., and Carol Karasik. 1988. *The People of the Bat: Mayan Tales and Dreams from Zinacantán.* Washington, D.C.: Smithsonian Institution Press.

Mattina, Anthony. 1985. *The Golden Woman: The Colville Narrative of Peter J. Seymour.* Tucson: University of Arizona Press.

— — —. 1987. "North American Indian Mythography: Editing Texts for the Printed Page." In *Recovering the Word: Essays on Native American Literature*, Brian Swann and Arnold Krupat, eds. Berkeley: University of California Press.

Miles, S. W. 1965. "Summary of Preconquest Ethnology of the Guatemala-Chiapas Highlands and Pacific Slope." In *Handbook of Middle American Indians*, vol. 2. Robert Wauchope, gen. ed.; Gordon Willey, vol. ed. of *Archaeology of Southern Mesoamerica*, part 1.

Nash, Manning. 1969. "Guatemala Highlands." In *Handbook of Middle American Indians*, vol. 7. Robert Wauchope, gen. ed.; Evon Z. Vogt, vol. ed. of *Ethnology*, part 1.

Orellana, Sandra L. 1975. "Folk Literature of the Tzutuhil Maya." *Anthropos* 70:839–76.

Recinos, Adrián, and Delia Goetz. 1953. *The Annals of the Cakchiquels and the Title of the Lords of Totonicapán.* Norman: University of Oklahoma Press.

Recinos, Adrián, Delia Goetz, and Sylvanus G. Morley. 1950. *Popol Vuh: The Sacred Book of the Ancient Quiché Maya.* Norman: University of Oklahoma Press.

Redfield, Robert. 1945. Notes on San Antonio Palopó. Microfilm Collection of Manuscripts on Middle American Cultural Anthropology, no. 4. Chicago: Joseph Regenstein Library, University of Chicago.

Rubio, J. Francisco. 1982. *Diccionario de Voces Usado en Guatemala.* Guatemala City: Editorial Piedra Santa.

Sapia Martino, Raúl. 1964. *Guatemala: Mayaland of Eternal Spring.* Guatemala City: River Plato Publishing Co.

Serrano, Manuel. 1970. *El Lago de Atitlán.* Coleción de la Casa de Cultura de Occidente, vol. 3. Quezaltenango, Guatemala: Tipografía Nacional.

Sexton, James D. 1972. *Education and Innovation in a Guatemalan Community: San Juan la Laguna*, vol. 19. Los Angeles: Latin American Studies Series.

———. 1978. "Protestantism and Modernization in Two Guatemalan Towns." *American Ethnologist* 5:280–302.

———. 1979a. "Modernization Among Cakchiquel Maya: An Analysis of Responses to Line Drawings." *Journal of Cross-Cultural Psychology* 10:173–90.

———. 1979b. "Education and Acculturation in Highland Guatemala." *Anthropology and Education Quarterly* 10:80–95.

———. 1982. "Ignacio Bizarro Ujpán: Thematic Analysis of a Tzutuhil Maya's Life Story." Paper presented at the Annual Meeting of the American Folklore Society, Minneapolis.

Sexton, James D., ed. 1985. *Campesino: The Diary of a Guatemalan Indian.* Tucson: University of Arizona Press.

———. 1990. *Son of Tecún Umán: A Maya Indian Tells His Life Story.* Chicago: Waveland Press. (First published in 1981 by University of Arizona Press.)

———. 1992. *Ignacio: The Diary of a Maya Indian of Guatemala.* Philadelphia: University of Pennsylvania Press.

Sexton, James D., and Clyde M. Woods. 1977. "Development and Modernization Among Highland Maya: A Comparative Analysis of Ten Guatemalan Towns." *Human Organization* 36:156–77.

———. 1982. "Demography, Development and Modernization in Fourteen Highland Guatemalan Towns." In *The Historical Demography of Highland Guatemala*, Robert M. Carmack, John Early, and Christopher Lutz, eds. Pub. no. 6. Institute for Mesoamerican Studies, SUNY at Albany. Distributed by the University of Texas Press.

Shaw, Mary, ed. 1971. *According to Our Ancestors: Folk Texts from Guatemala and Honduras*. Summer Institute of Linguistics. Guatemala.

Stephens, John L. 1969. *Incidents of Travel in Central America, Chiapas and Yucatan*, vol. 2. Mineola, New York: Dover Publications, Inc. (First published in 1841 by Harper and Brothers.)

Stuart, George E., and Gene S. Stuart. 1977. *The Mysterious Maya*. Washington, D.C.: National Geographic Society.

Tax, Sol. 1949. "Folk Tales in Chichicastenango: An Unsolved Puzzle." *Journal of American Folklore* 62:125–35.

– – –. 1968. "Descripción Sumaria de los Pueblos," In *Los Pueblos del Lago de Atitlán*, Sol Tax, ed. Guatemala City: Seminario de Integración Social Guatemalteca.

Tedlock, Dennis. 1983. *The Spoken Word and the Work of Interpretation*. Philadelphia: University of Pennsylvania Press.

Thompson, J. Eric S. 1970. *Maya History and Religion*. Norman: University of Oklahoma Press.

Townsend, Paul G., ed. 1980. *Guatemala Maya Texts*. Summer Institute of Linguistics. Guatemala.

Valdeavellano, Marcela. 1984. *Adventuras de Don Chebo*. Guatemala City: Editorial Piedra Santa.

West, Robert C., and John P. Augelli. 1976. *Middle America: Its Lands and Peoples*. Englewood Cliffs, N.J.: Prentice-Hall.

Woods, Clyde M. 1975. *Culture Change*. Dubuque, Iowa: Wm. C. Brown.

Acknowledgments

My research assistants Mimi Hugh and Gwenn Gallenstein helped me translate and edit portions of this book. My research assistants Ann Manning, Janneli Miller, and David Ortiz proofread the final manuscript and gave me editorial suggestions. My wife, Marilyn, read the manuscript and provided editorial suggestions. The editorial suggestions of Sallye Leventhal of Anchor Books were especially useful. Henry Hooper, academic vice president and graduate dean at NAU, and the Committee for Organized Research and the American Philosophical Society funded the project, including a field trip in 1988 while I was on sabbatical. Earl Backman, Dean of Social and Behavioral Sciences, made possible a new personal computer when I needed it most. Finally, my son Randy's belly laughter after reading portions of these tales was a source of encouragement.

Glossary

abogado — defender, lawyer
ajpop — supreme ruler, king
aguardiente — sugarcane liquor, firewater
alcalde — mayor, head
aldeas — villages
alguaciles — runners, attendants
arroba — 25-pound measure
asador — roasting rod, spit

baile — a dance
barranca — ravine
bombas — fireworks shot from mortars
botecito — small jar
bravo — pushy, mean, brash
brujo — witch, sorcerer, wizard, magician

cabacera — main town
caca — excrement
cacique — chief
cadejo — an imaginary animal or bad spirit similar to a *characotel*
    that lurks at night
caites — traditional sandals
campesino — rural peasant, or Indian
candil — a light, or an oil or kerosene lamp
caporal — leader
caracol — snail, curl
cargado — on their backs as cargo

caseríos—hamlets
Castilla—Castilian Spanish
characoteles—persons who turn into *naguales* and act as spies
chicha—corn liquor
chichicastes—nettles
chichín—maraca
chilacayote—very large gourd fed to livestock
chipilín—greens
chirimía—an indigenous oboe
chirmol—a sauce, eaten with or without meat
chiros—young goats
chompipes—common turkeys
coche—pig
cofradías—religious brotherhoods that have as a major obligation
    the sponsoring of saints
colorado—obscene; red
comadre—co-mother, or godmother
comal—earthenware dish for baking maize tortillas
compadre—co-parent or godfather
copa—glass, drink
corte—native skirt
costumbres—customs, rituals
cuadra—a turn; a linear measure of 275 feet
cuento folklóricos—folktales
cuerda—0.178 acre
culo—butt
curandero—a curer

dios—god
dios del mar—god of the ocean
dios del mundo—god of the world
dueño, dueña—owner, or god

ejemplo—example
encomienda—a colonial system exploiting the goods and services of
    the Indians
escrituras—title deeds

finca —farm
frijolar —field of beans

güicoy —medium-sized edible gourd or pumpkin with big grooves
  on its surface
güisquil —a climbing plant whose gourd-like fruit is the size of an
  orange

hijita —dear daughter
hijito —dear son
huevos —eggs, or balls (testicles)
huipil —blouse

indígena —indigene, or native inhabitant
indio —Indian
injertal —*injerto* tree, grove
injertos —soft, brilliant green fruit
invierno —winter

jefe —chief or head
jocotes —yellow, plumlike fruit
Joseños —people of San José
juez —vice-head, judge

latigos —whips
lavadero —public wash place
lebal —Tzutuhil name of a dance

maestro —teacher
malaya (or *malhaya*) —damn it
mayordomo —administrator; a liason between the *juez* and secondary *mayordomos* who are the rank-and-file members of a *cofradía*
m'hija —my daughter, my dear
m'hijo —my son, my dear
morería —store where costumes are made for dancers
mozo —helper, or servant
muchachito —little boy

mujer—woman

municipios—political and geographic subdivisions of departments

nagual—inseparable companion, sorcerer, wizard, animal form of a person, spirit

natural—native

nima rajpop achij—great military commander

nixtamal—corn cooked in lime or ash water

ocote—pine with a lot of resin

pacayas—palm fruit whose flowers also are edible

padrecito—dear father

pastor semanero—weekly pastor

pastorcito—dear, little pastor

pataxte (or *patashte*)—white chocolate

perrito—little dog

petate—weaving, sleeping mat

pícaro—naughty; a rogue

pisto—money

pita—a string made from the agave plant

poder—power, ability

potreros—wide open spaces between houses where children play and where the people keep chickens and large animals

principales—town elders

príncipe—prince

puchica—goodness (exclamation)

quilete—mulberry herb; a slightly bitter plant that is eaten cooked

ranchito—a small, rustic house

rancho—rustic dwelling

reales—money

regidor—councilman

resbalón—a slipup

rey—king

riqueza—wealth, or sex
ruda—a green plant that makes a yellow flower

Santo Mundo—Sacred World, Earth
secreto—magical or sacred rites
sitio—homesite
suerte—luck, fate, fortune, destiny

tacuche—elegant suit
taltuzas—rodents who dig long tunnels in the earth
tamalito—small tamale (ground meat with chili wrapped in corn
   husks and steamed)
tecomate—gourd, or gourd jar
temascal—sweat house
tenamastes—three cooking stones; three-stoned hearth
tepezucintle—wild animal the size of a pup that looks like a wild
   dog
tierra fría—cold country, above 2,000 meters
Título C'oyoi—ancient Quiché text
tituntes—the small rocks that keep the kettles from falling when
   placed on the *tenamastes*
tragos—shots of liquor; drinks
traje—suit
tules—a nonedible plant used to make mats
tutor—the guardian, or person in charge

veladora—short, thick candles
vieja—old woman
viejitos—little old folks

zajorín—shaman, seer, clairvoyant
Zinacantecos—people of Zinacantán
zompopos—macrocephalic ants
zompos—short for *zompopos*

About the Editor

James D. Sexton and Ignacio Bizarro Ujpán (a pseudonym) have been working together since 1970, when Sexton made his first of eleven field trips to Guatemala over a span of twenty years. He translated and edited a trilogy of books about the life and country of Ignacio: *Son of Tecún Umán* (1981, 1990), *Campesino* (1985), and *Ignacio* (1991). He has also written *Education and Innovation in a Guatemalan Community* (1972) and several articles on modernization and cultural change in highland Guatemala. Sexton has been teaching at Northern Arizona University since 1973, where in 1982 he received the NAU President's Award for excellence in teaching, research, and service and in 1991 was named Regents' Professor.